ANGELHUNTING

ANGELHUNTING

A SEAMUS CARON MYSTERY

JI HONG SAYO

Published by ECW Press
665 Gerrard Street East
Toronto, Ontario, Canada M4M 1Y2
416-694-3348 / info@ecwpress.com

Cover design: Caroline Suzuki

Quotes taken from *White as Milk, Red as Blood: The Forgotten Fairy Tales of Franz Xaver von Schönwerth*, translated by Shelley Tanaka (Knopf Canada, 2018).

LIBRARY AND ARCHIVES CANADA CATALOGUING IN PUBLICATION

Title: Angelhunting : a Seamus Caron mystery / Ji Hong Sayo.

Names: Sayo, Ji Hong, author.

Identifiers: Canadiana (print) 2025013974X | Canadiana (ebook) 20250139871

ISBN 978-1-77041-817-2 (softcover)
ISBN 978-1-77852-406-6 (ePub)
ISBN 978-1-77852-407-3 (PDF)

Subjects: LCGFT: Novels. | LCGFT: Detective and mystery fiction.

Classification: LCC PS8637.A997 A83 2025 | DDC C813/.6—dc23

This book is funded in part by the Government of Canada. *Ce livre est financé en partie par le gouvernement du Canada.* We acknowledge the support of the Canada Council for the Arts. *Nous remercions le Conseil des arts du Canada de son soutien.* We would like to acknowledge the funding support of the Ontario Arts Council (OAC) and the Government of Ontario for their support. We also acknowledge the support of the Government of Ontario through the Ontario Book Publishing Tax Credit, and through Ontario Creates.

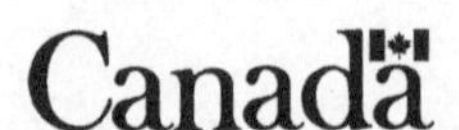

PRINTED AND BOUND IN CANADA

PRINTING: MARQUIS 5 4 3 2 1

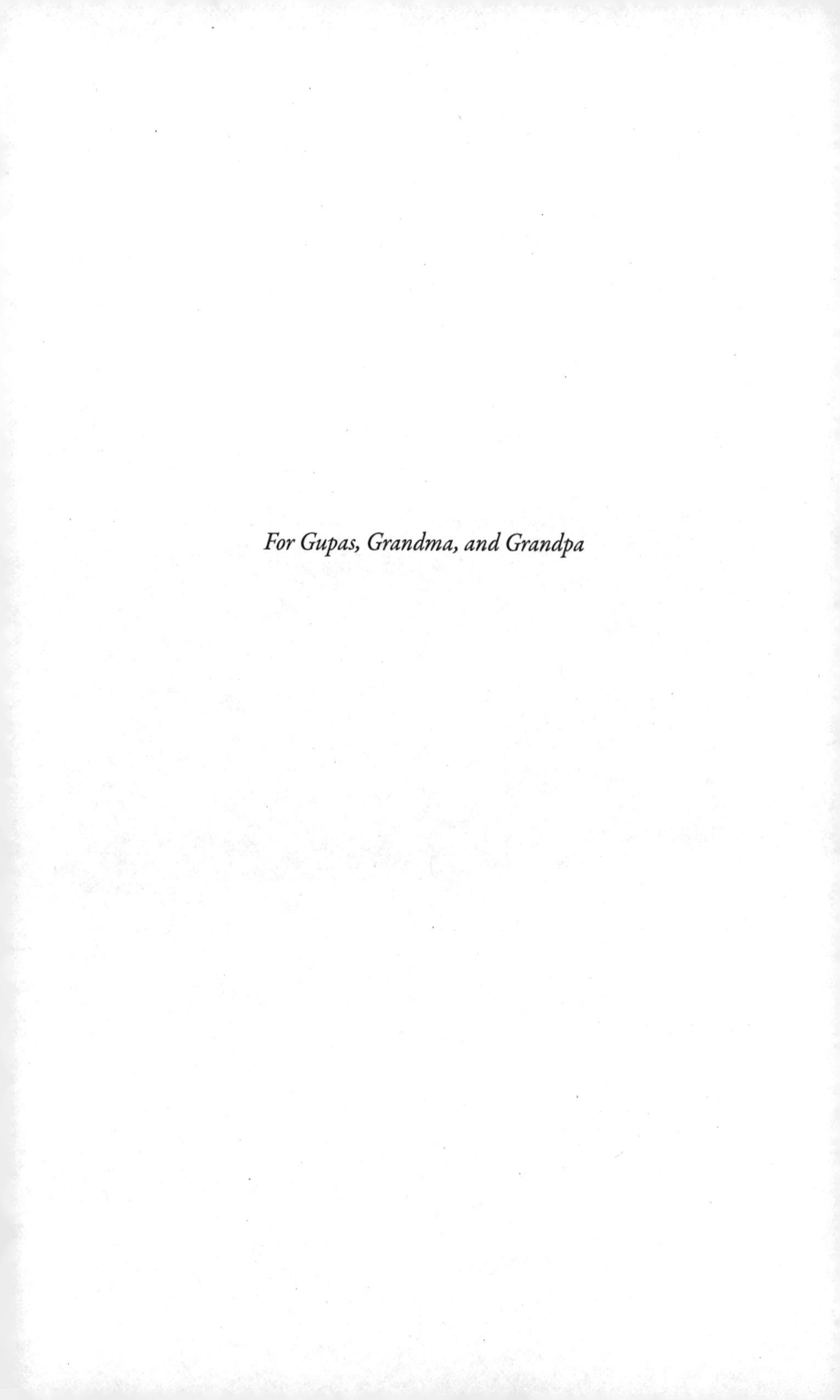

For Gupas, Grandma, and Grandpa

CHAPTER ONE

Business hadn't so much slowed down as curled into a ball and died, and Seamus Caron was about two hundred bucks away from cracking a few safes himself. He'd seen plenty of blood and tears in his fifteen years as a private eye, but he'd take either over boredom and a thin bankroll.

Seamus sat at his desk, oilskin coat loose over his shoulders, trying to plan. It was his least favourite occupation. Far more enjoyable to be in the morgue puzzling over half an ear or trolling Queen Street with a picture of a man who didn't want to be found or bloodying his knuckles dragging the same man back to his creditors. At this point, he'd even welcome an easy week of tailing some wayward husband to seedy motels. Trouble was, there wasn't enough crime and desperation for a man to make an honest living these days. And more than the money, whenever his life slowed down like this, that nameless, gnawing unease crept back in. It made Seamus's fingers twitch and pushed him into more bar fights than was strictly healthy.

Seamus had just decided that flying a kite off the balcony would take his mind off his troubles when a silhouette darkened the frosted glass of his office door. The knock came sharp and impatient, and Seamus opened the door to find a narrow-faced woman. In her heels, she was taller than Seamus, and she looked to be in her early forties, with pale blonde hair falling to brush a dark wool overcoat. Attractive in a severe way, with a sharp-edged figure and a face whose lines had been partially obscured by fillers and botox. Seamus nodded a cheerful hello and saw the woman's disdainful glance at the battered oilskin that hung off his shoulders.

"Nice to meet you too," said Seamus to a dry silence. "I assume you're looking for a private detective?"

"I am."

"Please, step into my office, Miss . . . ?"

"You don't need my name."

Seamus grinned slightly at this and moved to let her pass—standing just slightly in the door frame.

The woman carried a Birkin bag at her side—Seamus didn't know enough about fashion to guess how much this particular one might be worth, beyond the fact the answer would be obscene. He did, however, have other areas of expertise—pickpocketing, for instance, which he'd learned from a seven-fingered woman in Greektown. The very expensive purse the woman was carrying didn't happen to have a zipper and, being difficult to latch closed, was hanging open, a matching grey wallet tucked just inside. He slipped his coat off and slung it over his arm as he held the door for her, then snatched a "New Client" form from his desk. Producing a pen from one of his innumerable pockets, he stepped to the woman's side, then stood in place, feigning concern that she fill out the form correctly.

"Just a formality," he said. "If you don't mind. You don't have to put a name, but I *will* need a contact number."

She looked annoyed by the request but shifted her bag to her left arm, beside Seamus. It was always a gamble, but you could count on most people being right-handed. As she took the pen and darted out a cell number, Seamus blocked her line of sight with his bundled coat and light-fingered her wallet. He jostled her slightly as he did so and drew out her driver's licence with one hand as he apologized. Ontario licences were easy—you could feel the little square of lamination on the bottom corner. Seamus stole a quick glance at the card, and everything went back into the purse just as Arya Williams, resident of apartment 4761 in the Waverley complex, finished jotting her answers to the last few questions on the client form.

If it was for a case, Seamus had an excellent memory.

She sat stiffly in the client's chair, clearly unimpressed by his small office and affectedly bumbling manner. Seamus decided to take the opportunity to enjoy himself.

"So, what brings you here, Arya?"

She didn't quite jump, but she flinched hard enough that her chair rattled against the floor. Seamus just grinned wider, which he knew could be unnerving. He was, in his own disinterested estimation, fairly handsome, with his neat salt-and-pepper hair, his Lao mother's deep tan skin, and his father's oxygen-blue eyes. Or he *would* have been handsome, if it weren't for the scars. Faint white lines traced up and over his lips, jaw, and left eyelid—he'd been collecting them since he was eleven. A wide smile, with those scars and bright blue eyes, was often enough to make people flinch. Of course, Seamus's smile wasn't the main reason for the sweat now bleeding through Arya's makeup.

"How—" she looked furtively back at the door, as if contemplating an escape. "No one could have told you I was coming. You couldn't know my name. It's impossible—"

"For the properly trained mind, Ms. Williams, nothing is impossible. From a few observations—the brand of your shoes, the time of your arrival on this particular Tuesday, the specific brand of perfume on your wrists—it was simple enough to deduce your identity."

This was nonsense, but it was often useful to convince clients that he had some truly extraordinary deductive skills. In actual fact, quick fingers and a talent for picking locks were more useful to a private detective than the capacity to solve puzzles, but for some reason his clients were more impressed by the latter.

He watched the alarm on Arya Williams's face slowly melt away, replaced by a look of awe.

"Mr. Caron," she said solemnly, not quite recovering her composure, "I'm afraid I underestimated you."

"I don't blame you," he said. "We've just met, after all. I'll warn you, though, that it's a dangerous mistake to make."

"I won't forget that. Mr. Caron, I'd like to hire you to recover something of mine. Something . . . sensitive. Two days ago, my Tesla was stolen, along with a briefcase I had locked in the trunk. Of sentimental value, you understand."

Seamus held in a sigh. While some fast dealing was par for the course, he had rules, and he'd have to tell Ms. Williams up front if the case was legitimately impossible. Seamus always delivered, or at least always convinced his clients that he had.

"I understand perfectly well. In all honesty, Ms. Williams, if you lost a briefcase full of cash two days ago, the odds that I can recover it—"

"*Not* money," she said, looking pained. "I can't specify the exact contents, but I have reason to believe they wouldn't be easy to sell. The car itself was wrecked"—here she gestured unconcern—"but the briefcase is still missing. I want you to find it. And if you do succeed in recovering the briefcase, I'll ask that you not open it."

Seamus raised an eyebrow. "This is starting to sound expensive," he said. A find-and-recover job was one thing. Not too different from what Seamus had done before he'd gotten into the detective business when he used to work for loan sharks whose clients were slow making their weekly payments. Not a bad job, so long as you didn't mind hard work and a few red stains on your jacket. But if you didn't know what you were recovering—blackmail material, corporate secrets, pounds of uncut cocaine—you were putting yourself in danger. And danger meant a steep rate.

"The contact who referred me said you were a premium contractor. They told me specifically about your charging ten thousand dollars for a case which lasted a week." Here she leaned forward slightly. "If you can recover my briefcase inside ten days, I'll pay forty thousand."

She was watching for a reaction, and Seamus was careful not to give her one. Instead, he favoured her with a look of cool disinterest.

"That's a very generous offer. On the other hand, you're asking me to find a briefcase stuffed with some unknown—likely illegal—valuable, which has been missing for two days in the fourth largest city in North America."

"You refuse, then?"

Seamus grinned, showing her the points of his teeth.

"Of course not, Ms. Williams. I'm just surprised you think I'll need the full ten days. Remember what I said about underestimating me? I will, however, require an additional five thousand to take on the case. Up front. That won't be a problem, will it?"

It was, even though Seamus suspected Ms. Williams's wallet cost more than five grand. But Seamus could hardly run a case like this without a little something to grease the wheels, and the promise of a small windfall if it fell through in the end. Besides, he needed a secretary—he never took a job without a secretary if he could help it, although they rarely lasted longer than a case of instant noodles. A secretary was indispensable when you needed a lookout, or someone to keep the clients busy on the phone, or a witness with no criminal record. Five large would more than cover two weeks' salary, after which said secretary could be cut loose via a few delicately placed loopholes buried deep in the contract no one ever bothered to read.

At length Seamus came to terms with the woman, with her calm face and her desperate eyes, and gathered what details he could about the case. There wasn't much—Ms. Williams knew almost nothing, and she was willing to tell him less. She did leave him with a crisp five-thousand-dollar cheque, though, and that was as good a start to a case as any lead.

The afternoon was spent laying groundwork. Seamus dug into research on Arya Williams, printing off ground-view maps of the area where the car had been stolen and laying them out on the desk, building a picture of the woman who'd offered him forty thousand dollars. And he put an ad for a secretary up on the message boards, promising an hourly wage that would pay down rent on a very comfortable cardboard box in downtown Toronto.

But the picture he was trying to build wasn't fitting together correctly. Arya Williams, it seemed, was a junior executive at a downtown financial firm, with an estimated net worth in the tens of millions. Which explained why she'd offered Seamus such an exorbitant fee, but not why she was willing to take the risk of hiring him in the first place. Surely, she could swallow whatever loss that little briefcase represented—unless, of course, it wasn't just money she stood to lose.

Seamus looked up from his laptop and found he'd arrived at Jackson's Bar, although he didn't quite remember leaving his desk. Jackson Azizi was behind the counter, as always, stacking a tower of pint glasses.

Seamus glanced around as he came out of the silent focus of his work, swivelled to look out the bar front window. The streets were cooling as the sun fell, and a slight rain had started to patter against the sidewalks, but all was well at Jackson's, the glasses chilled and the radiators purring. A tumbler of bourbon sat untouched by his right hand, although Seamus couldn't say whether it had been there five minutes or an hour. He took his first sip as he resumed his focus through the window.

Out in the cold, the streetlights were casting haloes in the dim air, lighting a jacketed figure hurrying through the drizzling rain. The door swept open, and Seamus smiled to see his best and oldest friend.

"Seamus, how the hell are you?"

"Oh, well enough. Looking for a new secretary. Jackson, would you get Sandra a beer? On my tab."

"Generous. You can buy me some wings too."

"Since you asked so nicely."

Sandra Blair, chief of homicide of Toronto's forty-fourth police division, was dressed in her usual threadbare denim jacket, her long, black hair carefully braided back. Seamus didn't usually pay much attention to faces—it was the hands you had to watch, in case they were going for a knife—but even he recognized Sandra's soft-edged beauty and the way it jarred with her twice-broken nose. That second break had been the work of a drunk on the Yonge line, back when Sandra was a rookie cop and unused to dodging empty Molson bottles. Seamus had actually met the man—he was well-meaning enough when sober, and by the time they parted ways, he regretted his mistake with the heartfelt sincerity that only a broken leg can produce.

Seamus knew Sandra from Wiarton, back when they'd spend afternoons catching bullfrogs or acting out gunfights or just about anything to put off going home another hour. She'd come over to do her homework, get some dinner if what passed for her mother happened to be in a bad mood, and play with the rusty .22 Seamus had found in a barn up by Tobermory. The latter was the source of Sandra's nickname, after she shot out two of Seamus's windows.

"Have I ever told you what a great friend you are, Steady?"

She used to hate being called that—didn't seem to mind so much now that she had the highest firearm proficiency of any detective in the province.

"Buckle it, Trouble. If you want a favour, you'll have to buy it. Got a case I want your take on."

Seamus's nickname had a simpler story behind it: Sandra's mother had called him that so much it stuck.

"What, someone steal your donuts from the break room again?"

"If that'd happened, there'd be another murder to worry about, and I'd be hiding out south of the border."

"Murder again?" Seamus sighed. "Your job is awfully monotonous."

"This one might be more fun than usual. We didn't find a body."

Seamus raised an eyebrow. "Go on . . ."

It seemed that one John Ryba, at Michael Garron Hospital for an appendectomy, had triggered a code yellow that morning. Seamus wanted to ask why the chief of homicide was concerning herself with a missing patient, but he didn't say anything—Sandra had a story, and she'd want to tell it in order.

"So," said Sandra, "this lawyer's hospital bed is empty. Nurses can't find him, and the family gets called in. Police too. We've got a uniformed officer there telling them not to worry, that he probably just wandered off high on the pain meds. Happens all the time."

"Can't imagine why they'd be worried," muttered Seamus.

"Yeah, I'll be chewing that newbie out later. Gotta hit the next of kin with the 'we're doing everything we can,' and make sure they don't see you stopping for some all-dressed chips on the way out of the hospital, like Ryba's wife did. Rookie mistake—you've gotta keep the snacks stocked in the patrol car. But anyway, nothing much else happens till five, when a nurse goes to clean out his room. There was a plastic shower curtain under the sheets, and under that, a couple pitchers' worth of blood soaking through the mattress. Which means unless someone gave him a real quick transfusion—"

"Mr. Ryba's no longer with us. And you want my help on this one? You sure you can afford me?"

Sandra snorted. "Do it for free, and we'll say it's one less favour you owe me. At the rate you're going now, you won't have paid me back till we're both dead. C'mon, this one's perfect for you. No motive. No weapon. No body."

"And what's the real reason you want me to look at it?"

Sandra looked slightly embarrassed at that—subterfuge had always been Seamus's strong suit, not hers. Even the suggestion of deceit made Sandra's eye twitch.

"Alright. You remember Alister Carleton?"

"The doctor? He used to know my father—I remember him visiting after the funeral. Gave me a Mickey Mouse watch."

"'Sorry 'bout your dad, here's a fun watch'? That's kind of fucked, isn't it?"

"Never liked him much," said Seamus with a shrug.

"Neither do I," grumbled Sandra. She tended to get angrier about that sort of thing than Seamus did, which he appreciated. "But he remembered you when I interviewed him."

"He's working at Michael Garron now?"

"Part-time, I think. He came up to me just as I was leaving—think it took him about twenty minutes of staring to see if he could remember who I was. Said he wanted to get back in touch with you. Looked nervous."

Seamus frowned.

"How does that connect to the case?"

"C'mon, Detective Caron. Think it through. A murder happens on the floor where a doctor works, and he just happens to want to meet his old friend the private investigator? Something's off there. And he looked like he had something to hide."

"Maybe he misses my sparkling wit and personality."

"The last time he saw you was when you got out of juvie. I don't think that's it."

Seamus's jaw tensed. He had other reasons for not liking Carleton, ones he didn't need to rehash with Sandra. Carleton and his father had actually been quite close, worked at the same hospital. Thomas Caron had gone to him for advice on a few occasions, one of them being Thomas Caron's very last patient, Lauren Carres. Seamus had never found out what Carleton advised in that case, but given what his father did, and what happened to Lauren in the end, Seamus wasn't disposed to think very well of Dr. Carleton.

"I'll give him a call," he said reluctantly. "But it'll be my usual terms."

Sandra rolled her eyes but nodded assent. He'd helped with a few cases before—he was a lot closer to the criminal side of things than Sandra was, and that gave him a useful perspective. Jokes aside, he didn't charge for those occasional consultations, but he reserved the right to take a look at the crime scene himself. It kept him sharp, working actual cases after a few months of tailing husbands or, if he was really unlucky, some poor kid with neurotic parents whose GPA had dipped a quarter percent. Seamus could usually tell if a particular crime was the work of the mob and warn Sandra to get out of the line of fire.

Not that she ever listened to him.

"I need a favour too," said Seamus. "Pull in your contacts in narcotics. I'm looking for a black briefcase full of *something*."

It didn't sound quite right to him, but his best guess so far was that Arya Williams had misplaced a bunch of high-quality cocaine or heroin. Whoever had "found" it would be selling it on the street, so there were reasonably good odds the precinct would've heard about a jump in supply.

Sandra gave him a warning look.

"I can't pull a brick of cocaine out of evidence, even for you."

Seamus raised his hand in a warding gesture.

"I'm not asking you to. As a matter of fact, my client hasn't told me what the briefcase contains, just what she's willing to pay to get it back."

Sandra nodded slowly.

"A'ight. And you'll tell me if any of your colleagues stabbed Mr. Ryba to death?"

"You wound me, Sandra. They're friends, not just colleagues. But yes. And I'll be by the morgue tomorrow to look at whatever evidence you've got."

"That's not my purview. You'll have to take it up with Radner."

"Tell you what, Sandra," said Seamus, grinning, "if your boss objects to my visiting the morgue, tell him I completely understand and mention that he'll have his name in the paper soon. I'm sure his husband will be excited."

Sandra knocked back the last of her beer. She'd never asked exactly what dirt Seamus had on Radner, but Seamus suspected she'd crack soon. It wasn't anything personal—Herbert Radner just happened to have the bad luck to work in the jurisdiction where Seamus took most of his cases, and the bad taste to get in Seamus's way when he was made superintendent. When he was first appointed, Radner had made it clear that he was going to put an end to Seamus's tacit partnership with the forty-fourth, regardless of Seamus's connections to city hall and the mob.

Within two months of his appointment, Seamus had footage of Radner in a rather compromising position with a very young yoga instructor. Being a private eye, his discretion could be counted on—so long as he still had access to the morgue, of course, and the ability to run background checks on police computers. As Seamus had said the first and only time he'd been invited to speak at Monarch Park Collegiate, you could achieve almost anything with persistence, optimism, and a willingness to blackmail.

The conversation of the night ended as it usually did, Sandra clapping him on the back.

"I'd tell you to go to hell, but the devil doesn't deserve that kinda headache."

He answered her with a too-wide grin.

"Alright," she said, slapping the bar as she stood. "See you tomorrow, unfortunately. I'd better get back to Michael—he'll be worrying about me. It's a hobby for him. And we've still got to pick a date for the wedding, might even manage to do it tonight if I catch him in a good mood. Evening, Jackson."

As Sandra wrapped herself up in her old denim, Jackson reached for the bottle of Basil Hayden.

Seamus waved him off. "That's all for tonight," he said. "Still looking for a secretary, though. You know anyone who needs a job?"

"Sure," said Jackson with a smile. The big man was always smiling, whether he was listening to a regular's life story for the third time or cleaning up the vomit that had interrupted the fourth retelling. "Boomtown came in looking for a job and a pitcher of vodka again the other day. I gave him some soup and a dozen packets of saltines, same as every week. You want his résumé?"

Jackson reached under the bar and drew out an old paper napkin. Seamus took it from him, noticing too late that Boomtown had also used it to wipe soup off his mouth, and carefully read the ballpoint-scrawled qualifications.

"Old Boomtown's a Harvard graduate, is he?"

"And fluent in 'every language,'" said Jackson.

Seamus handed the napkin back.

"I'm afraid he's overqualified. Can't afford him. But give him a few sandwiches next time he's in, on my tab."

"Getting long, that tab of yours," said Jackson, still smiling.

"Don't worry. I've got a case now, and paying for my bourbon's the first priority."

That was true enough—and there were other advantages to keeping Jackson happy. Years ago, Seamus had bailed him out from under a pyramid scheme—although Jackson maintained to this day it was more of an obelisk—and it was useful having a friend who used to be in the confidence business, not least because Jackson still kept a basement bolthole stocked with clean bandages and ammunition. The first three hundred dollars off the cheque in Seamus's wallet would go to Jackson's Bar, with a fat tip to round it out. Jackson seemed mollified, leaning over the bar.

"Michael came by earlier," said Jackson. "He doesn't usually. Was asking if Sandra'd been in for lunch."

"That's nice of him," said Seamus, his eyes fixed on the endless tiers of bottles behind the bar. "He must've wanted to take her out."

Jackson's eyes were narrowed.

"I don't like him. You know the first time he came in here, he ordered a *Perrier*."

"Well, Sandra probably told him not to drink anything you gave him that didn't come out of a bottle."

Seamus bid his friend goodnight, wrapped his jacket tight around his shoulders, and headed back to the office. The rain had gotten heavier, painting the night sky solid black. Despite the cold, Seamus paused before he unlocked the door to the building and looked up at no stars. He let the rain trickle down his smile.

—

Seamus's office building was a squat mass of concrete just off Queen East. On warm nights the neighbouring park was a popular place to sleep, and you could hear the occasional drifter's midnight revelations in the alley below. The hallways were dark, but he'd long since memorized the steps and turns that led to his office. He flicked on the lights and shrugged off his jacket, the first time it had come off since he'd put it on that morning.

The long oilskin had been green once but was now more of a beige, with enough pockets to conceal everything he might need and a spare. It had been a gift from his mother on his seventeenth birthday, along with a few thousand dollars in the pockets. She'd handed it to him and told him to be out of the house by the end of the day. Ma'd always been strict, but after Thomas Caron died, whatever softness had padded her edges had worn off, leaving the cold steel core at her centre exposed. He remembered the night of his father's funeral, as he'd sat weeping quietly by the open hole in the ground, she'd come and put a firm hand on his shoulder. *You're always fighting*, she'd told him. *Never cry. Never let them see you're hurt.* Good advice in general, but perhaps a little stern for a twelve-year-old. Still, Ma had fed him and clothed him and only ever done what she thought was right—and in the final analysis there was nothing else you could ask of anyone.

Seamus gathered his shower things from an empty filing cabinet under the desk, snapped his office door shut behind him, and went downstairs to wash up.

The architects had planned to put in a gym, but all the builders had managed was a set of showers in the basement that no one was supposed to use and a few sealed-up rooms that the current owner couldn't find the cash to reconvert. Seamus had quietly hooked a single shower into the building's water mains, and the superintendent never could figure out why the water bill was just slightly higher than it should have been.

Moving through the hall past the shuttered offices, Seamus carried his kit: a towel, shampoo, and a single faded rubber duck.

When he emerged from the shower scrubbed pink, Seamus made his way back to his office, whistling tunelessly. He paused when he reached his door and grinned with pride: illuminated by the window-refracted moonlight, he could just make out the words cut into the frosted glass.

Seamus Caron
Private Eye—Freelance
When you have nowhere else to turn, come to Seamus Caron

He'd bought that door with the three hundred dollars from his last collection job. It had been entertaining work, but Seamus tried not to miss it. Sandra'd never thought much of his first career, regardless of the fact Seamus's targets generally deserved what happened to them. Now that he was a private eye, Seamus followed his Ma's advice and did what he thought was right, which sometimes even lined up with what was legal, and he was back on speaking terms with his best friend.

Of course, it didn't pay as well.

The office itself was spacious.

Toronto prices real estate prices meant Seamus had the choice between sleeping in his office and selling at least one kidney; after some debate, he'd picked the former. There was the main room, with plenty of space for Seamus's makeshift bed in front of the desk, and a second room that toed the line between storage and hostile wilderness.

Kicking off his slippers, Seamus rolled out the sleeping bag he kept tucked in the filing cabinet underneath his three pairs of pants. He lay down at precisely eleven o'clock—the last time he'd slept well had been before his father died, and while he'd long since adjusted to the nightmares, it was important to keep up his routines. It certainly wouldn't do to stop sleeping entirely again.

Seamus startled awake at six with cold sweat on his neck and adrenalin acrid in his mouth. Just like every other morning. His heart raced, though the images were indistinct, fading even as he woke. No sense in thinking about it too much—it was always the same nightmare anyway, or variations on the theme: a rigid body; blue skin, cold to the touch; the stink of dried urine. Seamus shook his head and took a swig of water. Enough. There were better things to think about.

Like how he was going to sort through the mass of applicants for the secretary position he'd listed only the day before. Apparently, anything above starvation wages and no required college degree got you the pick of the litter as an employer. Seamus downed a bowl of instant noodles, cooked with water from the electric kettle under his desk, and started organizing interviews—anyone who wasn't free that morning was out of the running.

Seamus was nothing if not optimistic, but by lunchtime he'd begun to despair for humanity. The applicants he'd managed to slot in were singularly underwhelming: there'd been the jittery boy who struggled with the esoteric mechanics of the door knob until Seamus had taken pity on him and let him in, the college student still slightly drunk from the previous night, and no fewer than three actors who'd moved to the big city from their hometowns up north and found the slow process of starving to death less romantic than it had first appeared. All these candidates had been thanked for their time and assured that they would receive a call if HR decided they were a good fit.

Seamus stood and stretched, suddenly aware of the hollowness in the pit of his stomach—a single bowl of instant noodles, though a nutritious and complete breakfast, wasn't enough to sustain him an entire day.

If he couldn't get a secretary, he'd work the case on his own, but that meant no one on lookout, no second pair of eyes on the suspects. Moreover, appearing with an assistant at his side tended to give the operation a sense of heft and legitimacy, and it put his targets on edge, which was exactly what Seamus wanted. With any luck, the next candidate, one Maxwell Moscovitz, would be just what he was looking for.

The applicant's profile was questionable, but Seamus didn't mind a checkered past—it usually meant leverage, if he could find the right place to apply pressure. Moscovitz had graduated from Glenn Gould with a bachelor of music and high honours, but who listed exactly no musical employment. As a matter of fact, Moscovitz didn't list any employment at all for the previous fourteen months, before which the only position seemed to have been senior camp counsellor.

The rap on the door shocked him out of his analysis, and Seamus put on his friendliest smile to answer it.

"Are you Seamus Caron?"

Standing at a slight lean in the doorway was a woman in her early twenties, shorter than Seamus, but still tall for a woman, with dark-ringed hazel eyes and hair a shade too dark for the natural world. She carried a black knapsack in one hand, which matched everything else she wore: black cargo pants, a black turtleneck, an ill-fitting black blazer, and old combat boots polished to a shine. It was a uniform of sorts, but not the type one would typically wear to a job interview.

"That I am," he said, adding after a beat, "and you must be Maxwell Moscovitz?" to which the woman at his door nodded. Seamus returned to his desk and gestured for her to sit. "Take a seat and we'll begin the interview."

She walked briskly across the room and pulled out the opposite chair in a single jerky motion. Nervous, but trying to hide it. Not rich, judging by her clothes, but she seemed steady. And wearing all black to an interview had to signify either confidence or fatalism, both of which were valuable in a secretary. She offered him a printed résumé, which Seamus set to one side as he leaned back in his chair.

"Nice to meet you," she ventured.

"That's not a common opinion," said Seamus. "But it's nice to meet you as well. No power suit?"

She shrugged and looked down, as though she'd forgotten exactly what she had put on that morning.

"It's what I always wear. Doesn't matter for this job, does it?"

"Fair enough. Let's get started, then. You graduated from Glenn Gould with a degree in classical violin?"

"Yup."

"Funny you haven't listed any jobs in the music industry. Why is that? And I wouldn't mind an explanation for the year-long employment gap in your record too."

She blinked and curled backwards, as though threatened.

"You're supposed to ask me about my greatest strengths and weaknesses and that shit first, aren't you?"

"I can, if you'd like," he said, "but in this line of business you'll find that people are rarely forthcoming about their greatest weaknesses. Mine, if you're curious, is bullet wounds."

Seamus eased back in his chair, smiling. He cared very little about Ms. Moscovitz's obviously defensive behaviour, and not at all about her unorthodox approach to workplace etiquette. But there was one absolutely crucial requirement for a good secretary: they had to be *unflappable*.

"So," continued Seamus, with an inviting gesture, "you were going to tell me what you've been doing for the past year."

The answer came quickly, with a practised wariness: "I wasn't. That's private."

"Fair enough," said Seamus, "but be advised that learning other people's secrets is what puts bread on my table. Moving on, I have a series of questions designed to test your problem-solving skills, aptitude for the job, and general worth as a human being. Please consider your answers carefully."

Seamus paused for effect. Maxwell Moscovitz set her shoulders, her eyes going flinty.

"First of all," he said, "have you ever fired a gun?"

"You're looking for a secretary, right? Why would I need to fire a gun?"

"Sometimes people leave you on hold a little too long," said Seamus. He pulled out a pad of paper and pretended to take notes, which he'd found an effective method for making clients more nervous.

Maxwell frowned, but she answered: "My uncle taught me to shoot a rifle when I turned fifteen."

"Excellent. Now, for a few more serious questions. First: if your bedsheets were made of deli meat, what meat would they be?"

She held his gaze resolutely, looking unimpressed. "Bedsheets are a total scam, you can just lie down right on the mattress and have one less thing to wash. But if I used them, and they were meat, they'd be pastrami."

"You can either fight a hundred duck-sized horses or five horse-sized ducks. To the death. Which would you pick?"

Maxwell contemplated the problem. "I'd take the hundred mini-horses."

"Good answer. Ducks are terrifying," said Seamus. "How many ten-year-olds could you take in a fight?"

"As many as you can find. I used to work as a camp counsellor, those little fuckers talk a big game, but they run when shit gets real."

Maxwell Moscovitz seemed willing to take things in stride, and her answer to the duck-horse problem was promising.

"The job's yours," said Seamus. "You've got a lot of potential, Ms. Moscovitz."

She looked doubtful—it's not like the bar was high—and Seamus reflected that he might have overdone it.

"In addition to the salary listed on the ad, there are a few other benefits," he said. "I'll cover your lunch every day. And dinner fairly often."

An extravagance, but the knife-thin Ms. Moscovitz didn't look like she'd be eating much. And it was a good way for Seamus to make sure *he* remembered to eat at least once a day.

The look of indecision faded from her eyes, and she nodded briskly.

"Alright, I'm in. When do I start?"

"As soon as you sign," said Seamus, handing her the new employee form. "After that, it's time for you to hear about the case we'll be working on. Over lunch, of course." Not waiting for her to finish scribbling her signature, Seamus moved to the door. As he pulled on his coat, Seamus noticed her squinting at him.

"Is it normal for the secretary to get all the case details?" she asked.

"I have an innovative approach to client confidentiality," said Seamus with a slight flourish. "It's part of what makes me such a great detective."

With that, Seamus raced out the door, leaving Maxwell Moscovitz trailing after him. He heard her swearing behind him as he hit a dead sprint down the stairs, but she was on payroll now, and Seamus wasn't about to foot the bill for a leisurely stroll down the street.

Ten minutes and as many blocks later, Seamus was standing in front of Minnie's place. The small partially lit storefront was lettered with the words *GOLDEN FISH—FINE CUISINE*, and a clip-art Italian chef smiling down at Seamus. Mandarin characters flashed in neon, the smell of hot oil and broth seeped out to the sidewalk.

Maxwell was still two blocks back, gasping and staggering and cursing at Seamus, but he wasn't overly concerned. A brisk run would do her good.

The Golden Fish was part of what little of East Chinatown still existed by Broadview; the big restaurants and apothecaries had all moved to the suburbs where the real estate was cheaper. But there were still survivors: across the road, a forty-year-old grocery store enticed passersby with plump winter melon and the faint, sweet smell of persimmon.

Seamus waited till Maxwell had almost caught up, then walked through the glass door and waved down Minnie. Dressed in her blue polyester polo and apron, she held two mighty stacks of plates with heavy, knife-scarred hands.

"Seamus! Good to see you. Who you bring this time?"

She'd run the restaurant for thirty years—she'd had her husband's help for the first twenty-five, but around the time Seamus met them he'd retired to tend his bonsai, which grew in the front yard, and his marijuana plants, which grew in the back. Seamus had helped smooth over the legal difficulties that arose from his selling both crops to church friends—although Seamus suspected the old man had always been more worried about a reprisal from the Toronto Bonsai Society than any drug charges those gweilo police might pin on him.

"I brought my new secretary, Ms. Moscovitz," said Seamus, nodding to the storefront window Maxwell was leaned against, panting. "I'll be here for lunch more often, now that I have someone to eat with."

"Good, good. You'll waste away otherwise. Like my grandniece, always something better to do than eat. 'Suan Yi,' I tell her, 'you'll never do well in your studies unless you eat plenty of sugar—it helps your brain, you know.' But does she listen? Hah!" Minnie paused to furiously wipe the counter while somehow simultaneously pouring a glass of milk tea. Seamus considered himself a talented pickpocket, but his hands weren't half as fast as Minnie's.

"Well," said Seamus, "I wouldn't want you to worry, so we'll eat well today. Give me food for four." He waved a quick hello to Qiao, one of Minnie's innumerable nieces, who ran the cash.

Minnie smiled and turned back to the open kitchen to shout her orders in rapid-fire Cantonese. She was answered by sizzling and the clatter of pans.

The lunch rush had died down, and only a few diners sat scattered around the Golden Fish. Seamus eased himself into a booth seat and gestured for Maxwell to join him as she staggered in. Then he leaned back, relaxing amidst the bubbling fish tanks and Formica.

"Alright, protégé, time to learn the crucial points of the job. First and most important: this is the best restaurant in the city. At any given time, I'll be here, Jackson's Bar, the police station, or my office.

You'll meet my friend Sandra at the bar. If you enjoy the use of your arms, don't annoy her."

Seamus reached into his jacket pocket and pulled out a bundle of loose notes, with a LinkedIn photo of Arya Williams he'd printed off pinned to the top of the stack. Getting the secretaries involved in casework was a risk, of course, but it was often helpful to have a fresh set of eyes on the problem. And if his clients objected, there wasn't much recourse available to them, considering they rarely wanted the police involved in whatever sordid mess they'd hired him to clean up.

"Yesterday, this woman came to me offering four times my usual rate, which, between you and me, is already exorbitant. Her name's Arya Williams, a high-powered something-or-other in the financial district. Her Tesla was stolen and turned up totalled, minus a black briefcase, which she asked me to recover. Now, she won't tell me what is in it, only that it is private and of great 'sentimental value.'"

"Drugs?"

"You're a quick one, Moscovitz. That, or blackmail material. Since you wouldn't keep nude photos in a black briefcase unless you were very, very ugly, it's either drugs or something else of concentrated value. The upshot is, if we recover an empty briefcase, we still get paid—after all, I don't even know what's in it. Got all that?"

Maxwell squinted at the photo.

"Honestly, boss? Not at all."

Seamus grinned. He appreciated directness, and "boss" was a nice touch.

"We're going to find a briefcase. My friends will help us."

"Better."

Seamus nodded. "Any questions about the case?"

"What would a detective want to know . . . ? Where was the car stolen?"

"In front of her apartment downtown," said Seamus, "one of those high-rises where the residents eat bread made from the bones of the poor. Tea? It's jasmine."

Seamus carefully laid out the teacups and poured two searing servings of amber-green tea. Maxwell flicked her eyes at him through the pale sheet of steam.

"If it is drugs," said Maxwell, "what kind?"

"Another good question. It must be something extremely expensive to worry our client."

"Must be fancy," she said, eyes slightly distant. "High density, I guess you'd say? It could be pills, but that's probably not pricey enough. Heroin, or coke early up the pipeline might do it."

Seamus raised an eyebrow. "You seem like quite the expert. Should have put that on your résumé."

"I've got a friend—a cousin, I mean—"

"It's fine, I appreciate a range of expertise. Just make sure you're alert on the job, hmm?"

For his own part, Seamus hated the mere sight of any chemical aids besides a good bourbon, and even that he used sparingly. But if someone were determined to make a ruin of their life, well, that was their own affair.

"Now, both cocaine and heroin would seem like good guesses, but there's a problem with that theory. Gram for gram, uncut cocaine would probably be the most expensive. She said the case was small, maybe fourteen inches long and three thick. You'd be able to carry at most two kilos of cocaine in a case that size, which would be worth a few hundred grand on the supply end."

Maxwell nodded. "So, she loses a half-million and hires you to find it for peanuts. Seems straightforward."

"Not quite. It's too big a risk—what if I just turn it over to the police? I've got a reputation, Maxwell, for going the extra mile for my clients. Do you know what I'm saying?"

Maxwell gave him a lopsided grin, the first smile he'd seen out of her.

"You mean you don't mind if your money's got a little smudge on it."

"Exactly. But shuffling around hundreds of thousands of dollars of illegal drugs is more than a *little* smudge. Arya Williams would know better than to hire me if that's what she'd lost. And her net worth is in the tens of millions—why not just swallow the loss?"

"What about acid? That shit's pricey."

"True, in the pure form. But why would a millionaire be moving lab-grade LSD? You'd expect her to be carrying blots. And if I found a million dollars of LSD in a briefcase, why wouldn't I just sell it myself and retire to Champasak?"

Seamus was cut off by the clatter of dishes hitting the table. Maxwell looked at him expectantly, but if she wanted to hear more about the Dadaist nature of the real estate market she was going to have to wait until after lunch. He'd inhaled his first pork bun before the server had set the last plate on the table.

Seamus had polished off a smallmouth bass along with a few plates of noodles before he glanced up to see Maxwell staring at him, only about halfway through the har gow on her plate.

"Hungry, boss?"

"Life's a battle, and you've got to eat quick when you get the chance. Let's head back for now—you can clean out your office."

As Maxwell popped the last couple of shrimp dumplings in her mouth, he pushed his chair out and called to the counter: "Delicious as always, Minnie. How much do I owe you?"

"This again? You eat here for free, Seamus, and if I find one of your bills in my pocket again, I'll burn it."

Seamus just laughed and waved her away. He leaned over the counter to chat with Qiao, practise his Cantonese a bit. Seamus caught Maxwell's eye—she seemed quite interested in Qiao herself, took the opportunity to flirt a bit, which Seamus would've thought impossible given that Qiao spoke a total of perhaps ten words of English, but Maxwell had a blush out of her in a minute flat.

Across the restaurant, there was a clatter as a toddler knocked her bowl to the ground. Qiao murmured an apology and bustled off to clean up the mess. Just what Seamus was waiting for—the Golden Fish existed in a permanent state of uproar, and a convenient distraction was only ever moments away. He glanced to the kitchen, where Minnie was busy yelling at the chefs. With one hand, he flicked open the cash register, which drew an inarticulate noise of outrage from Maxwell, but before she had time to say anything, he'd pulled a fifty-dollar bill out of his jacket with his other hand and tucked it into the cash drawer. It took maybe two seconds, all together, and the quick-fingered movements turned smoothly into him grabbing two guava candies from the glass bowl on the counter just as Minnie turned around.

Seamus tossed Maxwell a candy and raised a finger to his lips with a slight smile. Minnie, oblivious to the fact she'd been paid for their meal, went back to chastising Seamus.

"I couldn't charge a man who's done so much for us."

Seamus did a mock bow.

"You're too good to me, Minnie. If it weren't for you, where would I go when I'm luring my secretaries into crime and deceit?"

Minnie just laughed.

"Oh, don't listen to him," she said, offering Maxwell another guava candy. "He's a very good man, helped us more than once. And that last secretary, well, it's not Seamus's fault he didn't duck when Seamus said to, is it? Young people these days—always complaining. He wasn't even in the hospital a month."

Seamus had made a point of showing Maxwell her office *after* she'd signed the contract.

As Seamus opened that second room's door back at his office, a jar of assorted ball bearings that had been balanced just so fell over and made their escape across the hardwood. Maxwell kept her poker face, although she was going a bit pale. To say it looked like a bomb had gone off was unfair—detonating a bomb in the centre of the mess would've been an improvement, and probably their best bet for cleaning.

"Your last secretary worked in here, huh?"

"Yes, but he quit a few months ago, and the situation has grown far more dire. Don't worry, there's a desk in here somewhere," he said with a vague gesture at the sea of chaos. "And there's a window, I believe. You can start cleaning—just be sure not to open any sealed boxes or files."

"Confidential?"

"If you're lucky. I'm something of a hobby chemist, and at some point, you'll run into my missing bottle of nitroglycerin."

Maxwell nodded. "Sure, boss. I'll put things down gently."

Seamus raised an eyebrow. "You're impressively good at taking things in stride."

"I've eaten a half-a-box of macaroni for breakfast, lunch, and dinner every day this past week. You ask me to bite off my pinky finger, it'll be, 'Left or right, boss?'"

"Excellent. One word of advice, though, Maxwell? In the back you'll find some black suitcases. *Don't* open those. Trust me."

Maxwell nodded and shut the door. Seamus left her alone for a few minutes to hunt for the suitcases.

Some lessons you have to learn the hard way.

Seamus opened the door again and found Maxwell standing very, very still. In her hand was a black case. It was lined with impact foam, and nestled carefully in the grooves in the foam were three different handguns, along with extra magazines. She didn't appear to be breathing.

"That was very predictable of you," he said. "I'll need to lock those up tonight." Seamus's voice was cool and light, with no threat in it. His eyes were hard on hers, though. "I appreciate initiative," he continued, "to a point. But this is a dangerous business, and if you want to work here, you're going to follow orders. For your own safety. Are we clear?"

Maxwell's head jerked up and down. Seamus smiled and left her to her work. She clasped the case closed and replaced it. She went back to stacking the boxes, very carefully.

If she didn't quit, she'd make a good secretary.

After Maxwell had left, Seamus stayed motionless at his desk, thinking about what he'd found on John Ryba.

It'd taken him an hour on LinkedIn, but he finally found the Ryba he recognized—a criminal defense lawyer who worked for the Greene family and was generally seen hanging at the edge of the courtroom like a hungry ghost.

And that meant he had valuable information to bring to Olexa Greene, who either ran or knew about every racket in the province, in exchange for her help finding a certain black briefcase.

Seamus didn't sleep well that night, either, but it was excitement that kept his mind turning as he lay in his thin blankets. A case, a paycheque, and a fun little side-murder to keep him entertained—life was looking up.

CHAPTER TWO

Seamus kicked out of his sheets, rubbed most of the grit out of his eyes, and got ready for his visit to the coroner's office. Maxwell wouldn't be in till ten, so he'd have a chance to brush up on the evidence before they paid a visit to Olexa and went to see Sandra's crime scene.

He walked to the coroner's with a smile on his face. It was kitty-corner to the police station and was everything the station wasn't: a squalid mess of orange brickwork and shoddy concrete that had looked outdated the day it opened. Seamus found it more comfortable than the station, and he never needed to resort to blackmail to get in: he was the best friend of the chief coroner, Elial Crimps, a position for which he had exactly zero competition.

Elial was one of those people who, through no obvious fault of their own, was just slightly repulsive. He was sallow and thin and smelled of embalming fluid. In his forty-two-year tenure at the coroner's office, Elial might have smiled twice. When they'd first met, Seamus had helped him track down a deadbeat, absentee ex-son-in-law, although in the end all Elial had wanted to do was send him a handwritten letter expressing the fact that he'd known, ever since his daughter had first brought the little bastard to dinner, that he was a spineless, worthless, brainless individual with genitalia well below the global average size, and here was the proof. Said son-in-law's furious reply had alerted the police to his location, and he'd had to start paying alimony. Seamus remained unsure whether this had been a stroke of genius on Elial's part or simply the universe's reward for bottomless spite.

Seamus also happened to forget a few thousand dollars cash in the autopsy room every few months, which no doubt strengthened the relationship.

The office's receptionist wasn't there, although given that she rarely came in before two, the question of whether she was truly late was a philosophical one. Elial was a perfectionist when it came to his own work and cared not one iota for anyone else's.

Seamus found Elial eating a sardine sandwich in the autopsy room, looking as though he hadn't moved all night.

"Good morning, Elial," he said with a sunny smile.

"It's not. What are you here for?"

"Sandra told me you had an amusing little homicide on your hands. Wanted me to take a look at it."

"That one." Elial inhaled sharply and popped a menthol cough drop into his cheek. "I've got some hospital sheets, sure."

"I'll take a quick look, if you're not busy."

Elial shook his head and made his way across the lab at a speedy limp. "Never busy."

All he had to look at were the bloody hospital sheets, kept at a chill four degrees Celsius. They were formerly hospital-green, now stained an uneven brown.

"Did they already run the DNA?" asked Seamus. There wouldn't have been any trouble getting a sample, at least.

"Matched the hospital samples. There's a fair bit of John Ryba in these sheets."

Seamus nodded as he unfolded them on a sterile examination table. Elial hovered at his shoulder, pointing at the odd splotch and rip.

"Killer covered the sheets with plastic bags and made up the blankets on top of it," said Elial. "That's how it went so long without anyone noticing."

"How bad was the decomposition?"

Elial sniffed, looking unimpressed.

"I've seen a lot worse. There was this one time in '97, we found a body that'd been sealed up inside drywall for a month—and this during July in the middle of a heat wave. Let me tell you, it was scorching—"

"I'm sure it was very exciting at the time. But about *this* murder?"

"Well, I figure twelve hours, by how dry the blood was."

Seamus nodded. There were two sheets—one that would've covered the mattress, and a heavier one that would've covered John Ryba, and which was hacked almost to shreds.

"You have a count on the slashes in the top blanket?"

"Twenty-three tears," said Elial. "Clustered in the middle, where his abdomen was, most likely. Some faeces mixed with the blood there."

"Delightful. Well, there are almost no cuts in the bottom sheet, so the weapon wasn't long enough to penetrate the body completely."

"That, or they didn't push hard enough."

Seamus shook his head. "You don't stab someone a dozen times unless you've worked up some enthusiasm for it. Judging by the cuts, I'd guess a knife, or another metal object with at least one sharp edge."

"Professionals go for the neck," observed Elial, looking over the bloody sheets the way someone else might scan a lunch menu.

Seamus nodded, his eyes abstracted. "So this was an amateur. You stab him in the stomach, maybe a hand over his mouth, he wakes up and starts struggling—" Seamus pointed to the tension tear at the corner of the top sheet "—so you panic and start jabbing away. I'd bet it took a few tries before they hit an artery."

Elial murmured agreement, though he'd drifted off to look at the corpse on the neighbouring table. He seemed to prefer the cadavers to his warm visitors: occasionally, he'd even pour them a cup of water or turn his portable TV around so they could watch.

Seamus spent a few more minutes inspecting the sheets, but there wasn't much to go on, and there wouldn't be until they had a body.

Back at the office by 10:10 a.m., Seamus only had to wait about fifteen minutes for his new secretary to walk in.

"Morning, boss. Sorry I'm late—TTC's got more delays, go figure."

"Don't you live five blocks away?"

"Sure, but if everyone else gets to be late this morning, why do I have to be on time?"

Seamus smiled and gestured for the door.

"Well, you can't blame a woman for walking a little slow to the gallows. Let's head out—we're paying the Greenes a visit."

Maxwell was fidgeting with her umbrella as she walked. She looked like she hadn't had anything to eat that morning, which was a shame—never smart to go to the battlefield on an empty stomach. Before seeing Elias, Seamus had cooked himself double rations of delicious, nutritious instant noodles.

"I really want to believe we're not doing this." Clearly, Olexa Greene's reputation preceded her.

"Even mobsters don't go around killing everyone they meet," said Seamus as he marched down the pavement. "It's perfectly safe."

They made their way to the financial district, and Maxwell discovered just how hard the wind could pull on her umbrella as it ripped between the glass-edged high-rises. Seamus was letting the rain run through his hair and over a broad smile. This sort of a day, there was no point in trying to stay dry or warm—the moisture in the air would let the cold damp creep up your sleeves and down your neck no matter what.

"Just follow my lead, Maxwell. Greene's owed me a favour ever since I busted some rival gun runners."

"I'm gonna get stabbed to death at ten in the morning. For twenty dollars an hour."

"Don't be ridiculous. It's closer to eleven."

Seamus stopped and sheltered under the stoop of a green-blue office building, and Maxwell followed his lead. His eyes turned serious.

"Just remember: Keep a level head. Don't say anything unless you have to. This office is her front—she'll be here to do business."

Maxwell stared up at the skyscraper, whose peak vanished into the grey rainclouds.

"This is just her front?"

"The bigger the scam, the bigger the front," said Seamus. "Just look at city hall."

Maxwell followed Seamus into the lobby, hanging back a few feet. A good idea normally, but useless in this case—Olexa's men would be on them before they made it five steps if they tried to run.

Both of them dripped small puddles onto the marble floor as they stood by reception. A young woman with an unusually long face sat behind a white desk, and Seamus walked up to her with a smile.

"We're here to see Ms. Greene."

The woman dragged her eyes up from her computer screen, looking deeply unimpressed.

"I don't have a 'Ms. Greene' in this building."

Old habits—he always asked for Greene by name at her old office. He'd first met her back when he was working collections, and she'd liked him even then, or more accurately hadn't disliked him enough to send one of her men to slit his throat.

"Sorry, my mistake. I'm here to see Vasco."

"Do you have an appointment?"

Seamus waved this concern away.

"I'm an old friend. Tell him Seamus Caron is here to see him."

The receptionist looked incredulous. Seamus leaned in slightly over the desk.

"It's Company business," he said, lowering his voice. "The password is labor omnia vincit."

The receptionist was suddenly stiff and pale. She grabbed her key card and hurried over to the elevator. "Twenty-second floor," she said, tapping the card against the scanner set in the wall. "Please have a nice day."

Seamus nodded to Maxwell, and they slipped into the elevator. Inside, Smash Mouth's "Everyday Superhero" played, interpreted as slow jazz. Seamus turned to her as soon as the doors closed.

"Olexa makes a point of keeping up appearances," said Seamus. "That's why we gained entrance with Vasco's name. Officially, this is The Knife's office." He gave her a warning look. "That password I used is private—if you like your internal organs *inside* your body, I'd advise against trying to use it yourself."

"Sure. Secret passwords. A gangster named The Knife," said Maxwell, her eyes flickering rapidly over the blank walls of the elevator. "I've got a whole list of things I wanted to do before I died, you know."

"Pessimism. The Knife isn't so bad. After a while, you don't even notice those red blotches on his suit."

The elevator doors opened with a ding, revealing the most coordinated room Seamus had seen in his life. The walls were white, patterned with a perfect navy grid. Everything was silver, white, or a single shade of dark blue. Standing across from them, looking at an easel set in front of a window onto the city skyline, was a tall man in a suit the exact same dark shade of blue.

The tall man looked back sharply as the elevator opened, twitched, then marched over to his desk and jabbed a finger into the intercom. His sharp, petulant voice carried across the room.

"Susan. Why have you sent these people up? I am not to be disturbed while creating. It is paramount to the process that—they're here to see mother?" The man in the suit gave a put-upon sigh. "Well, I suppose that's acceptable. Strive do better next time, Susan."

Continuing his extended sigh, he sank his thin frame into the chair behind the desk, staring off into the distance with an annoyed expression.

Maxwell leaned towards Seamus to whisper. "What the fuck is this?"

"Vasco 'The Knife' Greene," Seamus whispered back, with an air of mock solemnity. "Ever since Olexa's old club got busted on health warrants, her son's interior design business has been her front. Got his nickname when his cousins came back from a hit and found him mixing plaster for a modelling project. They say there isn't a man alive faster with a palette knife."

"I *hate* you."

Vasco didn't deign to look at them, but he gestured flutteringly in their direction.

"Mother's office is through the door to my left. I was in a perfectly lovely creative mood—if you leave quickly, I might be able to salvage some of it."

With that, he closed his eyes and started muttering a mantra, sounding way more annoyed than Seamus figured you were supposed to while you did that.

Maxwell and Seamus crept along the wall to the door on Vasco's left, which opened onto a room much closer in character for the Company. Behind a huge mahogany desk, half in shadow, sat Olexa, a tall woman with eyes like broken jade. She wore a dark tweed vest with a small gold star pinned to the front and was speaking to a huge man with deformed ears who crouched at her side to listen.

The giant was Trelly—Olexa's right-hand man and her oldest employee. He was Russian—*Trelly* being short for something containing a profusion of *y*s and *k*s—and a former Olympic heavyweight wrestler. A knee injury had ended that career for him—he'd proudly told Seamus that the man who'd given it to him couldn't walk to this day—and sent him into Olexa's employ, silver star glinting on his chest in the gloom. Seamus tried to avoid getting close to Company men, but he'd always gotten along with Trelly. There were few better sparring partners in all of Toronto.

Raising a hand to her employee, Olexa Greene stood up straight as a crossbow bolt.

"Detective. You've brought a new one."

Her voice was quiet and precise, with a slight rasp.

"Olexa. It's good to see you again. Are you free to talk? I have news."

Her hard eyes traced slow paths over them. Seamus wasn't sure how old she was—fifty, maybe, but it was hard to say. Most faces softened with age, but Olexa Greene's had hardened, like petrified wood.

"I assume you've come here on business," she said. "Speak quickly."

"Two things. Have you heard about a murder at East General?" asked Seamus.

"I haven't."

It'd been worth a shot. Even if Olexa hadn't called in the hit herself, she might've known who was behind it. But then, most murders were passion projects, not professional work.

"Well, you'll be wanting to hire a new lawyer. Some enterprising soul stabbed John Ryba to death two days ago."

Olexa didn't show surprise—such weakness was beneath her. But she held silent for the space of a breath.

"He was a good lawyer. A good man. We used him for some of Timmy's—indiscretions. I'll send roses to his wife."

"It's a dangerous profession, protecting your Company from the evils of law enforcement," said Seamus. His voice was light and teasing, but he kept his eyes on Trelly, who was rarely enthusiastic about any perceived disrespect to his master.

"What did you come here for, Detective?"

"Information, actually," said Seamus. "I thought we might arrange a trade. Useful to know someone's killed off one of your lawyers, hmm?"

"It might be. And what do *you* need to know?"

"A Tesla was stolen on Spadina a week ago," he said. "Some valuables went wandering—my client wants them back. Heard anything?"

Olexa's eyes flicked sideways for an instant.

"Down by Baldwin Street, there's a group of children. They've been known to take Teslas."

"Do they answer to you?" asked Seamus.

"Not yet."

Seamus nodded at Maxwell—time to leave. He turned to go but paused with one hand at the door. He could always feel when he held the advantage—it was a shift in the air—the way you knew it was time to throw a punch as your opponent's guard fell.

"You know, Olexa," he said casually, "whoever did Ryba is probably after more than just your lawyers. Have you considered that hiring a detective might benefit you?"

Trelly growled and got to his feet, looming over him and Maxwell. Olexa gave a smile that didn't quite reach her eyes.

"Why, Detective. Do you imagine we can't deal with this sort of thing ourselves?"

"I have no doubt you will get your revenge. The question is, can you do it before the killer does more damage? You know finding is my forte."

Olexa walked past her desk and drew close to the pair standing by the door. Maxwell looked like she wanted to fold in half, but to her credit she forced herself to meet Olexa's eyes. Seamus approved of that—cowering never made a good first impression.

"The new secretary?" said Olexa.

"That's me. I'm—my name's Maxwell."

"Your employer *is* very good at finding," said Olexa. She spoke in a quiet, toneless voice that was at once very convincing and oddly terrifying. "In my city, people who find too much often suffer accidents."

"Don't scare her," said Seamus with a smile. "I've stayed alive so far, and I'm hardly even trying."

"Your help is not required, Detective. But I'm grateful for the information. Leave now."

Trelly lumbered over to open the door for them—Seamus nodded to him as they left.

"Good to see you, Trelly."

He scowled in reply, and Seamus caught sight of a small crucifix hanging against his neck. Strange—when Seamus had first met him, Trelly'd been shaking down a priest who wasn't making his payments in a timely manner. The man, it seemed, contained multitudes.

—

Back in the elevator, Maxwell let out the breath she'd been holding for the last few minutes and leaned against the mirrored wall.

"Not so bad, right?" said Seamus.

"I thought I was gonna piss my pants," said Maxwell. "She's terrifying."

"Yes," said Seamus cheerfully. "She certainly is."

"Where does someone like her come from?"

"Upper management at one of the rings of inferno, I imagine," said Seamus. "To be honest, I don't know that much about her. Which is intentional on her part, no doubt. I know one story, though," he said as he slipped out the elevator doors.

"No one knows how old she is, except that it's older than she looks. That one story is about how the Company started—back when Olexa Greene was still in grade school at some Ontario conservatory. Apparently, she had a good head for business back then too, moving smut magazines and cigarettes in the hallways. One day a gang from the boys' school across the road came and tried to move in on her business—pushed her into the wall, told her they'd be in charge from then on."

"What'd she do?"

"Nothing," said Seamus, "for two years, until everyone had nearly forgotten about it. She did what the older boys said, worked under them. Did so well for herself that she had her own little gang of kids from both schools. She trained them up—Olexa always has her men ready for action. Those older boys who thought they were running the show started getting sloppy."

"Let me guess," said Maxwell. "She ended up getting all those boys who'd pushed her around expelled?"

"No. After those two years, she had her own gang to corner them in an abandoned soy sauce factory, line them up, and beat each of them half to death, one at a time. Broke both the ringleader's legs with a two-by-four—I'm told he never stood up again. And no one was willing to talk to the police—Olexa had scared them too well. That's how the Company got started."

Maxwell was pale again.

"Holy fuck," she said softly.

"Exactly."

Seamus walked out into the rain humming tunelessly. The falling raindrops were thin as knives and about as pleasant on the skin, and as Seamus watched the street, a cyclist skidded by on locked brakes, narrowly avoiding a heap of trash by the roadside. Sandra would be expecting him at the hospital in half an hour, and now he had something interesting to bring her. And there was always a certain thrill to be had investigating a murder.

They took transit to the hospital, and Seamus passed the trip trying to guess which other riders might be headed to the same destination. The woman with the cough? Or the man who couldn't seem to see properly as he stumbled onboard?

"Remind me why we're messing around with a murder case, boss."

"I owe Sandra a few lifetimes' worth of favours," he said, "and she thinks an old friend of my father's might be tied up in this one. This is just a sortie—we'll go and see what we can see at the crime scene."

The interior of the subway smelled of old clothes and wet steel, but Seamus was still happy to ride. There was something distinctly comforting about the worn red felt of the seats and the quiet sounds of three dozen people breathing the same air, and if you had to contend with the occasional violent drunk, it was still better than the slow, creeping despair of their destination.

Seamus and Maxwell walked north from Danforth, past the residential streets and the gardens that'd bloomed in the summer and were shutting themselves up, deep green and brown, to wait for the snow.

Sandra was, as ever, slightly late, and along with her usual faded denim she wore a bright yellow hat that sprouted from her head. Seamus was not remiss in noticing this.

"Interesting hat there, Sandra. Were they all out of pylons?"

She rolled her eyes. "Shut up. It was a gift from Michael. It grows on you."

"Like a fungal bloom. A police officer should be more cautious in a hospital—you know there are people at risk for a spook-related death in there?"

"You're the expert, Mr. Fashionista. See you've got your oilskin on—I guess stains are in this year?"

Seamus cleared his throat.

"In more important news, I've got a lead for you on Ryba. You know he's a criminal lawyer?"

"*Was* a criminal lawyer."

"Right. You happen to know who he represented?"

Sandra squinted at him—she was good at reading his expressions. In this case it was easy: Seamus's smile was pure schadenfreude.

"Fuck. He worked for the Greenes, didn't he? They kill him off?"

"Not as far as I can make out. But they had him on retainer—they'll be quite interested in whoever did kill him, I suspect. Better get witness protection fired up."

Sandra set her jaw.

"I'll dance with Greene if I've got to. But between you and me, I hope I don't."

That worried Seamus. Sandra was tough—possibly the only person he'd admit could stay on their feet longer than him in a fight. But she was just one person. The Company was an army.

"Let's not get ahead of ourselves. Better find a body before we start fighting over it."

In the east wing of the recovery unit, the only sounds were the rustling of sheets and the occasional optimistic beep of a heart monitor. John Ryba's room had been taped off, along with the whole hallway—a major concession to the police, given the resource strain of leaving even a single bed empty. The air conditioning was running on full blast, and being late fall it kept the room icy. Sandra explained that they'd cranked it up to keep the bloodstains from rotting, which the hospital might've complained about. There was a uniformed officer posted by the door, warming his hands with a cup of Tim Horton's finest—he smiled at Sandra and paled when he saw Seamus.

Both Seamus and Maxwell drew their coats tighter as they stepped through the door—the cold bit, all the worse because it seemed so wrong to be running the AC with winter bearing down. Sandra looked smug.

"Looks like the hat was a good pick after all," she said. "The colour keeps me extra warm."

"I'd rather die of exposure," said Seamus. "But speaking of heinous crimes, how was this place when you found it?"

Sandra flipped him off as she glanced around the room.

"Figure you've already seen the sheets at the morgue," she said. "We found those on the bed; nothing else has been moved. I'm gonna keep this place sealed up tight till we've got a lead on the body. What else . . . forensics found blood specks all over the floor, like you'd expect. Place was clean otherwise."

"Fingerprints or DNA?"

"Nothing that didn't match Ryba, the doctors, or the nurses."

"So the perp wore gloves."

Sandra stalked through the room, glaring at the spare upholstery. She was a good detective, but her strong suit was interrogation—and a knack for making suspects think they'd have to have their jaws wired if she didn't get what she wanted. Sandra never actually laid a hand on them, as far as Seamus knew, but she was good at looking vicious and unpredictable when she had to. Unfortunately, that talent meant that she occasionally tried to stare down crime scenes, usually with less success.

"Alright, Seamus," she said finally. "How did they get the body out?"

"Judging by the sheets, the killer was determined, but untrained and unprepared. Why would you carry a knife if you didn't know how to use it? I don't know how they could've gotten the body out without a plan."

"I say the body left the building," said Sandra. "But we've already done a search."

"It's inside a very large box," mused Seamus. "Possibly gift-wrapped. To be delivered to an unsuspecting child on Christmas Day . . . are you taking dictation, Maxwell?"

Maxwell was leaning against the wall, fiddling with the hand sanitizer, having worked out that this wasn't relevant to the case they were getting paid for. She raised a middle finger. "Screw off, boss."

Seamus just grinned.

Sandra called in the uniformed officer at the door, who bowed his head to her slightly.

"Double-check the closets on this floor," she said.

"We already did the double-check," he complained.

"Oh, my bad—I meant triple-check," said Sandra, her voice hard. "And ask the orderlies how often each one's used and if any have been closed for more than three days. I want a list of answers about all of them."

Seamus followed the officer out the door and tried to wave down a passing doctor. The doctor carried himself with his chest rounded out, walking slow and prideful, his hair neatly done, though for all that his face had a funny weaselly look to it.

"Excuse me, sir. Do you have a moment? I'm with the police. Is there a floor plan I can look at?"

The doctor looked annoyed. "Ask a nurse. I've got work to do," he said as he brushed by.

Maxwell materialized at Seamus's side. "What a dickhead."

"Show some respect," said Seamus, with a pointed look at her. "*Doctor* Dickhead, please."

He found a nurse who didn't have the luxury of walking slowly—she was hurrying down the hallway with a tray of surgical tools, but she paused when Seamus caught her eye.

"Hello, ma'am. Do you know where I could find a floor plan?"

"At reception," she said, settling her tray on her hip and continuing on her way. "We've got one for evacuations," she called over her shoulder.

Sandra had caught up, and as the three walked down the hallway. Seamus found the floorplan thumbtacked to a wall and leaned in to inspect it.

"I've told you not to say that you're police," Sandra said.

"I said I'm *with* police, which is technically true." She gave him a sharp look. "A slip of the tongue," he acquiesced, as they sidled up to the reception desk.

Sandra grunted. "Do it again, and you'll experience the slip of my boot into your shin."

Seamus chose that moment to become very interested in the floor plan. There wasn't much in the way of hiding spots: three supply closets that had already been checked. The fire escapes both appeared empty, and a quick whiff by Maxwell confirmed the absence of a decaying defense lawyer in either of them. Of course, Sandra would've told you that all defense lawyers fell somewhere on the spectrum of putrefaction—it was only a matter of degree.

"Not on this floor, then?" said Seamus, as they completed their double-check and made their way back to the crime scene. "Even if it was two people, carrying a body through the hospital would've been hard work."

"What if they used a gurney?" asked Maxwell.

"Good thought," said Seamus, "but this is the recovery wing. You'd get odd looks wheeling around a corpse with a knife in its chest."

Seamus walked over to the bloody cot, frowning. "That's the hardest thing about a murder, actually. Getting rid of the body. Unless you've got plenty of lye on hand—"

He looked up to see Maxwell had turned slightly green and decided not to finish that thought out loud. Sandra joined him in pacing the room, which was comforting—it brought back some rare pleasant memories of childhood.

"I say we rule out the body getting melted—this isn't another Orangeville, thank God," she said, and even Seamus shuddered at that. "They must've gotten it out somehow. We'll just have to keep an ear to the ground."

"They might have gotten a body out if they'd had a getaway car and a plan. But I'm sure this was impromptu work. When you've just landed that last stab and the thrashing suddenly stops, your first instinct is to tuck the body out of the way and hope for the best."

Maxwell caught that. "You speaking from experience, boss?"

"No comment." Seamus laid his hand on the pale green wall of the hospital, looking over the chipped and repainted drywall.

"This is an old building," he said to no one in particular. "It must've been remodelled . . . more than once. Is there any empty room or a stairwell that's not in the floor plans?"

Sandra shrugged. "Real estate ain't cheap here," she said. "Why leave a room empty?"

Seamus exhaled sharply, wrapping his coat tighter. He found himself thinking about another consideration for the aspiring murderer—the smell. A good half of all murder victims were found when someone called the city to complain about that godawful stench coming from the house down the street.

"An old building," mused Seamus. "Air conditioning—"

Seamus cocked his head, then started digging through his coat. In the breast pocket he found what he was looking for: a folding screwdriver. Maxwell moved forward, her eyes bright again. "You think of something?" she asked.

"It's an old building, with low-pressure HVAC," he said, as he hurried to the wall. "A main vent might just be big enough to—here we go—hold a body."

Seamus knelt to the floor, wrinkling his nose. The blood spatters may have been partially dry, but they weren't exactly fresh. He felt along the wall until he hit a ventilation grate—that was the best bet.

With his usual dexterity, he undid the screws holding the grate to the wall and pulled it off to reveal a duct just large enough for a man to wiggle into. Before Sandra could stop him, Seamus popped a penlight in his mouth and jammed himself in to the shoulders.

That might have been a mistake. It had been very faint in the room, but the smell of death was strong in the darkness of the duct: not just blood, shit and rot too. But Seamus wasn't one to retreat with the answer close at hand. He slid himself forward, penlight tight in his teeth as he inched along. He kept moving, in the dark, towards a bend in the tubing, until he saw a toe.

He felt bile in his throat; having trapped himself in a dark tube with a dead man may not have been his best move, but it was a victory nonetheless. He retreated, which was just as well, considering Sandra had a hold of his left leg and was trying to drag him back.

When he emerged he spat his penlight into his hand, glancing at the now blood-speckled shoulders of his jacket—that'd need a wash.

"So, what's my finder's fee?"

Sandra's eyes widened, then narrowed. "You didn't touch the body, did you?"

"This isn't my first rodeo, Sandra."

She broke into a smile at that and clapped a hand on his shoulder. "I've got to hand it to you, Seamus, you get results."

Sandra wasn't smiling once they saw the state of John Ryba's body. Some of the younger detectives had to leave the room to collect themselves. They'd called in most of homicide, as well as the forensics specialists. That was a hard crowd to shock, but this was a nightmare even to the men and women who made nightmares their profession.

Seamus, usually just as hard to faze, had to force his eyes onto the victim. All twenty-three stab wounds were visible in his abdomen, dried and swollen in death to purple lines. Seamus still didn't look away. If a man had had to die like this, he could stomach to look unflinchingly.

Sandra's face was rigid, but she shook her head at the body, as if to express her displeasure. "Well, that's a whole new can of worms," she said.

Seamus stood beside her. They were the only two in the crowd who kept their eyes on the corpse.

"Your friend Greene do this? Maybe Ryba found out a little too much about his clients?"

Seamus shook his head. "Greene's a professional. We'd never have found the body. The killer couldn't have known you'd put the air conditioning on—they got lucky. If someone had cranked the heat instead, you'd have found this days ago."

Sandra let out a frustrated puff of air. "This whole thing's damn weird. Man like that's got plenty of enemies, sure, but why kill him in the hospital? Whole lot harder than grabbing him off the street or waiting for him at home one night. And that's a lot of stab wounds for hired work, not to mention—"

"They hit the stomach, not the heart or the neck." Seamus nodded, considering.

A woman from forensics called to Sandra, who hurried over. Seamus looked around and realized he'd nearly forgotten about Maxwell, who was now out in the hallway. She was deathly pale, he saw as he approached her, and Seamus felt a pang of regret for letting her watch as the body was extracted.

"You alright?" he asked.

Maxwell swallowed and set her lips in a line. "No problem, boss. I can take it."

Clearly a lie, but Seamus could appreciate someone who was willing to push their limits. "If you say so."

Sandra came out into the hall, carrying a plastic baggie. "They found the knife."

Seamus quickly pulled a fresh pair of nitrile gloves from a breast pocket and onto his hands.

"How—how much do you keep in that jacket?" asked Maxwell, pointedly keeping her eyes off of the baggie.

"Everything. And a spare," said Seamus, as he turned back to Sandra. "Let me see that knife."

Seamus took the weapon delicately in his hands and held it to the light. It was a butterfly knife, with the handle folded up to conceal the blade. It was, oddly, very clean, although there was a waxy smudge of what Seamus suspected was human fat along the hilt. The anodized blade shone like a rainbow when Seamus eased it open, and the brass handles were covered with intricate carvings: Seamus caught names, faces, crosses, skulls.

"Thought you'd be more interested in the body," said Maxwell, her voice a bit steadier.

Seamus's eyes stayed fixed on the blade, smiling faintly. "A body tells you about the victim; a weapon tells you about the killer. The second's more useful."

The smile slipped.

"This doesn't make any sense, though. Those carvings—the owner must've done them, they aren't professional. The knife's well maintained, but it hasn't seen use in several years. Look at the patina forming on the brass." Sandra, leaning in close, nodded. Seamus caught a slight hint of the cedarwood oil she wore in her hair, a welcome relief from the stink of decomposing flesh.

"The pivot joint's been greased," said Sandra.

"And the scratches show it's been sharpened by hand," said Seamus. They'd been trading observations long before either of them had to do it for a living. Back in Wiarton, they'd toss them back and forth while they sat on hay bales or ran from some farmer who was overly attached to said hay bales. There'd been plenty to notice, even up north—a fresh bruise imperfectly covered by foundation, the bulge of a flask under a jacket, a widow's quiet smile at the funeral. Lots to notice, and good reason to pay attention: life was dangerous, and if you didn't watch it closely, it was liable to jump out from around a corner and gut you.

"The killer loved that knife," Sandra said.

"Someone with a sense of aesthetics," said Seamus.

Sandra snorted. "I sure didn't see much beauty in what they did to the poor bastard in the air conditioning vent."

"It's a performer's weapon," said Seamus softly. "But this was an efficient, ugly murder."

Sandra shook her head and turned back to the hospital room, now bustling with uniforms. "We'll know more when we get it to the lab."

The last of the senior detectives were arriving to glare at Seamus. He might have been untouchable with the chief's protection, but they couldn't hide that they didn't like him. Especially when he scooped them like this. Sandra was the only one, he found, who put solving the case ahead of her ego.

"I'm gonna give some orders," said Sandra, glancing at Seamus as if to warn him down. "Then I've got interviews. Potential witnesses. The widow."

"May I join you?"

"Sure, if you keep quiet and hang back."

Potential witnesses, thought Seamus. Olexa had been tight-lipped when it came to John Ryba, but it was her nephew who Ryba had most often represented: Timmy Greene. If there were a chink in the Company's armour, it was that perpetual screw-up. If memory served, he had seen Ryba at Timmy's most recent DUI hearing. Maybe dear nephew would have something useful for Seamus.

Seamus generally didn't think about anything else when there was a case turning over in his mind, so he didn't realize Maxwell wasn't all there until she stumbled down the main entrance steps as they were leaving the hospital and he had to catch her arm.

Seamus pulled her aside. "Feeling good there, secretary?"

"Sure. I just—haven't seen a body before. Not like that shit—gave me the shivers. Give me a few minutes to catch my breath, and I'll be fresh as a daisy."

Seamus gave her an appraising look. "Why don't you go home and get some rest? I don't need a secretary with me to listen to Sandra grill witnesses."

She bristled. "I'm fine."

Seamus gave her a droll look. "That must be why you're not walking straight." Determination was good, but not if you couldn't get the job done. He softened his voice: "I'll tell you what. I'll pay you full wages tonight to work from home, do some research on Timmy Greene for me."

Maxwell looked positively alarmed at this, but at least her eyes lost some of their glassiness. After a moment she nodded and stumbled off homeward, shoulders hunched.

By the time Sandra had finished giving her orders and come out of the hospital, night was falling. The hospital was busy—the hospital was always busy—but the sky was clear and quiet. Looking up, Seamus could make out the first stars. It would be a cold night, without any cloud cover to keep any lingering warmth of daylight trapped.

Sandra blew in her hands as they started walking, then stuffed them in her pockets. The yellow hat was gone, presumably stuffed in a pocket as well.

"Cold snap," she said. "Killer had a lucky break."

"Very lucky," agreed Seamus. "This'll be a hard winter."

"Good thing I like it cold," said Sandra, her breath curling white around her head. Seamus hated the cold, which Sandra knew well and delighted in reminding him of.

"You ought to put on your hat," said Seamus. "I didn't mean—"

Sandra gave a rough laugh at that.

"When in hell have I ever changed what I was wearing on account of your opinion, Trouble? But I've got to admit—the thing looks like it grew in Chernobyl. You were right. First time for everything, huh?"

Seamus grinned at her.

"That's a lot of lip to the person who just cracked your murder case wide open. When's homicide going to get around to firing the rest of your detectives and hiring me to work for you?"

"As soon as the mayor pulls together a few million to cover all the ethics suits you'd pull in."

"Frontier justice, Steady," said Seamus, trying for an Albertan accent. "You want to clean up this here town, you gotta get your hands a little dirty." Sandra grinned at him—she'd long been of the opinion that the only movies worth watching were old Westerns. She answered him in kind: "I'm the sheriff round these parts, Trouble. You'd best keep those irons in your belt and mosey along."

Seamus laughed. His mood was suddenly light, despite the horrors of the hospital. "You probably shot me at twenty paces in a past life. And don't worry, I'll tell Mike you loved your hat. Even if it isn't a ten-gallon."

"*I* wouldn't lie to my fiancé. I suppose it ain't my business what *you* do, though," she said with a wink. "Speaking of, we're thinking of a date next fall."

"Oh? Will I get an invitation?"

Sandra rolled her eyes. "You know I haven't got any other friends, don't make me say it."

"It would break Jackson's heart to hear that," said Seamus, picking his way over some fractured asphalt.

"Jackson likes everyone," she said. "Not like the two of us."

"I'm a friendly guy. Mostly."

Sandra laughed. "Can't lie to me, Seamus. You remember high school. Your valedictorian speech was just a half hour of insults. I'll never forget the look on Clyde's face when you pointed at him, Mom and Dad on either side, and said he was a brainless, spineless, heartless sonofabitch."

"Honesty is the best policy, Detective Blair."

Seamus could just make out Sandra's soft smile in the artificial twilight of the streetlights.

"We've had us some good times, huh?" she said.

"*I've* had good times. *You've* grabbed me by the collar and foiled all my plans."

"I've always held you back, Seamus." Sandra bowed her head in mock remorse. "If it weren't for me, you'd have gotten your way and been a bloody paste on the sidewalk years ago."

"I can admit that if it weren't for you, I'd be dead about ten times over by now. But I have the consolation that whatever happens to me, it'll be my own damn fault."

They were headed west, into the rich residential neighbourhoods nestled along the Don Valley. For the most part, they took residential streets, walking past blocks of soft-glowing windows, all shut tight against the cold.

There were three witnesses to interview, but first, there was Ruby Ryba. It was Sandra's habit to visit the next of kin herself. It was a courtesy—but Seamus also knew she'd gotten a few confessions when an allegedly loving parent or spouse cracked under the pressure of a surprise visit. For his part, family murders left a slight chill in Seamus's blood. It was one thing to get shivved in an alley—Seamus had tried it himself, in fact—but being smothered by your daughter in your bed held a special sort of horror. That said, when familial spite went far enough to make a person pick up the knife, the killing was usually well-earned. Sandra's parents, for instance, would've been greatly improved by a few perforations.

Ruby Ryba's house was perfectly ordered, from the porch furniture down to the pale lavender growing in the rock garden. Sandra absently plucked one of the flowers—the last, Seamus guessed, before the frost got them all—and crushed it slowly between her hands. It was a ritual he recognized from their childhood—when he caught sight of her face again in the twilight, she wore a look of sombre professionalism.

"Let's get this done, Seamus."

He rang the doorbell and was immediately answered by a tall, statuesque woman. She wore a blouse, a skirt, and a full face of makeup.

"Hello, Mrs. Ryba," said Sandra. "We've met. I'm Detective Blair. I just wanted to check in, see if you were doing okay."

The woman blinked and retreated into herself. "I've already spoken to the police."

"I understand," said Sandra, "and I don't want to give you any trouble. I just wanted to check in, and—"

The *blam* of the door slamming shut broke the stillness of the night and was swallowed by it just as quickly.

Sandra turned to Seamus with a sigh. "C'mon. Let's go."

Seamus answered quietly enough that nobody would be able to hear him through a shut door. "That's it? I'd say we could get some information out of her."

"She's mourning, Seamus. And I don't think she likes cops much—her husband was a defense lawyer, remember?"

Seamus calculated for a moment. Then he raised his voice: "I don't care what you say, Blair! That woman has a right to know the truth."

Sandra whipped on him, but the door clicked open before she could reach for his throat.

"Who are you?" Ruby Ryba was squinting at him. Seamus straightened his jacket and made a show of looking indignant, put some distance between him and Sandra. The glare she was giving him helped complete the scene, although he worried it might leave a burn.

"I'm a private detective, investigating the circumstances of your husband's death."

"Who hired you?"

"No one. I was a colleague of his," said Seamus, improvising. "John would hire me to gather evidence for his cases from time to time, and I've been lucky enough to call him my friend. Now he's gone, but I thought there might still be something I could do for him—so he could rest easy. You can't always trust the police to investigate the death of someone they considered an enemy." This with a pointed look at Sandra. "I'm sorry to say it, ma'am, but I found your husband's body today. I've been working with the police—though I can't say I approve of their methods. Very inefficient."

Ruby Ryba staggered, but she didn't fall. She held herself up on the door frame and nodded to Seamus. "I—thank you, Detective. Perhaps you'd like to come inside. I'd like to speak to you."

"Of course."

Seamus turned as he stepped through the door and winked at Sandra with his back to the widow. Sandra glowered at him as he entered the dim glow of the house and clicked the door shut gently in her face.

The interior was impeccably furnished, with tchotchkes and delicately displayed china lining every spare inch of space. A dozen red roses sat in the hallway, still wrapped in the florist's plastic, slowly dying of thirst. Seamus made it to the living room and took a seat amidst an assortment of cushions and throw pillows. Ryba sat opposite him, trying diligently to suppress her tears.

"I'm sorry for your loss, Mrs. Ryba."

"It's— I'll survive." She said. "I just haven't gotten used to the thought of him being gone yet. You said . . . you worked on cases with him before?"

Seamus gave her an apologetic look. "I can't tell you much more than that. Confidentiality, you understand. But when I heard his body hadn't even been recovered—well, let's not mince words. I was furious."

Ruby gave a sharp, bitter laugh, stifled as she pressed a Kleenex to her face. "So was I. How could they take so long? Oh, John."

Seamus nodded and made sympathetic noises. After taking another few moments to compose herself, she looked back up at him. The makeup, now running wet down the contours of her face, the perfect housekeeping—Seamus saw someone who was falling apart and trying to sew herself back together as it happened. Despite himself, he felt some sympathy for the enterprise.

"Are you going to continue investigating on your own?"

"I'm afraid it's not an option for me," said Seamus, arranging his face into a picture of regretful sincerity. "I want to see justice done here as much as you do, but I don't have the time or resources to run a full murder investigation on my own. Besides—"

"No. No, I need—*we* need—to find out who did this," said Ruby, a sudden intensity coming into her voice. "Listen to me. If you can find the man who killed John—would fifty thousand dollars be enough?"

Seamus started to make denials. Then he considered. Ruby Ryba had a very nice house, and life insurance payments to cash, most likely—she could afford some custom work.

"Well, Mrs. Ryba, I think something can be arranged. Is there anything you can tell me about your husband that might be relevant to the case?"

It took about twenty minutes, but Seamus walked out of the claustrophobic cleanliness of Ruby Ryba's house with a better picture of John Ryba's business, not to mention a lucrative new client. The last thing she'd said as he left caught in his mind: "Check his office," she'd told him. "I don't know if someone threatened him, but if they did—John always kept records of everything, in case he'd need them in court."

Seamus walked down the block spinning the keys to Ryba's office on his finger. Much easier when they just gave them to you—it saved you on picklocks.

He found Sandra on the street corner two blocks down. She was trying to glare at him, but Seamus knew his friend well—she wouldn't object to Seamus's methods if it meant a lead.

"How'd scamming the widow go?"

"I had to tell her something or neither of us would've gotten past that door."

Sandra snorted.

"Just make sure you tell me everything she tells you."

"Of course, Steady. I'll bring you up to speed on the way."

She pushed off the streetlight post she was leaning against.

"Can't argue with that. Let's get moving—we've got a little bit of night and a lot to do."

They walked south, away from the luxury of the valley houses and into the permanent noise of the city.

Two of the nurses who worked at Michael Garron lived in the same apartment complex by the lake, and the one who'd found Ryba was across the street, just north. The neighbourhood was in the east end, at the edge of the water, where the smell of algae and the water treatment plant rolled off the lake along with a wind that stirred the crushed coffee cups on the beach. A place for people who made a living but couldn't afford a place anywhere you'd really want to live. Sandra's badge got them past the front desk, and Seamus memorized the addresses she pointed out.

In the elevator up, he turned to her. "What are we dealing with here?"

"Jim Taylor and Selena Garcia," she said. "We've got Mariah Lopez in the next building over."

"Lopez. The one who called in the alarm, right?"

"Yeah. Seeing all that blood must've been a shock, and her colleagues say she's been sick for the last few months. She's just quit."

They met Garcia first: a rotund woman with puffy eyes in her late fifties. She was excessively polite and eager to please, which probably meant she'd hidden something illegal on the premises. Seamus did see an interesting baggie of mushrooms on the counter, before she hastily covered them with a tea towel. But neither he nor Sandra had the time to torment aging hippies, and Selena relaxed once she realized their visit wasn't a raid. Unfortunately, she didn't have anything she hadn't given them in her original statement.

Taylor was a tougher nut to crack: he wouldn't even open the door until Sandra put her badge up to the peephole. Once they got in, he answered in monosyllables and wore a permanent angry squint, whether it was Sandra asking if he'd seen anything or Seamus commenting on the weather. He all but pushed them out the door. Once they heard the bolt thrown, Sandra sighed and leaned back against the slightly grimy wall.

"Fucking door duty. No one saw anything, everyone hates cops. Always the same old story."

"Do you think Taylor seemed suspicious?"

"Nah, just seemed like he had a stick up his ass. But we saved the best for last—got an actual witness to interview."

The apartments on the other side of the freeway were slightly brighter, if just as cramped. Sandra's knock at the door was answered with a slow, limping walk, and when the door creaked open, Sandra and Seamus both looked down—Mariah Lopez was a head shorter than either of them, smiling up with warm, lined eyes.

"Hello! How can I help, officers?"

"I'm the only officer," Sandra clarified. "He's my associate. I'd just like to ask you a few questions. Are you Ms. Lopez?"

She chuckled as she waved them inside.

"Please, Detective. Call me Mariah. I remember you now—I saw you at the hospital. Would you like something to eat? I have some candies . . . or something to drink?"

"No, thank you," said Sandra, as Seamus slipped in behind her. "I understand you've worked at the hospital for the last few years?"

Mariah made agreeable noises and, undeterred by Sandra's refusal, went to fetch an ancient tin of butterscotch and a bottle of Coke from the kitchen. Seamus scanned the apartment: the furniture seemed like it had all been thrifted twenty years ago, but it was lovingly maintained, cracks and tears carefully plastered over with scotch tape.

The contrast to the Ryba household struck Seamus. This was a place worn bare by necessity, the sort of house that was usually empty while its inhabitants were out trying to earn enough to keep it. There were traces of care—ancient lines marking a child's height on a door frame, pictures of friends, and, inexplicably, a collection of colourful rocks and minerals in little plastic and glass bottles. Seamus picked one up, crystals glinting gold under the fluorescent tubes overhead.

"Pyrite?"

Mariah glanced over, looking slightly embarrassed.

"I collect them," she said. "Rocks, minerals. Ever since I was a girl, I loved them. Even wanted to be a chemist when I was younger. Nursing's good work though—good to help people."

Seamus nodded, carefully replacing the sample in its glass ampule. His eyes drifted over the wall and the dustless framed photos that hung on it. There was one in particular that caught his eye—a beautiful woman and a man with hooded eyes and a small child smiling between them.

"Yes . . . good to help people," said Mariah as she limped back from the kitchen and settled heavily on the faux leather couch, "I worked at the hospital this last seven years. I took a break, when I first got sick, but I went back, of course."

"I'm sorry to hear—"

"Oh, it's nothing, nothing. I'm only old, that's all." She smiled, all her teeth still in place, worn though they were. Seamus narrowed his eyes at her slightly—she was lying. It was a liver illness, judging by the yellowness of her eyes and her cracked fingernails, and an advanced one, the bilirubin stains deep in her skin. But she wasn't yet frail: he'd seen cases like hers. The body remembered the strength of youth and didn't surrender it easily.

Mariah's eyes alighted on his, and her grin sharpened.

"Ah, you're staring at me, young man. Do I seem very suspect?"

Seamus was surprised, but he covered it with a smile.

"No, not at all. You remind me of someone, that's all."

"Oh? I've often been told I look just like that one actress, Vergara," she said with an air of grave seriousness, throwing her hair to one side. Then she smiled and gave a loud laugh, and Seamus found himself smiling with her. Mariah leaned forward, a flashing intelligence in her eyes.

"You aren't an officer? Just an 'associate'?"

Seamus nodded. "I'm a consultant but not a member of the force. I'd be happy to wait outside if you'd like to talk privately with Detective Blair."

Mariah waved that away. "No, no. Stay. Have a butterscotch, Mr. Associate. Do they pay you well?"

"Only in favours."

Mariah *tsked* at that.

"I was paid like that, too, once. Groceries: you can't buy them with favours."

"Seamus doesn't need groceries," said Sandra. "He gets by on bourbon and instant noodles."

"I live off the suffering of your homicide detectives. And my clients. And secretaries."

"Right," said Sandra with a crooked grin. "Can't forget your main nutrient source."

"Ah!" said Mariah, clapping her hands together. "I see. You brought your boyfriend, Detective? That's not against the rules?"

Sandra flushed and looked down. Seamus would've once ribbed her about that, but he knew it would bother her that anyone was thinking it now that she had a fiancé.

"No, Ms. Lopez. He's just a colleague. But we came here to talk about you—at the hospital, they said you just quit?"

"Oh, I have some trouble getting up in the morning," said Mariah, looking faintly embarrassed. "You know how it is. I have money saved—enough to retire, I think."

Sandra nodded. "It's too bad you had to retire in these circumstances. The people I spoke to at the hospital all said you were an excellent nurse and coworker. But I can understand why you'd want to leave. Must have been a shock, seeing a murder."

"Well, I only saw the blood."

Sandra liked her little traps, but it looked like Mariah was nimble enough to avoid them. "We found the body just today."

Mariah pursed her lips. "Very sad news. He was a successful man, yes? Very sad."

Seamus nodded. "We just visited his wife. She . . . found it difficult to accept that he was gone."

Lopez's eyes widened, and she looked down at her folded hands. "It is hard. I lost my husband ten years ago. I know."

"Do you have any children?" asked Seamus.

"Ah, I had a son. He passed two months ago, God keep him."

"I'm so sorry to hear that."

Mariah smiled, face tight with pain, and shook her head, closing that line of questioning.

After allowing a moment's pause, Sandra continued, her voice soft: "Did you notice anything out of the ordinary, the day it happened?"

"No, everything was normal. I told your police before. I didn't see him in bed, but I thought he was at the toilet. He was only on light monitoring."

"When you pulled the sheets back, did you move anything? Was there anything on the floor?" Sandra leaned forward. Seamus smiled inwardly to see it—she kept her voice calm, and it took someone who knew her well to see that she was practically vibrating with curiosity.

Mariah just shook her head again. "No, no. And I would have noticed, I've worked there so long. Everything was clean. Maybe the bed was made wrong? I thought, at first, that the man had made it, so I didn't think it was so strange."

Sandra deflated a bit but nodded to Mariah. "Alright, that's all, then. Thank you, Ms. Lopez. Please call me if you remember anything else."

She smiled at both of them.

As he and Sandra stood, Seamus drained his Coke and smiled back. "You take care, Ms. Lopez. I hope you feel better."

"Such a nice young man. Tell his wife for me, things get better. In time. She should see her friends as much as she can. And be careful walking home—the city isn't as safe as it used to be."

They left her apartment and took the elevator down to the deserted lobby. Sandra stood there a moment, looking out into the inky night.

"Lopez was right," she said, watching a hollow-eyed man shuffle endless figure eights through the dark outside. "Not a neighbourhood for a stroll at night."

"We're the two worst things you could run into," said Seamus cheerfully, "and I have three and a half illegal firearms hidden in my jacket in case I'm wrong."

"One day you'll run into a cop who takes you seriously. I'll bring you stamps and smokes on visitation days."

"If there's one thing you should know by now," said Seamus, "it's that you should take *everything* I say seriously."

The walk home was windward facing, and Seamus arrived at Jackson's with his cheeks scraped red by the cold air and road salt, Sandra rubbing her arms at his side. Seamus tapped the bar with numb fingers, and Jackson spun nimbly around to snap a shot glass of something clear onto the bar in front of him.

"This'll warm you up, Seamus!"

Seamus reached for the glass, and the grimace that came on as he knocked it back developed into a full-body shudder. "We've already got a stabbing to deal with," he said, "what makes you think we want a poisoning on our hands too?"

"I just got it in," Jackson protested. "It's the latest from LA."

"Ungodly. Is it . . . mustard-flavoured vodka?"

"Hotdog, actually."

"It's a wonder we let you near the drinks at all."

Sandra rapped her knuckles on the bar.

"I want something to warm up as well. It's too cold for beer tonight."

Seamus and Sandra sipped bourbon, and Jackson polished his glasses. Seamus sat in silence for a time, turning the facts of the Ryba murder over in his mind. When he spoke, his eyes stayed fixed on the bar in concentration. "Ruby Ryba was willing to put down a lot of money to find out who killed her husband," he said. "I think we can rule her out as a suspect. That leaves someone with a connection to him from work—an unhappy client, maybe."

"I've already pulled files on every former client on his register," said Sandra. "I figured there might be some recent releases with a grudge, but the man was good at his job. Everyone he represented in the last ten years got off not guilty, or with a slap on the wrist. You don't kill your lawyer 'cause he got you community service."

"Then it's someone who thought he was doing his job *too* well."

"Could be. But there's something about all this that doesn't fit right," said Sandra, frowning into her glass. "Gang war usually means the leaders go down, not the lawyers. Either Greene was lying to you when she said she didn't know who did it or this is a whole lot more complicated than some rival trying to hamstring the Company. Anyway, you've gotten us started, finding that body—I'll buy you some Pocky." That was a surefire bribe for Seamus. "I've gotta get going. Michael's coming to pick me up."

"Good luck with the wedding planning, Steady."

"Got my eye on this one dress. You'd like it."

Seamus couldn't recall anything Sandra wore that she didn't look quite nice in, but this wasn't the occasion to say that. The door swung open, and in walked a tall, slightly paunchy man in jeans and torn plaid, winter rain soaking through the carefully worn-out shoulders of his jacket. He crossed the bar with a light step and kissed Sandra.

"I missed you."

"You saw me this morning, idiot," said Sandra with a smile.

"I'm still allowed to miss you," Michael said with a pout.

"Well, miss me some more. I've gotta hit the can before we go."

As Sandra got up for the washroom, Jackson came over with a smile. "Michael! Get you a drink?"

"I'd love one. A Perrier would hit the spot."

Jackson kept smiling, although Seamus could swear he heard his teeth grating together. Seamus, for his part, gave Michael a smile and raised his glass in greeting.

"Not drinking?" Seamus asked as Michael took his seat at the bar. "You've got my respect."

"Oh, it's not that. Between you and me—" he said, affecting to lower his voice, "—I'm not sure the glasses here are always clean. I found a spot on mine last time."

Seamus made himself grin and nod. Seamus had never understood Michael's appeal, but he trusted Sandra's judgment if he trusted anyone's, and he *tried* to be civil.

"How's the anthology coming, Michael?"

"Oh, it's slow work. Not easy. Just the other day I had to throw out three poems. It was a major setback."

"Sorry to hear that."

"Well, I have to bear it. These kinds of struggles really enliven my verse—I've always thought that a poet's got to *lead* a great life, not just write about one."

"Is that so?" Seamus said and knocked back the last of his bourbon. Jackson, doing his part to keep the conversation rolling, poured him a double as soon as the crystal hit the bartop. "You should talk to

Sandra about her work—there's lots of interesting material there. We were just investigating a lawyer's murder. Ever heard of John Ryba?"

"Well, I tend to avoid that field. Law is so stilted," sniffed Michael. "What was it Wordsworth said? 'Poetry is the spontaneous overflow of powerful feelings'. Writing has to be organic, above all else. It's that philosophy, as a point of fact, that won me fourth place at the Tobermory Writer's Derby . . ."

Seamus stopped listening and began noticing things to pass the time—Michael's black beanie, that awful plaid jacket, and a single black earring—he knew from experience that Michael rarely needed a response once he got started on the topic of his accolades. There were odd smudges on his neck, Seamus noted, some of them blue. Intrigued, he stood abruptly.

"Michael, it's too hot in here, let me grab that coat for you."

Michael shrugged off his jacket and turned to continue talking at Jackson, who was looking a little battle-weary.

As Seamus took the jacket from Michael, he took a closer look at the marks on his neck, blue smudges of what looked like paint. The fact they were only visible on the back of his neck suggested he'd made a conscious effort to wipe them off. As he crossed the room to hang the jacket on a coat hook, Seamus investigated further: the same bright blue stained the collar of his coat. When he quickly ran a finger along the stains, they came off on his skin, waxy. Not paint, then—some sort of makeup. He paused for a moment and glanced back at Michael, who was still engrossed in his own story. Sandra was in the washroom, and she'd be a few minutes. Seamus ran a deft hand through the pockets of the coat, feeling a phone, loose receipts, and two sets of keys. One he recognized by touch, Sandra's apartment keys with a little quill keychain Sandra had given him. Pulling out the other, he saw a flimsy pink plastic tag that read *23 Carlaw Ave*. Seamus memorized the address, replaced the keys, and hung the jacket on an empty hook.

Michael remained oblivious, which was hardly shocking.

After a moment, Sandra came out and said goodnight to the bar, and the couple walked off into the night, Michael's arm around her waist.

"Jackson," said Seamus, after they'd left, "give me a hot chocolate."

"You want something in that?"

"Marshmallows."

"You alright? The last time you asked for marshmallows, the Costa Ricans had broken three of your ribs." Jackson narrowed his eyes slightly. "Michael getting you down?"

"You could say that."

Seamus drank his chocolate in silence. It was good, though lacking in marshmallows. Back in the day, Sandra'd come over to his house fairly often. She'd liked to try to cook for him and Ma, but all she knew to make was hot chocolate, and twelve-year-old Sandra'd never seen the necessity of adding sugar. Ma drank it straight, uncomplaining, but Seamus had got in the habit of stuffing his mug with marshmallows to compensate.

He was only vaguely aware of Jackson watching him with interested eyes—he had too many other things to think about to be much concerned by it.

When he left, it was with his jacket zipped up tight to his neck, moving down the street without seeing it, completely preoccupied.

Seamus didn't recognize the address on those keys. It might've been something harmless, but Seamus was in the business of secrets, and instinct told him Michael had something he wanted to hide.

And that meant Seamus was going to find out what it was.

Back at the office at last, with the lights out, he nestled his blanket between Maxwell's piles of junk. He didn't fall asleep easily.

CHAPTER THREE

Lauren was making pancakes.

The smells of caramelizing sugar and browning flour hung sweet in the air, pulling Seamus out of the daze of sleep, along with the sunlight that came sifting through the living room windows. He woke slowly, calmly, his heart steady in his chest, and pulled his hands out from under the cream covers. When he curled them into fists it was soft tan skin that pulled taut over his knuckles, not layers of silver scars and arcing veins.

Seamus kicked off his blankets—he'd fallen asleep on the couch—and stumbled over to the kitchen, where he found Lauren cheerfully prodding pancakes on the stove.

Lauren's face had a blurred look, but not from lack of memory—he'd recalled her so many times the memory had bleached and faded. She towered over him, although a distant bit of Seamus's mind realized she should've been a good deal shorter. Her voice rang clear and familiar.

"Morning, Trouble. Sleep well? Sandra there's already got herself some breakfast—why don't you join her?"

Something moved Seamus's legs to continue to the kitchen, where he'd find Sandra with a gap-toothed grin and an unbroken nose.

Maybe he'd even see his father there, or Ma, as she was back when she smiled.

Seamus shook himself, and the dream wavered. He drew anger about himself like armour and counted the fingers on each hand, feeling his vision sharpen as he did.

Lies, illusions, comfort: weak men needed them. Not Seamus. He gritted his teeth and forced his eyes open.

All at once the dream dissipated and he was staring up at the ceiling of his office in that special darkness that you only saw an hour before dawn. Seamus sat up in his sheet and rubbed his eyes.

It had been a long time since he had dreamed of Lauren. Those had been terrible nightmares back in the day, on waking if not in the dream itself, but time had run on. Either the wound killed you or it closed in the end, and Seamus had been alive long enough that that grief had long since scarred over. He had work to do on the Williams case, which he ought to finish off before he got any further tangled in the murder.

Two hours at the gym burned off the lingering scraps of the dream and put him in a much better mood, and he made it back to the office only to have to wait for Maxwell, who at last wandered in at ten thirty, explaining that her washing machine had sprung a leak

They walked downtown, arriving at the locale Olexa had given him in time for an early lunch. Unfortunately, this being the start of the lunch rush downtown, the best he could find was a set of worn cement steps beside an overfull ramen restaurant on Baldwin. They sat on the cracked pavement with their disposable chopsticks, peeling the soft plastic lids off their bowls. Seamus set to work on a bowl filled with extra-thick noodles, pork-fat broth, and, at his request, three times the standard quantity of pork. University students flitted around him and Maxwell, eating and flirting and giving a wide berth to the strange pair eating on the steps.

"Tricks of the trade, Maxwell: enough sodium chloride will get your blood flowing better than any amount of caffeine."

Maxwell stared as Seamus attacked the delicious mountain of noodles.

"Christ, that'll plug your arteries. You eat in the last week?"

"Barely. And I need the calories. Things could get tense in the next few minutes."

"How are you gonna find them, anyway? Greene barely told you anything."

"She told me exactly as much as the information I brought her was worth—she's strict like that. But I've already heard of a little pseudo-gang out of Baldwin. Small-time kids."

They seemed to be college dropouts, mostly. Rogue engineering nerds turned petty thieves. Seamus had overheard Sandra complaining about a colleague having to track down some idiots who'd hacked the public library websites, which had also been traced to an apartment on Baldwin. Seamus had suggested the death penalty: in his opinion, anyone who caused trouble for the public libraries was a demon out of hell and ought to be returned there. His views hadn't prevailed with the prosecutors.

"Jacking Teslas isn't small time," observed Maxwell, turning a beansprout with her chopsticks.

"I suspect Olexa Greene would agree with you. She'll be offering them employment soon enough—not her usual line of work, but she's never been one to let the trends get ahead of her. Very forward-thinking woman, Ms. Greene."

"And if they say no?" asked Maxwell.

"I hope they don't. The suicide rate's high enough as it is."

Seamus and Maxwell finished lunch and made their way to the apartment slowly—Seamus was letting his noodles settle, and he suspected Maxwell didn't mind taking her time walking into trouble.

The building itself was small, probably crammed with students. Seamus pushed open the front door to reveal an expanse of wall-to-wall carpet that stank of mould and grain alcohol and stale Chinese takeout. Behind a plywood desk sat a grizzled landlord who smelled about the same, with just a touch of desperation added into the mix. Seamus sold him on a story about meeting old friends, and they made it into the elevators. Seamus wasn't picky when it came to music, but the techno blaring from the speakers jangled even his nerves. Maxwell winced and covered her ears.

"God, this stuff's horrible. The baseline is way too high—sounds like they produced it on a two-bit synth."

This was interesting—evidence of that music degree—but Seamus found himself wondering about the gaping hole in her résumé too. Something to do with the music industry, but why keep it a secret? He'd figure that one out sooner or later, regardless of Maxwell's opinion on the matter.

But he silenced those thoughts for the moment—the next few minutes would be delicate, and he needed to stay sharp.

The fledgling hackers had rented a large unit on the top floor. Maxwell raised her eyebrows when she saw the door left slightly ajar.

"That looks like a trap, boss."

"Maxwell, these young idiots spend their time on video games, porn, or some ungodly combination of the two. I'm not surprised they'd forget to lock the door."

He knocked hard, forcing the door to swing in, and winked at his secretary.

"Always knock first. Makes it not-trespassing."

He heard her mutter some disagreement, but his thoughts were already with what they'd find in the apartment. If he found *anything* illegal, that meant leverage, and the possibility of actually recovering Williams's briefcase. Seamus cleared his throat.

"Hello, there! Anybody home? My associate and I are conducting a poll for the National Anime Society, and we need just a minute of your time."

There was a slight wheeze from deeper in the apartment. Seamus stepped in, ignoring Maxwell's glare.

"You hear that, Maxwell? We've been invited inside."

As he walked into the living room, the friendly smile he'd been wearing slid off his face. The place was a catastrophe. Scattered around him were the ruins of several pizzas, boxes overturned and crushed into the floor. No fewer than six near-empty litre-bottles of Mountain Dew were dripping their dregs into the shag carpeting, and a seventh had been thrown through a computer monitor. Two keyboards were snapped clean in half, letters scattered across the floor like the world's most vicious game of Scrabble.

"Something's wrong here."

Maxwell had elected to follow him in, and he could almost hear her eyes rolling. "No shit, Sherlock."

"I'm serious. This place hasn't just been ransacked—someone's gone off the rails. I've seen things like this with PCP users. Get ready for a fight."

"What—"

Seamus bent his knees slightly and put his weight on his back foot, moving into the old stance he'd learned first from his mother, then refined in a dozen Muay Thai gyms and more street fights than were worth remembering. He counted his fingers—a quick gesture to steady him before a fight. From one of the rooms off to the left was the faint sound of dialogue, someone talking too fast and too low.

Seamus called out again: "Is there anybody home? We're here if you need help."

The murmuring continued without a pause.

Maxwell drew in close and whispered to Seamus, "Do you have a gun?"

He shook his head. He did, in fact—a small, illegal automatic pistol he kept hidden in his inner chest pocket. But he wasn't about to draw it. If they found someone who'd gotten high as a kite and lost the plot, a gun would only make things worse. And Seamus didn't want to deal with a manslaughter rap at the moment.

"We'll talk them down. Speak slowly. And if he comes at you, watch for the teeth."

Maxwell swallowed and nodded.

Seamus knocked on the door the muttering was coming from behind. He made his voice as gentle as he could. "Hey there, are you alright? Do you need help?"

There was an indistinct murmur in response.

He pushed the door open, hands not in fists yet but up at his chest, poised to dance back and shatter someone's jaw the second that someone charged him. But once he took in the room, Seamus let his hands fall to his sides.

"Shit."

The bedroom was devastated, worse than the common room: broken glass that had once been a coffee tabletop poked out of the carpet along with scattered bits of shredded computers. Curled up in a corner was a pale young man, mostly naked, his head against the wall. His eyes flashed back and forth, his breath came in gasps, and a disturbing amount of blood spread from his nose to his bare chest.

Seamus's first thought was that it served him right—chase your high and OD in the corner if that's what you want, it was none of his concern—but he pushed it away. Those were old memories talking.

Instead, he gritted his teeth and knelt by the young man, who shivered as Seamus came close but didn't pull away. At least he was alive.

"Hey," said Seamus. "Can you hear me?"

He shivered again. Seamus eased the kid's head to the ground.

"Maxwell. You've got a phone, right?"

Maxwell blinked hard, twice. "Yeah. Yeah, I'll call an ambulance."

"Do that, then go to the kitchen and get water." Seamus pulled a thin pair of nitrile gloves out of one of his pockets as he spoke. "I know a thing or two about toxicology. I'll see if I can figure out what happened."

Seamus scanned the young hacker, little more than a boy, and felt a reluctant bit of sympathy. The kid was shivering, his pupils dilated and his skin bloodless pale. Might've just been blood loss, though. When Seamus felt the boy's hand, it was hot enough that Seamus flinched back. The holes in the drywall nearby matched the newly forming scabs on the hacker's fists, and his fingers were discoloured, purple-blue at the tips. Very odd.

Maxwell ran back in with a grimy glass full of water. Seamus propped the boy against the wall, and he managed to stay sitting up. Although he was shaking too badly to hold the glass, the hacker gulped water when Maxwell raised it to his lips.

"Medic's gonna be here in ten minutes," said Maxwell. Her eyes were wide as she stared at the streaks of blood running from the boy's nose, but her voice was steady enough. "We should haul ass. Ambulance can take care of this dude."

"No need. I have a story for the paramedics. You take care of him while I look around."

Seamus surveyed the room. A faint smear of white on the floor caught his eye, and he crouched to trace swirls of it over the carpet. Flipping over a shredded pillow, he found a vial, unsealed and half-full of white powder, and left it where it was on the floor. He moved to dig under a few IKEA pillows and a mountain of bedding.

Behind him, the boy moaned slightly, and Maxwell's voice murmured, "You'll be alright. It's, uh, it's not that much blood."

Her bedside manner left something to be desired, but Seamus had more pressing concerns. He bent down farther, and a glint of chrome caught his eye.

Beneath the overturned couch was a small black briefcase with silvered clasps. Seamus drew it up with a quick motion, making sure his body blocked anyone's view. He doubted the boy would remember this, but there was no point in taking the risk.

Maxwell's voice came from behind him, more nervous this time. "Any idea what to do with this guy? He's getting worse."

"I've always found that chamomile helps me relax."

"Great, thanks."

His back to them both, Seamus flipped the briefcase latches, which were sharp-edged with burrs, as if the locks had been forced with a screwdriver.

Inside were thirty-four plastic vials, lab-grade, unlabelled, filled with a white-pink powder. Nothing Seamus could identify on sight, meaning he still had work to do. He weighed his options: he'd get paid if he returned the briefcase empty to Ms. Williams, and he'd avoid any legal discomfort that might arise from moving drugs himself. And if this was what had put the hacker they'd found into his current state, it was probably for the best that whatever this was didn't hit the streets. Seamus carefully took the vials out and laid them in a pile on the floor, partially covered with a blanket, where they'd be easy to find once the police arrived to search the place. He did that with each vial except the last, which he tucked carefully into his padded breast pocket beside his pistol. Then he turned back to Maxwell, who was trying to keep the boy from sliding down the wall with limited success. He'd stopped making noise and was shivering violently. After a moment, Seamus sighed, picked up a greasy hoodie from the floor, and wrapped it around the kid.

"Do you recognize these symptoms, Maxwell?"

"I mean, PCP gives you a fever."

"It's not PCP, not with those blue fingers. Something's wrong with his respiratory centre. Could be an underlying disorder, but I've never seen anything like it before—"

Seamus was cut off by three sharp raps at the door.

"Paramedics! We're coming in!"

"Don't say much, Maxwell," said Seamus. "Just follow my lead."

Seamus ruffled his hair and put on a worried look.

"Thank God you're here! We were just conducting a poll for the National Anime Society when this man called for help—"

After about fifteen minutes of questioning, Seamus and Maxwell strolled out the way they'd come in. It was possible the landlord would've contradicted their stories, but he'd made himself scarce as soon as he'd heard about the possibility of an overdose on his property. No one would have found the cache of drugs just yet, and Maxwell and Seamus wouldn't even be suspects by the time the police were involved. Likely, the paramedics would mention something about helpful strangers, and no one would miss a briefcase they weren't looking for—the briefcase that Seamus kept tucked under his coat as they left the apartment and didn't take out until they were four blocks away, under a cluster of chestnut trees.

He and Maxwell continued on their way towards the office, pushing through what had started as rain and since turned into a bone-chilling mist.

"So, what was he on?" asked Maxwell. She looked shaken but had recovered enough to be worrying about her boots as she dodged puddles and mud.

"It wasn't any ordinary downer. His body temperature was extremely high, which isn't normal for opiates. And his blood oxygen was low—blue fingers tell you that, but I also saw it when the paramedics put the monitor on. Low blood oxygen even though his breathing was unobstructed. The strangest thing is that the wounds on his hands were scabbed over, and the pizzas were dry—I'd estimate at least eight hours between him wrecking the place and us finding him. No pharmaceutical I know of would produce an altered state for that long without a second dose—and why would you take another hit when the first one did that to you?"

Maxwell was staring at him.

"How d'you know all this stuff, boss?"

"I went to med school. Way back when."

"Wow, can't imagine you being a doctor."

Seamus's smile hardened. Out of high school, Seamus had worked his way through university and signed up for med school out of a strange sort of compulsion: Possibly a desire to prove that he could survive what had destroyed his father. Possibly because he liked the idea of playing God. Either way, he'd realized that it was a mistake after burning through three years of his life and all his savings. While he was on rotation, a man had come into the ER with a broken fifth metacarpal. It was an injury familiar to Seamus—often called a boxer's fracture, you got it by punching something hard enough that the bones in your hand broke if you hadn't trained properly. The man's wife had come in too, with a broken jaw, and adamantly refused to speak to a social worker, begged them not to call the police. Her husband loved her, you understand, and she'd just fallen down the stairs, clumsy as usual.

Seamus's supervisor had explained to him that it would be a violation of ever-sacrosanct patient confidentiality to call the police without her permission. Seamus had listened carefully, walked out of his rotations, and broken both of the man's arms on his way home, leaving him lying in an alleyway, making that funny noise humans produce when they are past screaming, with a warning that if it happened again he wouldn't get the privilege of being able to walk away from their next meeting.

Seamus had decided then that any job where you are supposed to follow some code rather than do what is obviously right is a bullshit job. In retrospect he should have seen that beforehand, given what had happened to Lauren. Would've saved him a lot of money and three years of his life.

"Yes. Well, we all have our little fuck-ups, don't we? In any case," he said, brightening again, "the important thing is that we've got the briefcase, and that means I'm going to get paid. Forty thousand dollars."

Maxwell's mouth dropped open with a soft noise. Her boots were lace-deep in a mud puddle, but she didn't seem terribly concerned anymore.

"Forty grand . . ."

"I told you I was working at a premium. All in all, not a bad day's work, and we might've even saved that idiot's life—"

Maxwell froze mid-step and blanched.

"Cameras. There might've been cameras—"

"Relax," said Seamus. "I'm not an amateur. Any cameras outside that apartment would confirm our story: we knocked, heard something, went to help, and didn't take a thing when we left. I covered the briefcase on our way out for a reason. And as for inside the apartment, even the most obliging criminals aren't so kind as to leave a bunch of security cameras rolling to record evidence against themselves."

Mollified, Maxwell walked in silence for a few blocks. If Seamus had to guess, she was thinking about what she might do with an extra forty thousand in her pocket. If he was going to keep her around—and it looked like he'd have to, if he was going to work the murder after he collected from Arya—he'd have to give her a commission. Nothing bred dishonesty like desperation.

When they could see Seamus's office building down the street, she turned to him and cocked her head. "One last question: Why don't you have a phone, boss?"

"My mind, of course. Those five-G waves cause brainworms. Keep an eye on the office, I've got to go visit a friend."

Seamus was in fact more concerned with the fact Sandra's colleagues could use cell tower connections to trace the location of a mobile phone, but there was no reason to admit this to Maxwell. He turned and walked off into the mist. Insubstantial as it was, it let the cold seep in, and Seamus drew his jacket tighter around his chest. The vial in his pocket pressed tight against him.

Seamus walked until he found himself at the forty-fourth. Anyone could walk into the station's lobby—usually, the problem was keeping people in, not keeping them out. It looked to be a slow day, only a few drunks staggering past, escorted by annoyed beat cops. A single man crouched in the holding cell, slowly, incessantly rubbing the torn skin of his knuckles.

Strictly speaking, civilians weren't supposed to go up to the higher floors, but Seamus had lifted a keycard from one of his least favourite detectives months ago. Said detective—Seamus couldn't quite remember his name—had been so slow to report the card missing that Seamus had spent a week moving in and out of the evidence lockers as he pleased. When the detective finally realized his keycard had been stolen, not misplaced, Seamus helped him to see that reporting the lost card this late would mean a scandal that would likely lose him his job. That it was in everyone's best interests that Seamus keep the card, just their little secret.

Homicide had a floor to themselves. It was a bullpen-style affair, with desks separated only by low plywood barriers, the air filled—as usual—with the noise of a dozen rolling chairs and the smell of stale bagels being over-toasted. While Seamus respected his best friend, he'd never understood why Sandra would want to do more or less the same job he did with the addition of paperwork, meetings, and petty rules about exactly what she was allowed to do to suspects.

The other detectives quickly looked away as they caught sight of him, but Sandra waved hello.

"Good to see you, Trouble. Finally decided to join the force?"

"The city would burn inside a week," said Seamus. "I'm just on my way to see Elial, but I thought I'd be an upstanding citizen and give you an anonymous tip. I heard a man was found over on Baldwin, unconscious. An overdose, but an unusual one. I know that's not your jurisdiction, but keep an ear to the ground anyways—I'm curious if any of his friends are going to turn up with the same sort of symptoms."

"I'll ask my buddies downtown about it. Unusual how?"

"This anonymous source doesn't know what he overdosed on. It doesn't look like anything I've seen before."

Sandra's eyes softened.

"You found him yourself? You feeling alright, Seamus?"

"Perfectly fine, as you can see." Seamus wasn't proud of the sharpness in his voice, but even after all these years he couldn't quite manage to soften it. Besides, it was like anything else in life—it got easier every time.

Sandra frowned and looked away. "If you say so. Anyway, we got Ryba into the morgue. Probable cause of death is getting stabbed a bunch of times."

"Shocking. You find anything else?"

"Just one thing," said Sandra. "In her statement, the wife said he'd have been wearing a wedding ring and a gold chain. The body you found had the ring—no chain."

"You check the vent?"

"Thoroughly. No leads yet—could be the killer figured they could get a little money on the side."

"Or they took it as a trophy. You don't do that to a body because you want a few hundred dollars' worth of gold."

"Well, I'll still have the boys keep an eye on the pawnshops, see if any gold chains turn up nearby." She glanced towards the frosted windows of the superintendent's office—Herbert Radner was pretending to watch his monitor, glancing up at Seamus every few seconds. "And now you better get the hell out before Radner shits himself."

That got a grin out of Seamus.

"Now, I can't imagine why he'd feel nervous—"

"Can it, Seamus. It's more fun to chat somewhere people don't want to shoot you, not that you'd know. How about you come over for dinner Friday? Michael's cooking. Show up at six; you'll have a good time," she said, deciding for him. It was something she did a fair bit. Seamus didn't mind, considering her decisions were usually better than his.

Seamus waved agreement. Say what you would about Michael, he was a good cook. Seamus gave himself a little mental jab—no matter how much money there was to be made, he'd make time for a visit down to Carlaw tomorrow morning.

Seamus dropped off the vial he'd taken with Elial, then headed back to the office. He found Maxwell sifting through dusty piles of papers, electronica blaring out of her laptop at a volume that was definitely hazardous to one's eardrums and possibly a threat to the structural integrity of the building.

"Evening, Maxwell. Lovely day outside."

"It's been raining for hours."

"Never said otherwise. When you get the chance, give Arya a call—we're going to get paid and strongly suggest she take a nice long vacation."

"Okay, and why are we doing that?"

"I'm not convinced that losing some money could make Williams desperate, but coming to me is a desperate move. She had to know that it was a Hail Mary and that the odds of getting her merchandise back were slim. Now, what makes people desperate?"

"Fear," answered Maxwell immediately. It seemed that was a question familiar to her.

"Exactly. The market's competitive, and there are many people in the city who'd object to Williams moving in with some new drug. People who would be happy to visit her and express their displeasure in small-calibre rounds. Even Greene—she doesn't deal in narcotics, but she doesn't take kindly to people trying to do business without paying their respects."

Seamus abruptly stopped, then stretched and yawned. It was fine and good to talk through his plans, but he did have to be careful: the secretaries all knew his clients' secrets, but it wouldn't do for them to find out too much about *him*.

"But that's enough for one day," he said. "Go home and sleep—I'll do some more research on my own."

Maxwell didn't need to be told twice—she grabbed her jacket and disappeared out the door. That was curious—he could imagine her looking forward to the end of the workday, but her expression as she left the office was businesslike, with an underlying sense of urgency.

There was definitely research to be done, and one of his subjects would have to be this mysterious new secretary who had business at night. But right now, it was time for a drink.

Ten minutes later he was sipping bourbon at Jackson's. His laptop rested on the bar, emails sent to what few friends he still had in the medical profession. Old classmates, mostly—there were a few who hadn't heard about the incident on his last day of med school. There were also a few who had and were glad there was someone like Seamus slipping in and out of the cracks in the system, someone who understood the distinction between *legal* and *right*. They came in handy on occasion, those old contacts, and he suspected that what he'd found on Baldwin Street was above his pay grade.

The replies so far weren't promising: one old drinking buddy who'd made a name for herself as a researcher pointed him to a paper where a misfolded brain protein produced similar effects in twenty lab mice. The connection was tenuous at best. Hopefully tomorrow would bring better news: the kid would probably be awake, and a first-hand account of the symptoms would be helpful.

Seamus was slightly startled to realize that he was still working Arya's case, even though he'd already done enough for his paycheque. He was curious about just what Williams had been importing, but there was something else—he felt at the possibility gingerly, the way you probe a broken tooth with your tongue. Seeing the kid shaking on his apartment floor had gotten to him worse than he'd thought, and he wanted to do something about whatever had been in those vials.

It was stupid, and he knew it. One man could never make any particular dent in the overdose deaths in a city.

He shook his head to clear it and moved on to a more sensible line of inquiry. His new secretary was a tangle of contradictions—secretive but brash, and surprisingly competent. And the music—there was a connection there. Seamus spent a half hour digging through old bookings around Toronto, looking for performers who'd recently quit or gone to ground. No one that looked like Maxwell—but he did find one long shot. Something to look into tomorrow.

He drained his glass with a long draw and held it up for a refill. Jackson sidled up, smiling as always.

"Sandra came by earlier—planning for her big day. Seems excited."

"Good for her," said Seamus with a forced grin. "If he makes her happy, that's good enough. I've never seen her even think about a ring before, and now she's asking me whether I think a princess cut or a cushion cut would suit her better."

"What'd you tell her?"

"When it comes to marriage, any sort of cut will do, provided it looks like an accident and you're the primary beneficiary."

Jackson chuckled slightly, leaning his heavy forearms against the bar. "You two came down to the city a long time ago, didn't you?"

Seamus inclined his head in agreement.

"You two ever together?"

"It would've been hard to drive here in a single car otherwise."

"*Together* together, Seamus. Have you ever dated?"

This, at last, made Seamus look up, an expression of pure bewilderment on his face.

"Sandra *Blair*?"

"Guess that's a no."

"The mind reels," said Seamus. "Sure, she's the best person I know—tell her I said that, and I'll call the health inspector on you—but . . ."

"Not your type?"

Seamus waved that aside. "Anyone with one working eye can tell she's beautiful, Jackson. No, she's stitched me up too many times. She knows I'm just a bag of blood and tissue; it's not conducive to romance."

Jackson shrugged and went back to polishing his glasses. Seamus kept his eyes narrowed on his back—it wasn't like Jackson to get close like that. He must have noticed something, but Seamus knew from experience that if Jackson didn't volunteer information, you weren't going to pry it out of him.

As he lay down in his blankets that night, Seamus found his mind drifting back to Jackson's question. He'd exaggerated his surprise to it—he and Sandra had grown up together, after all, and a few misadventures were inevitable. There was no need to mention that to Jackson, though. Discretion was the better part of valour, especially as far as engaged best friends went.

Still, whatever he told Jackson, there was a twinge of unhappiness whenever he thought about her upcoming wedding. Protectiveness, maybe. Michael, the alleged poet, wasn't much of a specimen in Seamus's estimation, but it was her life. Seamus would go and wish them happiness, whenever they managed to agree on a day. There was a tuxedo in the storage room, but maybe he'd buy a new one. One without knife holes.

CHAPTER FOUR

Arya Williams arrived the instant Seamus unlocked his office for the morning, and before Maxwell, who was supposed to have come half an hour early to help open up. Arya wore a shimmering puffer jacket and tight, perfectly tailored clothes that might have drawn the eye of another man. Seamus looked at those custom-made pants and wondered about their price tag.

"So, what is this status update you called me for? It's of great importance that the briefcase is recovered—I'm not sure you understand the urgency here."

Her tone was slightly frantic, and she'd refused the offered seat, preferring to stand and vibrate with anxiety. Seamus sighed and leaned back at his desk.

"I understand better than you'd think. I have your briefcase right here." Seamus lifted the black briefcase onto the table and watched all the tension go out of Williams's shoulders. "It's empty," he warned. Williams crumpled but tried to rally. "We did our best, but the contents proved irrecoverable," said Seamus.

Her eyes flashed. "If you have my delivery hidden somewhere—"

"This is a matter of professional conduct, Ms. Williams," said Seamus, with an edge in his voice. "I run a business. I was not at any point aware of what this briefcase contained, but if I *had to guess*, I would imagine something very expensive, and very illegal, which might or might not have already landed one person in the hospital. If I found this thing, I would be obliged to turn it over to the police, along with your name. Luckily for you, all I found was an empty briefcase, so you can pay me for services rendered and go on your merry way."

She looked as though she was still tempted to bargain, so Seamus added in a soft voice: "I look the other way for my clients, but not when I think there may be a train coming when I've got my back turned."

Arya Williams stood stock-still for a moment, then sank to the empty chair and put her head in her hands.

Maxwell chose that moment to stick her head through the door.

"Morning, boss! You wouldn't believe what the green line was like—woah, those clothes look expensive as all fuck."

Maxwell was smiling at Williams, looking slightly starstruck. Williams raised her head. She didn't deign to glance in Maxwell's direction but pulled a cheque from her purse and laid it on the desk. Forty thousand of the best.

"In that case, Mr. Caron, we have other business to discuss. In private."

Seamus glanced up at his wayward secretary. "Go grab three iced coffees from the Vietnamese place beside Minnie's. I've got a tab there. Don't take the TTC—I want you back inside fifteen minutes. And have them put tapioca bubbles in mine."

Maxwell looked disappointed, but she slipped back out the door. Seamus waited for her footsteps to fade down the hall before he locked the door and put his business face back on.

"You've lost a lot of money," he said, "but I gather that isn't your main concern."

"No. I can swallow the losses."

"You're worried someone else is coming after you. You should be. There are too many interested parties in this city for you to move in with your own . . . product." There was a glint of desperation in her eyes again, and Seamus knew he'd hit his mark. It would've been easy to shake her down for some extra money for "protection"—and, honestly, Williams probably deserved it if she'd been importing poison. But Seamus had his rules—he ran a detective business, not a confidence game.

"You're a millionaire, right? Disappear. If you go far enough, they won't bother coming after you. Spend your days getting fat on grilled pork on a beach in Thailand."

"I can't leave."

"I've heard that before," said Seamus. "People usually figure differently once it's too late and they're bleeding out on the linoleum in the back of a dive bar."

Williams paled but, to her credit, didn't flinch. "My business needs me, Mr. Caron. My people need me. And . . . and I'm not a woman easily beaten. I won't run. Timmy won't—"

"Timmy Greene?"

Seamus's attention sharpened on her, but Arya had snapped her mouth shut as if to forcibly seal any incriminating words inside.

"I'll need you to forget that."

"You mean that *Timmy Greene* is involved in this?"

"Please, Detective." Her voice was shaking. "If he finds out I came to you— I'm already behind . . . please just forget it."

Seamus was not inclined to forget case details. Timmy, involved in drug imports? The Greenes had never moved drugs. They specialized in weapons and protection rackets, which was why Seamus got along with them so well. Possibly Olexa was moving into new territory, in which case Seamus would have to move against her and probably be crushed in the process. He stopped his thoughts running too far down that dark avenue—if Olexa were behind whatever was in the briefcase, she wouldn't have fed information about it to Seamus. So Timmy was acting on his own.

Olexa Greene ran things by understanding the web of power and alliances that connected every illegal interest in the city—her Company was built on a million subtle threats and unspoken alliances. Timmy Greene had inherited all of his aunt's brutality and none of her deftness. Seamus wouldn't have been surprised if Timmy were just strong-arming people like Arya into smuggling for him. People who could move easily across borders.

"How'd he get you to make the first shipment?"

Arya just shook her head, but Seamus was looking more closely at her now. When she raised her hands, her fingers trembled. Her eyes were lined deep under her makeup, no miracle considering she was being targeted by the mob, but those muscle spasms in her lip didn't look to Seamus like the product of stress alone. He thought about the kid in the hospital—he'd clearly had a seizure, and the resulting brain damage would likely leave his muscles shuddering and disobedient the rest of his life, if he even regained consciousness.

"He got you hooked on it first, didn't he?"

She gave him no agreement, but the absence of denial was enough. So that's how Timmy was running his business—the first trip's free, but you'd better work for me if you want another hit. A crude strategy, bound to implode when competitors or an underling with a few spare neurons broke your monopoly, but just the sort of thing Timmy would try.

Arya wasn't giving Seamus anything else, but he might manage to scare her into spilling more details on Timmy's involvement. It was for the case, after all—and Seamus could be very scary when he wanted to be. She stood in front of him, tense as a set mousetrap. Seamus considered her—the appearance of strength, the abundance of vulnerabilities. Finally, he let out a sigh.

"If you need help getting out of the city, I know people. I'd even be willing to offer this aid gratis, since I failed to completely recover what you were looking for."

She just shook her head, put on a pair of black sunglasses, and stood to leave. Seamus made no effort to stop her, but he called after her: "Life is short, Ms. Williams. Don't make it shorter than it has to be."

At that she stopped and looked back, framed in the morning light sifting in through the window. Seamus caught her eye as she turned. Desperate, sure, but not yet beaten. A dangerous combination.

After a moment of quiet, Maxwell walked back into the office balancing three coffees and visibly deflated when she realized Williams had left. Seamus happily grabbed two from her and began drinking from both straws.

Seamus sipped from the oversize tubes of condensed milk as he held his cheque delicately, letting it catch the morning light. Forty thousand dollars: not bad for four days' work.

"Meeting went well then, boss?"

"Not for Arya Williams."

Maxwell nodded absently and turned to set down her coffee.

It was time to start on the second task of the day—testing hunches about the new secretary. "Shulker," he said, almost under his breath. The stage name of a rising star in the electronica scene, who vanished from any bookings about a month ago, and who'd always appeared masked. Maxwell went rigid and whipped around, eyes blazing.

"How did you—"

"I didn't," said Seamus with a grin. "But if you hadn't responded, I could've passed that off as a mutter."

Maxwell glared at him, eyes blazing.

"You've listed no employment for the last fourteen months," he continued, "but your primary residence is a downtown apartment. So you used to have an income stream." He took another sip of the strong sugary coffee. "Now, I don't peg you for the trust fund type. But I checked the brand on those headphones of yours—they retail for almost two thousand dollars. Put that together with the synth gear you've got in your backpack—I didn't open it, just watched when you did—and we know you're in the music industry. I couldn't find any performers in Toronto who matched your description, but the masked DJ Shulker first appeared about a year ago and was quite popular before they disappeared less than a month ago. Why'd you quit?"

Maxwell continued to glare, her arms crossed tight over her chest. "You had no right," she spat.

"My mother once told me," said Seamus airily, "*You've got a right to anything you can take in your hand, and no right to anything you can't.*"

Maxwell turned without a word and grabbed her backpack. Seamus didn't move from where he was leaned against the desk, but he called after her.

"I'm guessing, Maxwell, that you didn't give up a job you loved because you woke up feeling funny one morning. Something pushed you out—or someone. That someone could be a case for us. A little vengeance might be in order, don't you think?"

That stopped her at the door. "It's— That's a hell of a proposition."

Seamus nodded. Maxwell was steady—he'd seen that on Baldwin Street yesterday. He was willing to gamble a bit on her.

"Listen," she said, "I don't mind this job. The pay's okay, and I gotta admit it's interesting. But let me make one thing crystal-fucking-clear: You stay out of my business. What I do when I go home, and all that shit."

Seamus gave a rueful grin. "I'm a detective, Maxwell. Other people's affairs are my business."

"Not mine. Or you'll find yourself a new secretary."

Seamus considered. He nodded. He didn't have time to play around with job applications right now.

"Alright, Maxwell, you've got a deal. And to help with your motivation, you'll be working on commission along with your wages. Ten percent of every case goes to you."

Maxwell appeared to have a complete brain malfunction at the thought of earning four grand after a week's work. Seamus was worried she'd stand there staring and sputtering for the rest of the day, but abruptly she composed herself. "Alright. What are we doing today, boss?"

"That's more like it," said Seamus with a grin. "You're going to dig into that research on Timmy Greene—I want you to find out *everything* about him. Ryba was his lawyer, after all—maybe there's a connection there. I've got an errand to run." He had to take a look around at 23 Carlaw, and there was a chance it'd be safer for everyone if he found out what was there before Sandra did.

The place on Carlaw was a nightmare, and Seamus grimaced internally to think of how well it matched that grubby plastic key tag. The veranda had at one point contained a number of potted plants—these had been killed so thoroughly that the neglect went beyond benign and verged on malice aforethought. Maybe a pothos had killed the renter's parents when she was young.

Seamus rang the doorbell and ran rapidly through his cover story, which involved the Eastern Ontario Sport Fishing Society and a runaway carp. After a few seconds of stumbling noises from inside, a woman threw the door open wide. She was young, not a day past twenty-five, with blonde hair and drooping blue eyes and a T-shirt that just barely covered her chest. On her lips was a smudge of blue lipstick.

Seamus set his jaw so hard it ached. There were fourteen bones in Michael's face, and he was going to break every one of them.

"What's up?" asked the woman, in a slightly lilting accent.

"I was just looking for a friend of mine," said Seamus. It was easy to keep his voice light—he was long in the practice of hiding rage. "Do you know Michael Timmons?"

She smiled and stepped back.

"You're friends with Mike? Come in!"

Seamus was slightly taken aback, but he followed her through the door. The studio they entered was a maelstrom of laundry and gritty half-full mugs with paintings of cats on them. Seamus gingerly closed the door behind him, while his host happily flopped onto the bed in the centre of the apartment, joining a truly impressive collection of pillows.

"So, you're a friend of Michael's, Miss . . . ?"

She seemed to consider this.

"Well, we're like, fucking. I don't want to say we're *friends*, that seems so intimate. And my name's Evey."

"Ah." Seamus had lost his rhythm. He was used to extracting secrets like stubborn teeth: having them handed to him with a smile was disconcerting.

"I mean, he's kinda my type physically," Evey continued happily. "The dad bod's in, you know? And he's great in the kitchen. Brought me these little cookies one time. But let's be honest, he's a little clingy. And in bed, well, there's this weird thing he does—you've gotta understand, he hangs way to the left—"

"Nice stuffed animals you've got there," said Seamus.

"Right? What was I saying . . . ? Anyway, the poetry's kinda shit, y'know? He wrote one about me where my hair was seaweed or something. He said he was putting it in a book, which would probably embarrass me to death—"

Seamus, despite his best effort, couldn't bring himself to dislike this bubbly blonde girl who lived in a mess. But he found himself thinking about his best friend, with her broken nose and her sure hands and her true laugh, the one that sparkled, that he only heard rarely. He cleared his throat.

"You're aware, of course, of his fiancée?"

Evey sat up quickly. "Fuck."

Seamus gave her a dry look. "Precisely."

She scooted off the bed and, much to Seamus's bemusement, took his hand. "So that's why you're here! God, I'm such a moron. I never meant to come between you and Mike—"

Seamus used his free hand to rub his eyes. He was getting too old for this shit. "Not *me*. I'm a private detective, just doing my job. It's nothing personal. I fear, though, that this might change your feelings towards Mr. Timmons?"

"Like, no shit. I've had my boyfriend screw around—well, my ex, mostly—and I know how it feels. Tell them I'm really sorry."

"She won't blame you," said Seamus, which was a colossal lie even by his standards. He'd have to keep an eye on Sandra, particularly if she ever said she was going hunting and wound up near Carlaw. "I should be getting back. If Michael comes by again, I think a good solid slap in the face would be warranted—you didn't hear that from me, though."

Evey gave him a big, slightly blue grin.

"Absolutely."

Walking along Queen Street back to the office, Seamus sat on a rainbow-enamelled bench, avoiding the ice cream smears and cigarette butts. As he thought, the engine noises and multi-language babble surrounding him faded into a blur.

It was a definite fact that Michael was a lying cheating sonofabitch who needed some bones realigned. On the other hand, Sandra was the one person in the city whose judgment he trusted above his own, and possibly the one person in the city whose life he was genuinely reluctant to ruin. If she was happy with him . . .

He sat trying to unspool his thoughts but didn't get anywhere. Sometimes, it took a few nights for his brain to unwind a knot, and this was a difficult one. Sighing, he stood again and continued towards his office—there was still work to be done that day, and money to be made. By the time he opened his office door, he'd sealed away Evey and Michael and successfully turned back to the case.

Maxwell was lounging back in his office chair, working on a chunky black laptop. She looked up when she saw him come in but didn't stand.

"Hey, boss. Nice chair you've got here."

"That it is, Maxwell. Did any work happen to get done while I was out?"

"Sure did. Timmy Greene—three DUIs. John Ryba defended him in all cases, and none of the charges stuck."

"Of course they didn't. His last name's Greene, and there aren't many judges in the city with a death wish."

Maxwell fixed her eyes on her laptop, with an unusual intensity in them that bordered on anger. "Another two cases of aggravated assault. Had to do community service for one of them. Plus something where he was accused of poisoning someone, but it looks like that never went anywhere—I could only find one article. A certified shitspoon."

Seamus raised an eyebrow. "Not to pry, but it sounds like you weren't the biggest fan of Mr. Greene to begin with."

Maxwell glanced up at him, then back at the computer screen. "That's personal."

"Of course."

Seamus let the silence hang a minute—it didn't matter that much to him if Timmy was a former lover or dealer of Maxwell's, and he'd promised not to go digging on his own. But the thing about silences was that people usually felt the impulse to fill them with information they didn't mean to give you, if you could just wait them out. After about a minute, Maxwell cleared her throat.

"Is there anyone who'd go against her?"

Seamus cocked his head. "Who?"

"Olexa Greene."

Maxwell wasn't one to fall for the simple tricks—he'd have to remember that. And wanting to gather intel was a good instinct on her part.

"There are gangs with enough power to. The national organizations, the bikers. And Chinatown—nobody fucks with Chinatown. But the Company is better trained and better armed than anyone else in the city, and Olexa doesn't deal with drugs, which keeps her out of most of the turf wars. There *were* challengers, but there haven't been many more people stepping up since she left the ones who did with their chests split open in an old school bus."

Maxwell looked away from her laptop at last and stared into the gloom of the office. "Funny about Timmy Greene," she said, abruptly, "pissing away his life like that, when he's got all the money a person could ever need."

"He's a rich kid with an inferiority complex. Oldest story in the book."

"If I had that kind of bankroll, I'd get a Steinway. And a penthouse downtown, paid in cash."

"That's less exciting than I might've expected," said Seamus.

"I wouldn't mind buying some peace and quiet. Ever since I had to go back to being Maxwell Moscovitz all the time, things've seemed a lot louder."

Seamus nodded, his eyes distant. "Not too different from Arya Williams. All the money in the world, and still trapped by the little chalk lines she's drawn around herself. It's a common mistake."

Thomas Caron had made that mistake, and it had killed him and Lauren.

When Maxwell met his eyes, hers were almost mournful. "Do any of the fuckers actually make it out?"

"Not many. Once you've got money and status, the high road seems a lot less appealing. I know one man, though—made a fortune selling real estate that, strictly speaking, wasn't actually there. But then he ran into some real gangsters, the sort who know how to find you and your family wherever you try to hide. They sent one of their thugs, who kicked his door in one day and found him sitting by a half-empty bottle of sambuca, wife long gone. He gave everything he had to the man who kicked his door down, along with some useful information on their enemies. And they let him live."

"Where'd he end up?"

"Well," said Seamus, with a glimmer in his eye, "can you keep a secret?"

Maxwell caught herself nodding and rolled her eyes instead.

"Legend has it," said Seamus, "that he retired to a small bar in this very city and spends his days in peace, mixing undrinkable cocktails. The guy who kicked open his door was working freelance at the time—helped him smooth everything over, sent the money down the right channels. I hear he got out of the loan business and became a private detective. Drinks bourbon at Jackson's Bar, most nights."

Her eyes widened. "Do you know anyone who *isn't* a criminal?"

"Sandra," said Seamus without missing a beat. "And my mother's always been a law-abiding citizen, if you don't count the man she buried in the woods by our house up north."

"Scary thing is, I don't even know if you're joking."

"Maxwell, I never joke. Now get ready, we've got some snooping to do."

As he'd promised Ruby, they made it to John Ryba's office, the key Ruby'd gifted him in hand. It was a rented office in a squat building just east of downtown.

The office itself was garishly decorated with gold highlights and a few risqué plaster casts of water nymphs that earned a disapproving glare from Maxwell. That probably said something about the taste of his clientele, but then Seamus wasn't there to pass judgment on the dead man's professional life.

The police had already been through, of course, but they hadn't sealed it, and Sandra would've told him if they'd found anything useful. Seamus ran two gloved fingers over the desk—cheap wood, lacquered a dark brown to mimic mahogany. There was a desktop, of course, but he had no password to unlock it, and Seamus had never been one for computers.

"You think you can crack that?"

"Just 'cause I'm not old as dust doesn't mean I'm a hacker," said Maxwell, though she dutifully went and tapped at the keyboard. "Any guesses what this guy'd have as a password?"

"Try *Ruby*."

"No dice," said Maxwell, though she kept typing.

"What else are you trying?"

"*One-two-three-four* and *password*."

Seamus left her to it and continued his search for some clues that would be more recognizable to him.

Looking closer at the office accoutrements, he read the faint grease stains on the wood of the desk, noted the leatherbound law textbooks sitting dusty and forlorn on the shelves, discovered the bottle of scotch in the bottom drawer. That last was intriguing at first, but it was only a third empty and the cork stuck grittily as he pulled it out—a treat for clients, Seamus guessed, not a mark of some personal desperation. Not interesting, not useful.

There was a drawer of bills, receipts, and legal briefs, and Seamus took his time diligently reading through these, though his eyes practically fell out of his head with boredom. John Ryba had kept several clients, and Seamus filed the unfamiliar names away in his head, but going by his invoices, Seamus saw he'd served the Greenes exclusively in the last year, and Timmy most of all. Seamus set the last manilla folder back in its place, frowning to himself. He was wrong to expect anything more, of course. Hoping that the victim's office would hold some clue to his murder had always been a long shot. But he couldn't shake the feeling there'd be a motive here, if he could dig it up. Ryba might've had enemies, but the MO was so strange and distinctive, and it spoke very clearly of a hatred that Seamus felt sure would've left some trace on Ryba's life before he died. Then again, some men had lives outside of the office, and there'd be other places to look for those traces.

Seamus was about ready to leave, but he gritted his teeth and knelt down to see if he'd missed anything on the floor. No sense in doing a job if you weren't going to do it thoroughly. There was nothing on the floor, just a half-full waste basket that smelled of rot. He glanced at this reluctantly, then sighed to himself as he went to rummage through garbage.

The source of the smell was a half-eaten breakfast sandwich—Seamus decided to take a major risk and assume it didn't have a clue hidden in it. Tossed receipts, for coffee and beef and gasoline. Diligently he dug to the bottom of the basket and pulled out a single crumpled napkin. He'd have passed it over, but something about it caught his eye. In one corner was a logo—a cherry—that snagged at his memory without catching it. Seamus smoothed the napkin out.

Scrawled in ballpoint was a simple reminder:

next meeting: 1 a.m.
platinum

This last word was circled twice in red ink. Seamus sat back on his haunches and puzzled over it.

First off, the time was strange. Ryba would've worked his own hours, but meeting a client past midnight wasn't some slight eccentricity—it hinted at concealment. There was an old human instinct to do illicit things at night, no matter how brightly lit the city was at every hour. Then there was *platinum*—the topic of the meeting, Seamus would guess. He held the possibility that John Ryba had been in the illegal jewellery business, toyed with it, couldn't quite make it fit. For one thing, if there were evidence of financial distress on Ryba's part, Sandra would've found it. Desperation was a key ingredient of almost every murder, and she would've been looking for unpaid debts or a gambling problem. The John Ryba Seamus had built up in his mind had plenty of cash in his bank account and a house in Rosedale—he wouldn't be hustling precious metals in the wee hours of the morning.

So maybe it was code. You might meet a mistress at one a.m., which would make *platinum* a pet name perhaps. An odd one, though, and odd also that you'd need to write yourself a note reminding you what to call her.

Maxwell, having abandoned the computer, rolled over to him on the office chair.

"Hey, those are the same napkins they have at the Montmorency."

The Montmorency—Timmy's bar. It wasn't shocking that his lawyer would've visited him there, but midnight visits and codewords spoke of something more than just legal counsel.

"What do you know about the Montmorency?"

Maxwell eyed him suspiciously. "Been there a few times—it's way east. Didn't like it much. Dance floor's half-empty, and it's full of handsy dudes who are either gonna puke on you or start crying when you turn them down. All the cute girls go drinking on Queen West."

Be that as it may, Seamus would have to go pay Timmy Greene a visit at his bar. Conveniently, he wouldn't even have to break in.

They returned to the office and kept working into the afternoon, dredging up information on Timmy Greene. His connection to Ryba was clear—whether he'd been involved in the murder was less obvious. More likely it was a rival gang trying to shut down one of the Greenes' most effective get-out-of-jail-free cards, or the supply of whatever Timmy was importing.

The Company had professional hitmen, but other gangs approached cleanup jobs differently. Some pushers preferred to grab some shivering kid off the streets and tell them that their debts would be paid and they'd have all the coke they could dream of if they just did them this one favour. That approach was less reliable, with messier results. What Seamus had seen at the hospital had certainly been messy.

If Olexa decided one of her rivals had put a hit out on Timmy, it would mean war, and this thought raised the hair on the back of Seamus's neck. A gang war would be tough on him, but he'd be fine if he hung out of the way and took whatever bribes people saw fit to give him. It would be deadly for the famously honest Sandra Blair.

Maxwell broke in on his thinking.

"I've got a meeting tonight, boss. With—an old friend? Anyway, do you think I could go a little early?"

"Sure. I suppose it balances out, since you came in late," said Seamus. "But you're a terrible liar," Maxwell flipped him off and went to gather her things. Normally, he'd complain about his secretary's penchant for a six-hour workday, but he didn't have anything else for her to do, and there was no sense keeping her around to stare into the middle distance. He'd work alone tonight.

Once she left, Seamus waded into the mess of the storage room and dug out a brown suitcase with the words *dress-up* scrawled over the front panel in permanent marker. On went ripped white jeans and a short-sleeve Hawaiian shirt, then a puffer jacket that might've been designer, if you didn't look too closely. Then he started layering on concealer, thick enough to hide his scars, which people tended to remember. He checked a pocket mirror: he looked brash, uncertain, maybe five years younger. And unfashionable, but it would have to do. After a moment's consideration, he added a silver clip-on earring.

Seamus realized he'd forgotten to eat that day, so he put the kettle on and inhaled a few bowls of instant noodles to pass the time. At ten o'clock he set out into the cold, missing the comfortable weight of his oilskin on his shoulders.

The Montmorency was Timmy's base of operations and his main income stream. It was deep in the east end of the city, practically to the end of Danforth, in territory shunned by the trendier, brighter-lit nightclubs. Seamus had been there before, collecting. The music was tinny, the smoke machine spat out cod-scented fog, and the drinks, though cheap, tasted of runoff water. Despite this, it had been there for twenty years—long before Timmy came to own it. The Montmorency was an institution.

Mostly, this was because you could do anything once you got past the doors. Olexa Greene had given the club her blessing, and patrons of the Montmorency could get away with anything short of murder—or even that, as long as they didn't make too much noise. After a pleasant chat with a drunk in a Mardi Gras necklace, Seamus weighed the odds of a fight on the bus ride there as he rolled his knuckles in his hand, trying not to hope that someone would see him as a target. It wasn't the point of the night, but damn if it hadn't been a long time since he'd seen some action. He wasn't armed—there was a chance the bouncer would find a hidden pistol if he got patted down, and even if they weren't going to call the cops, Seamus didn't want to have to fight his way in.

When Seamus finally left the warm damp of the bus to meet the cold damp of the street, rainwater was making the lights dance on the concrete. A bright neon cherry shone over the shaded glass front of the club—that logo again—its light glinting off puddles of water and piss on the pavement outside. There wasn't a line yet, though the bouncers were already lining up ropes to corral the evening crowds that might or might not materialize, following the principle that the appearance of success often attracted customers as well as the genuine article. Seamus gritted his teeth at the twenty-dollar cover charge, though only out of principle, considering his recent windfall, and made his way to the bar. To his back was the dance floor, and a DJ producing some noise that Maxwell might've recognized. Seamus, contemplating a night that was likely to be pointlessly annoying, did the philosophical thing and ordered a bourbon.

Timmy Greene was there, as he was most nights. Down the bar, towards the back—Seamus could see his retinue around him, polo shirts and bottles of Grey Goose. Seamus knew what to expect from that crowd—they were former frat types, lost boys who'd just begun to realize their own mortality and huddled together for warmth and comfort. One in particular stood out: a short, muscular man in a Playboy-logo hat, who squatted on a barstool and watched his surroundings with a focus uncharacteristic of your typical parasitic hangers-on.

Seamus eyed Timmy carefully from across the club, watched him scare a waitress into sitting on his lap. Unfortunate, but Seamus had larger concerns. If Timmy had angered one of the other players in the city, whatever he was doing, he'd be operating out of the Montmorency. Figure out what exactly he was doing, figure out who might've killed Ryba as retaliation, collect fifty thousand dollars. Simple.

Across the bar, Timmy laughed at the woman's fear, swigged a tumbler of vodka. If Ryba's murder had been a threat, it didn't look as though Timmy had gotten the message.

The question now was how to get in close. A direct approach would be too suspicious and give the game away before Seamus was ready to move. Seamus would start from the assumption that Timmy was dealing out of the club but avoid staking anything valuable on that guess and spend the night gathering information.

The layout of the bar was strange, a collection of anachronisms built up over decades of shoddy renovations. A long marble-top bar spanned one wall—walking away from that, you'd hit the dance floor, sparsely populated this early in the night. A few wide-eyed women and swaying men gyrated on it, but their attempts at flirtation looked desolate rather than sexy with so few people dancing. Across from *that* were the private booths, upholstered in stained blue velour, and hanging above it all was the DJ box, a half-storey above the action, walled with Plexiglas to ward against the inevitable crushes and riots.

By eleven thirty the club was almost full, and it was a good time to start working. No one had approached Timmy's circle by the bar while Seamus watched, so it seemed he wasn't selling directly. Seamus tipped the bartender generously, despite the fact the bourbon tasted of drywall plaster—a taste he remembered well from that fight with the construction workers—and left his seat to check the corridors that led to the bathrooms. As he did, a thin man with sores on his lips nodded at him from a corner. Seamus idled over, aiming for a drunken stumble.

The voice that came was low and cracked: "You looking to take the edge off?"

"I dunno," said Seamus with a slight slur. "What's on sale?"

"I can get you anything you need. H, Molly."

"I'm looking for some new shit," said Seamus, with a conspiratorial smile. "My buddies told me there's something fun, just hit the market. Can you help a guy out?"

The man blinked, too-dry eyes betraying his incomprehension. No dice. In an instant, the pusher had recovered and started saying that he knew exactly what Seamus wanted, if he'd just follow—but Seamus was already gone, melting away into the crowd. Once he'd made sure he was out of sight, he sat down at one of the greasy mirror-top tables by the back of the club. Three tables down, taking small quick sips from her drink, a woman with her back to him, dressed all in black with an oversize suit jacket, caught his eye.

Seamus swivelled to take a closer look: it was Maxwell, arguing quietly with an elfin woman opposite her. Maxwell was tapping her fingers rapidly on the tabletop, not meeting her companion's eyes. As for that companion, she was delicate and small-boned and her face was coloured by anger and alcohol, gesticulating so heavily she almost knocked over the glasses stacked at her end of the table. Maxwell was curling back into herself with every flourish of the woman's green-painted nails.

After another moment's observation, Seamus shrugged and called for another bourbon. He had, after all, promised not to pry into her business, and if she was involved in some sordid affair of her own, that information didn't seem very profitable to Seamus. He contemplated his drink, trying to gather the courage to sip it.

His attention snapped back to Maxwell's table when he saw three men in too-tight polos encircle her. Seamus recognized a man in a Playboy hat from Timmy's circle—the other two were dressed in garish red and blue. All of them were well-muscled, Blue and Red just starting to get paunchy. Maxwell's tapping got faster, and she tried to stand and move away from the table. Red grabbed her wrist and fixed her in place, and Seamus felt a rush of ice in his blood. But he glanced to the door—he could take those three, but the rest of Timmy's men would swarm them. He might fight his way past the bouncers, but Maxwell and her friend wouldn't. Seamus held his glass and bided his time instead, watching the three men herd Maxwell and the other woman, whose flush had given way to a bloodless pallor, towards the back of the club. He'd need a distraction.

The bouncers who waited by the back door waved the men past, with ugly grins at their captives. Seamus waited for the door to close, then moved quickly towards the bar, hanging just close enough to the dance floor, partially hidden by a concrete pillar, to stay out of view of the bouncers.

Hidden, he weighed the glass of bourbon in his hand, then threw it at the bar, shattering a few vodka bottles. The two bouncers who'd been guarding the door immediately pushed off the wall and into the panicking dancers, and Seamus, who was well accustomed to disappearing after starting trouble, ducked low and moved to the back. By the time the dance floor was clear, Seamus had made it to that back door, now unguarded. With one quick glance at the chaos behind him, he pushed it open and strode into the gloom.

He found himself in a dank corridor, the tang of rotting cardboard heavy in the air. Dully glowing exit signs dotting the walls were the only sources of light. Seamus checked his pockets—gloves, picklocks, a single nylon to obscure his face, nothing useful for a fight. It was always the day that you didn't wear your jacket that you needed it. He sighed slightly to himself and counted his fingers once.

A whimper came from the hallway to his left: Seamus followed it. As he reached the door he thought it had come from, he heard a pleading voice, the words indistinct. There was a snapping sound then, a soft cry, and then nothing.

Seamus pulled the nylon over his face and a picklock from his pocket. He worked slowly, patiently, careful not to make a sound. Picking locks was perhaps his most useful skill—he'd learned it back when he worked collections. When someone came home from a long day of work, had a drink and a rinse, and lay down to sleep only to find that you'd been waiting behind their bedroom door all night, they rarely needed any more convincing to settle their debts.

Male voices came from past the door, low and threatening. Seamus pressed at it gently, the door opened with a soft click, and he put his eye to the gap. Beyond the door was a small room, stocked with liquor bottles and plastic cups. Maxwell and the blonde sat in stained folding chairs, dollar-store rope tight around their wrists. Maxwell was silent, her head raised in furious defiance despite the streak of blood on her face. It seemed she couldn't decide whether to glare at the woman or her kidnappers, so she was trying to do both. Despite everything,

Seamus smiled to himself—his secretary had nerve, you had to give her that. He'd get her out of this.

The elfin woman had been the one pleading—this had subsided into silent gasps of misery, although from her upright posture Seamus didn't think she'd been hurt very badly. Playboy Hat was rounding on Maxwell, his movements slow and mocking, with the grandiosity of the slightly drunk. Seamus made out the word *Shulker*. He looked at the card table pushed to the corner of the room, on which a phonebook, a crowbar, and a pair of pliers rested. Playboy Hat grabbed Maxwell's face with a heavy hand, a parody of a caress. Seamus felt a bit of bile rise in his throat at that—the man was enjoying it, her fear. Maxwell snapped her teeth at his fingers, and the man drew his hand back to swing.

Seamus shoved the door open, hard enough to rattle it against the wall. Bounding into the room, he had to cross the distance while they were disoriented—Red was closest, yelling something Seamus didn't hear, swinging wide at him. Seamus ducked and drove a straight left into the bridge of his nose, feeling the bone fragment under his knuckles. A broken nose wasn't enough to stop a man, so Seamus snapped his other hand down on Red's neck, bringing his head down as Seamus brought his knee up, slamming it into the man's face. Blood spurted, and Red fell to the ground.

As Seamus started to turn, Blue grabbed him from behind in a bearhug. Seamus exhaled as the grip started to tighten, nose filling with Blue's body spray, and saw Playboy Hat reach into his pocket—no time, he needed to go through them faster. Seamus broke Blue's grip, along with three of his fingers, and sent him reeling back. Playboy Hat roared and flipped open a switchblade, lowering himself into what he must've imagined was a fighting stance.

Seamus grinned at him.

Blue was still clutching his broken fingers, off balance—Seamus spun him around by his neck, pivoting his hips, and released him just as Playboy Hat rushed in—the raised switchblade sank into Blue's back. Blue curled into a ball, whimpering and bleeding. Seamus curled his lip at this and shut Blue up with a swift kick to the head, then turned to face Playboy Hat, who was now empty handed, his eyes wide and twitching.

"I think," said Seamus, "your friend has your knife."

Playboy Hat gave a high scream and swung wildly—easy to side-step and leave him stumbling forward, grabbing at air. Seamus was behind him before he could turn and had his arms around Playboy Hat's neck in a deep, tightening rear naked choke. For all his muscle, the man was slow. Weak and undisciplined.

Seamus had seen so many people lose their heads in fights, and he had never understood it. Despite the heat of the fight, he felt, finally, perfect clarity—that old familiar ice water in his veins.

The man stood and pushed back, trying to slam Seamus into the wall. Seamus gave a scornful laugh as they bumped gently against it. Playboy Hat took a stumbling second try, then crumpled forward, released by Seamus to fall directly onto his face, unconscious.

A rear naked choke could kill a man if you did it properly and left it locked long enough. Seamus had held it longer than was safe, but finally unclenched his arms and came up on his toes. Playboy Hat—who, incidentally, had lost the eponymous hat when hitting the floor—seemed to still be breathing, and that was good enough. Better than he deserved, probably. Red was unconscious, and Blue with the knife in his back wouldn't be standing again any time soon, if ever. Seamus pushed the nylon up over his face and turned towards the two women, whom he'd almost totally forgotten about. The elfin woman was staring at him in horror, feet scrabbling along the ground as she tried to push away. Maxwell was smiling and trying not to look too relieved. After a few breaths to come out of the fight, Seamus smiled back at her.

"I thought I told you not to get tied up in this, Maxwell."

"Nice timing, boss."

Seamus cut her ropes—she was shivery and pale, but steady enough to stand on her own. Seamus then turned to study the other woman, who had given up trying to get away in favour of curling forward to make herself as small as possible.

"Friend of yours?" he asked.

"Used to be," said Maxwell, her smile falling instantly away. Her tone was angry, her eyes, worried.

The woman's voice came high and reedy: "Please, Max. I didn't know they'd do this."

"Doesn't surprise me, Rei. You don't know shit." Maxwell turned on her heel. "Let's go, boss."

"Please don't leave me here, Max. Please. They'll kill me."

Maxwell didn't look back, but Seamus could see a tear running down her cheek. She said nothing.

Seamus gave Rei a cool look. "Betrayal's a serious mistake," he said dispassionately. "And I've always believed in facing the consequences of your actions. It builds character."

Maxwell's voice came very quiet then. "Let her go."

Seamus shrugged and cut the ropes. Rei bolted for the door, shoving him slightly to the side—Seamus had a moment's impulse to grab her wrist and slam her to the ground, but that was just the adrenalin talking.

Rei disappeared through the door, not looking back. Seamus nodded to Maxwell, and they both sprinted for the back door.

Ducking low and heading away from the crowd, Seamus made it out into the alley and held a hard sprint for four blocks, before coming to a stop and crouching behind a dumpster. He'd kept an eye on Maxwell, pushing just hard enough that she'd be able to keep up. His breathing was fast but steady—hers came in ragged gasps as she fell to her knees beside him. She clearly wanted to let go and cry but to her credit had managed to keep the sobs suppressed.

He waited till she'd recovered enough to fix him with a suspicious glare.

"What were you doing there?"

"As it happens, total coincidence. Timmy was clearly involved with Ryba beyond being his client, and that's as good a lead as I've got. You'd rather I'd have stayed home tonight?"

Maxwell hugged her knees.

"Thanks," she said at last. "Where the hell did you learn to fight like that?"

"I was home-schooled."

It was true enough—after his father died, his mother's training had gone from tough to properly insane. Seamus had never once complained, and some of his oldest scars were on his shins and knuckles where he'd broken the skin against the heavy bag. The brutality of it had kept both of them going back then. And he'd still taken the occasional break when Sandra came to visit.

He stood to listen to the icy night air, waiting for the guttering of an engine or shouts of pursuit. Neither one came: the three polo shirts probably wouldn't be in any hurry to report to Timmy that they'd been beaten half to death by a single man.

Seamus kept his eyes moving, checking his blindspots, but the roads were quiet enough, only the garbagemen and a few insomniacs walking their dogs. He stepped out onto the Danforth and hailed a cab.

Maxwell knelt behind him still, eyes closed, breathing too quickly. Seamus helped her to her feet and got her into the cab, but her eyes only really focused once he'd sat her down in Jackson's backroom and put a mug of hot chocolate in front of her. Jackson was about to close, but the backroom was always open to Seamus.

"Drink, it'll help."

"Did you put something in it?" asked Maxwell hopefully.

"Cocoa. And cream. And sugar."

Maxwell took a reluctant sip while Seamus sat down beside her and swirled his bourbon in his glass.

"So," he said, "I think you ought to tell me what you were doing at the Montmorency tonight. In exchange for me saving your ass. Oh, and you should give that girl you were with a call—if those men know where she lives, she won't be in the business of it long."

Maxwell stared at him. "What business?"

"Living."

She looked down into her mug. Seamus figured she was looking for guidance—he'd often found some there, in the whorls of foam and chocolate.

"Rei's an ex," said Maxwell. "And she was my manager, back when I was doing shows. And she's the reason I can't work anymore.

"Montmorency management had been looking to scale up operations, turn the place into a real club, not just a place you go to buy shitty X. They'd been getting talent from all over the city to come play, and it was a fucking good deal for them. I heard it from my friends in the business how they'd come to you with an offer to play a week there, for free. If you said no, you'd wind up in the hospital. I couldn't stay far enough away from that shit, but Rei was *ambitious*." Maxwell's voice had been calm, but she spat that last word.

"I knew Rei from back when I was playing at indie beat sessions. She was really sweet back then, just this dropout who liked Wagner, but she wanted to be a big producer—thought I was gonna be her ticket up, I guess. I went along with it because she knew a few guys who could get us bookings, and the shows did get bigger. Plus, she had a car. But then she started trying to live the lifestyle—private booths, Hennessy, lots of coke. Not really my scene—I like to party, but you've got to be careful with that shit. Problem was, she was as broke as I was, so she ran up a pretty big tab."

"At the Montmorency," said Seamus. The events of the night were fitting together.

"Yeah. The deadlines to pay came and went—Rei figured she'd only need a little longer, till we signed a record deal. I was close—a few more months would've done it. Then someone smashed all her car windows. And the last show I did, some of those men showed up. One of them had a gun. They said I ought to talk to my manager about paying her debts—luckily, I still had my mask on, and I decided to get out while I could."

"You were always anonymous then?"

"Yeah," said Maxwell, taking a shuddering breath. "It was a gimmick at first, and an old one, but I kinda liked it, and it worked. Rei's idea. So was this meeting tonight, but that one didn't work so well. She said we had to talk, that she'd already settled up her debts so there was nothing to worry about, and basically dragged me to the Montmorency. Must've been trying to set me up—I didn't know that was Timmy's home turf. At least she didn't manage to tell them *I* was Shulker—she basically lost it when those three guys came at us, and I don't think she said anything that made sense." Maxwell winced at the memory and rubbed her wrists where the rope marks were fading. "They took me along I guess because they didn't want me to call the cops."

Seamus nodded and laid a consoling hand on Maxwell's shoulder. "Don't worry. Rei will get what she deserves. I'm sure Timmy's men will have her feeding the trout of Lake Ontario within a week."

Maxwell started to cry silently. Seamus reflected on the fact that he'd never been very good at comforting people.

"Or," he said, thinking fast, "she could get out of town. Call her and tell her to go visit some relatives in Alberta. Or, even better, in Mozambique. Couch surf for a month. Timmy doesn't have the reach to follow her."

"Rei's not a fucking millionaire," choked Maxwell. "Her life's here. And Timmy, that shitspoon, is still gonna be here in a month."

"Oh, a month's longer than you might think," said Seamus, grinning slightly in the half-light of the backroom. "And Timmy's in a dangerous profession. For now, tell her to get out of town. Then—who knows what might happen in a month?"

Maxwell stared at him in what Seamus might have called blank astonishment. She grabbed the glass of bourbon he had left on the table and drained it. Then she stood and wobbled towards the door. There was one more thing, though—Seamus didn't want to say it, but it was the right thing to do.

"Maxwell," he called, "these are deep waters we're in. I'm not going to tell you it'll be safe. If you want to back out, get a job at Starbucks, now's the time."

Maxwell paused, her face reflected in the frosted glass of the back door. Her jaw was set, and a grim smile flickered over her face.

"Fuck that, boss."

CHAPTER FIVE

His knuckles burned. His arms were heavy, dragged down by hours of fatigue. He couldn't see his mother, but that was fine—her voice was there, same as always.

Again, Seamus.

His fist hit the heavy bag. A smear of blood stained the black leather, and a fine mist of it hung in the air.

Again.

He struck with his shin, despite the bruise on it. The bag crumpled where the blow landed, like a body buckling at the waist.

Again.

He was weighed down, bile in his throat. The air stank of urine, his legs burned under the dead weight of the body. He tried not to look, but when he couldn't avoid seeing the body's skin—anoxic blue. He cried out for help—there was no help. He took another step forward.

Again.

"Yo, wake the fuck up."

Illusions.

Pushing quickly out of his blankets, he came up onto his feet, still blind with sleep, but into the fighting stance that he'd had beaten into him as a child. There was a figure in front of him, but he was too damn slow—not sharp enough for striking, he snapped a hand out, caught a wrist—he'd throw them into the edge of the desk, that'd give him time to focus—

"Boss! It's me!"

Seamus blinked. Maxwell was standing in front of him, looking worried but not afraid. Sunlight was streaming in through the office window. Seamus dropped her wrist, suddenly embarrassed.

"Sorry, Moscovitz." Now he remembered giving her the extra key.

"You always sleep in your clothes?"

Seamus glanced down. He'd managed to take his shoes off, but not much else—he'd gotten to the office and all but collapsed.

"I try not to make a habit of it."

Seamus shook it off, stretching and yawning. Pushing away the nameless dread that came with sleep. Maxwell kept him fixed with a worried look.

"You alright, boss?"

"Better than alright." One of the upsides of your mind grinding endlessly even while you slept was that you got lots of extra time for solving problems. "Now we have an in with Timmy. We still need to know about his connection to Ryba."

"How does massacring three of his friends and trashing his bar add up to an in?"

"That sort of pessimism won't get you anywhere," said Seamus. "They don't know you're Shulker, right? As far as those clowns know, they picked up Shulker's *former* manager and some bystander, then some madman came in and did a bit of reconstructive surgery. Do you have a way to contact him as Shulker?"

"I have a burner, still. And a business email."

"Excellent. Give Timmy a call—let him know you've reconsidered and be sure to mention that you fired Rei a few weeks ago. You can't be accountable for her debts, after all—but give him a fake lead to keep him happy. You've got a new manager now, and he's ready to do business."

"The fuck?"

"Then," said Seamus, pacing around his office, almost tripping over the pile of bedding he'd left out, "you say you want to arrange a meeting, to flesh out the extended run of shows you'll be doing, free of charge. You're out of town, unfortunately, but this slick new manager can meet him and hammer out the terms."

Seamus gave her a considering glance. Maxwell was just staring, looking torn between rage and admiration.

"I'd advise you to be very polite," he continued. "Grovel a little."

"You've lost your damn mind."

"Don't speak that way to your manager," said Seamus, flopping into his office chair. "And don't worry. We'll go over the specifics of the plan at Minnie's."

Maxwell opened her mouth to protest, then closed it. Her eyes were suddenly thoughtful. "You think he's behind that shit we found at Baldwin, don't you?"

"I know he is. The question is whether Ryba was involved, too, and if that was what got him killed."

Maxwell opened her mouth to ask another question, but Seamus had already gotten up and disappeared down the hall. The lunch crowd would eat all the fried breadsticks if they didn't move quickly.

Maxwell was reluctant, of course, but Seamus knew he'd win out in the end. He had leverage, after saving her last night, and Seamus wasn't above using it to move forward on the Ryba case. It'd be good for her too—she'd be earning a year's salary in a week if they pulled it off. By the time Minnie came around with the almond-mango pudding, Maxwell was nodding.

"Alright, boss. What's the plan of attack?"

"First, give Timmy a call. Tell him your manager wants to meet, tonight. You can't make it, of course: even if you wear your mask, chances are good you get recognized."

Maxwell pointed an accusing spoon at him. "Same goes for you, Sherlock."

"*If* those men are out of the hospital—which they shouldn't be, I felt those bones break—they haven't seen my face, and what they did see of me they only saw in dim light. I'm safe. Give him the name Dominic Terrazzo—if he takes the bait, then I'll go in disguise."

Maxwell fixed him with a hard stare. Seamus expected an argument so he was surprised when she finally said, "Be careful, boss. You want me waiting outside?"

"No. Timmy's a moron, but he's dangerous, and you've seen enough excitement for your first week."

In Seamus's experience, bullet holes substantially reduced secretary performance. He opened his mouth to continue but paused for a moment—there was a smell in the air, faint under the omnipresent tang of five-spice powder and fryer oil, but there—cedarwood. Seamus turned towards the front with a smile and saw Sandra leaning over the counter, talking to Minnie. She received a tall glass of grass jelly and coconut milk and brought it over to take the empty seat beside Seamus.

"Still alive?" she said to Seamus with a grin. "Had a feeling I'd find you here if you were." Maxwell waved a hello, mouth full of fried noodles.

"Even in death, I'll still manage to crawl to Minnie's."

"Any leads on Ryba?" she asked.

"Maybe," said Seamus. "Too soon to say."

"Or too soon to tell me . . . but have it your way. That was Sam Ewe by the by, that kid in the hospital—don't think he's woken up yet. What about Carleton?"

Seamus winced. "I haven't gotten around to it."

Sandra raised an eyebrow.

"Thought we had a deal."

"What, finding the body wasn't enough?"

"No rest for the wicked, Trouble. Tell me when you've made contact."

Seamus nodded and mentally moved it a few slots up his to-do list. Calling Carleton to hear his insincere nostalgia and that he had nothing to do with John Ryba's murder now hovered somewhere in the two-hundreds on that list.

Sandra cleared her throat. "Anyway, I've got some news of my own. The overdose you tipped us off to? Someone in the department's doing a magic act, 'cause the evidence disappeared."

Seamus leaned forward, frowning. "That's extremely not good," he said.

"The drugs—which you never heard of, of course—never made it to the evidence locker."

"Do you know who took them?" asked Seamus.

"If I did, I'd be arresting them, not sipping on red beans here. Sure, there are people in the department who'd sell drugs out of evidence, but it'd be a hell of a risk to take."

"This isn't some desk jockey's side hustle, Sandra. If my guess is right, that stuff's valuable. I wouldn't be surprised if someone had been hired just to recover it."

"Yeah? Radner's been trying to keep a lid on it, doesn't want it going to the press."

"Which you don't agree with," put in Maxwell.

They both turned to face Maxwell, who just shrugged.

"I mean, you wouldn't be saying all this in public if you were worried about it getting out, right?"

"Good catch," said Sandra. "I don't think it's smart to hide this sort of thing. People deserve to know, and someone might have a lead."

"Unless Radner himself is involved," said Seamus. "It'd explain why he doesn't want it getting out. Be careful, Sandra. There are powerful people tied up in this."

"Who you don't know anything about, and who you haven't mentioned to me. Because if you *did*, I'd have to testify." Sandra stirred her drink. "But I hear you."

Maxwell offered her opinion: "Your jobs are fucking dangerous."

Sandra gave a short, harsh laugh. "Occupational hazards, kid," she said. "It's Seamus you've really got to worry about; he collects enemies the way some folks collect spoons."

"Nonsense. I'm universally beloved."

"Thought you were supposed to be a better liar than that," said Sandra drily.

"Not to you, Sandra," Seamus responded quietly. Sandra's smile in answer was different than the usual brash grin she put on like armour—it was soft and slow, and though it was one Seamus didn't see often, he was always happy to.

"I know," she said. "I guess we're both in . . . call them high-risk professions. Hell, Michael worries about me all the time. Talks about me quitting once we get married."

Seamus willed his eyebrows back down. "What do you say to that?"

"Hell no. I'm a damn good cop, and this city needs all of those it can get. And I don't wanna live off sawdust and charity."

Seamus grinned. "I'm sure you'll be in the lap of luxury once the poetry takes off."

Sandra suppressed a smile and tried to look angry. "Lay off him. He's putting everything he's got into this anthology—he's a good guy."

Seamus stiffened. Maxwell didn't notice—she was idly folding her napkin into a fortune-teller—but Sandra frowned.

"What's wrong?"

"Nothing. I'll see you for dinner—Friday, was it? Tell Michael I'm looking forward to it."

Back at the office, Maxwell made the call. She was nervous, but she had a way of deepening her voice—probably a trick she used while she was performing, come to think of it. After a tense few minutes of muttered conversation, she hung up and grinned at Seamus. "Dominic Terrazzo, just like you said. I got you an appointment tonight at twelve."

"Nicely done. You couldn't have gotten something earlier, though?"

"I was talking to this dude Braydon. Said his boss didn't get out of bed till nine, and it takes him a couple hours to get ready."

"It's these irresponsible bedtimes that cause crime and depravity, you know," said Seamus.

Maxwell fixed him with a squint, her coal-black eyes drawn to slits. "What's up, boss?"

"What do you mean?"

"You're talking on autopilot. What were you doing when you ran off yesterday?"

"Seeing my mistress," quipped Seamus, then winced slightly at how well it matched the situation. Maxwell snorted.

"Fine, don't tell me. I'm more interested in my five grand, anyway."

"I think there's a relevant saying about counting chickens."

"What, you don't think you can figure out who killed Ryba?"

Seamus frowned. "Who do you think you're talking to? If anyone in Toronto can—"

"Like I said, it's my five grand. Just waiting to collect. Now, let's see that disguise."

Bested, Seamus went to the storage room and dragged out his *dress-up* suitcase, then dug through the clothes and costume jewellery. He pulled a tight black turtleneck over his shirt, then withdrew a shimmering grey jacket from the depths of the suitcase.

"Is that real silk?"

"Of course. Just the thing for Dominic Terrazzo, vaguely European man of mystery."

"Doesn't sound airtight, boss."

"It doesn't have to be. Timmy Greene isn't the sharpest spoon in the drawer. Besides, I'm a shady manager looking to buy some drugs—you wouldn't expect me to be entirely honest about who I am. Some cosmetics and accessories will do the trick."

Seamus pulled a fine gold-plated chain from the suitcase and fastened it over the turtleneck.

"Maxwell, dig out some dress shoes. I know there are some in the storage room. Somewhere."

Grumbling, Maxwell went forth into the wilds of the storage room, and Seamus did his makeup. With a small mirror propped on the desk, he put on a layer of concealer, then made some specific changes: a layer of pale foundation over his tan skin, circles of grey under his eyes.

He was adding a long latex scar down the curve of his left cheek just as Maxwell came back with a pair of snakeskin loafers he'd stolen from a particularly garish racketeer. "Thought these'd match the aesthetic," she said. She leaned in close, inspecting the makeup. "That's a big-ass scar."

"One easy-to-remember detail," said Seamus. "Makes it unlikely he'll recognize me without it."

Seamus coated his hands with a gel that stank of petroleum distillates and slicked his hair back.

"How do I look?"

"Like a used car salesman who just won the lottery," said Maxwell.

"Excellent. You can head home for now, but I'd appreciate it if you kept your phone on tonight. If I get shot, I might need a pickup."

"If you get shot, how are you gonna call me?"

Seamus shrugged. "Payphone."

Seamus got to the Montmorency slightly early and did a lap of the bar, enduring the jaw-rattling music and the sweaty crush of young bodies. Seemed like business was pretty good every night of the week. He considered ordering some of what passed for bourbon but realized that's not what Dominic Terrazzo would be drinking anyway and ordered an appletini instead. Timmy was planted in the same spot at the bar he'd been at last night, glancing around the club every few minutes. He looked excited, or nervous.

Seamus checked his watch, an expensive-looking knock-off Rolex that ran exactly three minutes fast on the hour. Midnight was a good time for the meeting: enough time for Timmy to get a drink or two down, but not to the point that he'd forget what they'd discussed by the morning. At the bar, one of the many well-groomed men who surrounded Timmy was clapping him on the back, gesturing at a knot of girls on the dance floor. As Seamus had guessed, none of the three men he'd fought were in Timmy's entourage, whether that was due to injury or disfavour. Seamus narrowed his eyes, taking in the details.

Timmy was a handsome man, but undermined: puffy around the eyes, and pale, with the sort of well-fed emaciation you normally see only in successful actors. He had the look of a man with a stylist, a nutritionist, and a personal trainer who'd all told him he needed to stop doing three grams of coke a night. Seamus watched him take a long pull from his blue cocktail, then walked over.

"I'm looking for Mr. Greene," said Seamus. He didn't hit the accent too hard, but he made sure they'd remember it. Timmy looked him up and down, his hazel eyes half-clouded.

"Who the fuck are you?"

Seamus slid down into a seat beside him and put his hand on the bar, showing off every ring he'd managed to cram onto his fingers.

"Dominic Terrazzo. Shulker's a client of mine—asked me to represent him at this meeting, told me he'd made an appointment."

Timmy stared for a moment, then he lit up. He gestured for his cronies to clear the bar, and they moved back instantly, all grinning. Not one of them looked like he'd last fifteen minutes in Olexa's office without sending their boss up the river.

"I am a new arrival in this city, Mr. Greene," Seamus said. "I've been told that your family, and you in particular, are highly respected here. The people to know, if we're going to do business. My client has reconsidered your offer and wishes to accept—he'll perform two weeks of shows with a special promotional rollout, free of charge."

Seamus waited, listening to the gears grind in Timmy's head. This was a gamble: catch him in the wrong mood, or with something better to do, and Seamus would find himself out in the alley with nothing to show for the evening's work but a few sips of apple-flavoured kerosene.

"Good choice," said Timmy at last. "On his part. We actually ran into some trouble with the little bitch who used to manage your guy."

Seamus inclined his head. "My client terminated his connection with Rei several weeks ago, but we apologize deeply for any inconvenience. Between you and I—" Seamus leaned in with an ugly smile "—Shulker got a bit tangled up between those legs, let her stay longer than he should have. But my boy has learned better."

Timmy nodded—Seamus had thought he might relate to that. "So, we just need to set a date, dude?"

"At your convenience. As you might have noticed, Shulker has taken a bit of a—hiatus. But with this, he will return to the scene, bigger than ever."

Timmy nodded again, his smile slightly glassy. Up close, it was apparent he was awfully drunk, or medicated, for this early in his night, and his skin shone with sweat, almost as if he had a fever. Not important—Seamus could adapt, and it would be all the more convenient to sell Timmy on this lie with him off his guard.

"You know, I'm fucking glad to hear this," said Timmy. "It's been a messy week over here."

"Oh? I'm sorry to hear that."

Timmy took another long swig, draining his glass. As soon as he set it down, the bartender put the bottle to its lip.

"I wish I could tell you my boys have it under control," said Timmy, sending a dark look at his men, whose smiles suddenly looked hollow, "but I dunno if that's the case, after what happened last night. I had three guys pick up Rei—she was dumb enough to come here, along with one of her friends—but then everything goes pear-shaped. Apparently, five dudes with crowbars came down and kicked the shit out of my guys. No idea why. And that's not the worst of it—my supply line's all fucked, I've got delays, and one of my top guys suddenly turns up dead in the hospital."

Nice to hear he'd been rated as five vicious attackers by Timmy's men. And more importantly, that it wasn't Timmy who killed Ryba, unless Timmy was lying much more cleverly than he had any right to. Seamus pulled a sympathetic face. "Success breeds resentment. Do you think you're being targeted?"

"All I know is someone's putting their fingers in where they don't belong, and when I catch them at it, they're gonna get cut off."

Better men have tried, thought Seamus. But it was a lead—Timmy's rivals could have killed Ryba. Normally, Olexa Greene would've scared off any challengers, but that protection no longer applied if Timmy was moving drugs. Which meant Seamus needed more information about his import operation. No harm in gathering a little more evidence since he was here anyway.

"I did have one more issue to discuss," he said in a low voice. "I work with a number of artists, many of whom need encouragement, many of whom need to relax. It's a very stressful line of work. I understand you are also the man to deal with when it comes to—chemical inspiration?"

"For sure—wait, I'm not looking for someone to undercut me, okay?"

Seamus put up his hands, placating, and shook his head internally. Even if she hadn't known him, Olexa Greene would've seen through his story, and his disguise, before he'd gotten a word out. Timmy Greene would've been smarter to stay at the kids' table where he belonged.

"I didn't come here to make enemies, Mr. Greene," said Seamus, his voice oily. "I find friendship is far more profitable. The fact is, I have a number of clients, both here and in Europe, who are very rich and very bored. They are willing to pay for quality."

Timmy squinted, trying to wrap his small mind around this.

"To put it plainly," continued Seamus, "my client is willing to perform for free. But he would appreciate some . . . reciprocity. Two weeks of performances are very draining, and Shulker will require something to help him stay motivated. And if you can give him something interesting—sell it to me at full price, and I guarantee I can tap a market you couldn't otherwise access."

At last something clicked in the backwaters behind his eyes and Timmy nodded. "You want some merchandise, is what you're saying."

"Yes. Not just anything—my clients are discerning. I will require extremely high-quality product, and I don't doubt a man of your reputation can provide. I'll pay a premium, once Shulker's had a chance to test drive it."

"Course," said Timmy. "We can't have our boy stressed before the show, right?" Suddenly magnanimous, he threw an arm around Seamus's shoulder. Seamus stuffed down a sudden twinge of nausea as a wave of Axe body spray washed over him. "We'll plan something, for sure. I'm thinking January. He's going to help us go big-time, man. I'd be more than happy to send him a treat—and some for your friends too. What's he like? Coke?"

"I'd be interested to hear what offers you can make me, Mr. Greene. I'd buy cocaine, yes, but everyone has it these days, don't they? I'm looking for something new . . . I'm sure you'd find my price satisfying . . ."

That was laying it on a bit thick, but Seamus doubted Timmy would notice. Sure enough, he just smiled. "Dominic, I think I know just what you're looking for. This is what I've been busting my ass for."

Timmy waved to his nearest crony, one with a heavy gold chain nestled in truly luxuriant chest hair, and they both stood.

"C'mon, man."

The two of them walked Seamus past the bouncers, towards the stockroom where Seamus had found Maxwell. Seamus's shoulder started to twitch with the desire to knock them both unconscious before they could jump him—he couldn't show any hesitation. There was a chance he'd underestimated Timmy; if they'd planned an ambush, things could get messy—even Seamus could be overwhelmed, and he was going in blind.

But when they opened the door there was no mob waiting to burst out. The chairs Maxwell and Rei had been tied to were cleared away—the room was grimy as ever, but a table was set out, and two men sat at it, staring at their phones. Seamus recognized Playboy Hat from the previous night—his nose was bandaged, and he was speaking quietly into his phone—Seamus made out the words *delivery ready* before he glanced up at Seamus and quickly hung up. Another gamble. Seamus steadied his breathing as Timmy threw his arms wide.

"Gentlemen! We've got a customer. Shulker's new manager is looking for a supply."

Playboy Hat looked up, scowling.

"Shulker? That fucker who nearly killed Daniel? He's still in the ICU, man."

Timmy waved him off.

"If Daniel kicks it, he got himself killed. That Rei you fuck-ups got last night? She hasn't worked for Shulker in weeks."

"My buddy told me—"

Timmy slapped him hard with an open palm, the crack echoing around the small concrete room. Seamus winced internally, not at the injury but at the poor management. When you worked under the table, there was nothing more valuable than loyalty—something Olexa understood. As long as they obeyed, she treated her men like her own sons, and they loved her for it. Timmy, it seemed, treated his men like junkyard dogs. Playboy Hat sat down, and as Timmy's face was turned he shot him an interesting look—not hatred, but disdain, if Seamus read it right. There was some cunning behind those dark eyes—more than Timmy had, anyway.

"Braydon, what your buddy needs is a hole in his head," Timmy spat, then he turned to Seamus, looking slightly embarrassed. "Sorry 'bout that. Braydon's got a stick up his ass—still mad he got jumped, probably. Forget him—let me show you what I've got."

The phones in his men's hands disappeared, and one walked over to the wall, pushing back a dusty poster of a woman wearing a yachting hat and little else. Behind it was a wall safe, presumably where Timmy stashed the week's take from the bar as well as money from his less legitimate ventures. The crony pulled out a black steel box and set it on the card table, unclasping the top before he stepped back.

Inside were several thousand single-use plastic vials, the kind they use in biotech laboratories. They were small: each vial couldn't have held more than two millilitres of the opaque pinkish-white fluid that filled them. Gleefully, Timmy pulled out a few vials, rolled them in his palm.

"This is what you need, Dominic. It'll be the next big thing."

"What is it called?"

"Platinum," said Timmy triumphantly, and Seamus concentrated hard to keep his expression from changing. "Brand new stuff, fresh out of the lab. I'm the only one in the whole world who can get you this stuff."

Ryba was involved in this, and one of Timmy's rivals killing him suddenly made a whole lot more sense. They weren't just killing some lawyer to send a message, they were targeting the supply chain.

"What does it do?" asked Seamus, keeping his voice cool and skeptical.

"Beautiful shit. It's like Molly, but better. Gives you all the energy you need, and everything's smooth-fucking-sailing. Keeps you going all night off just one hit."

"Is the comedown bad?"

Timmy grinned and shook his head. "Best fucking part. There's no crash, just a slow, steady buzz down, lets you fall asleep nice and easy. It doesn't fuck you up too bad either—I did tests, slipped some to my buddy before he drove to Sauble with his girlfriend, and you know that's a three-hour trip. He made it just fine."

Seamus nodded. "Platinum . . . I like the sound of it. Allow me to buy a sample—if it's as good as you say, I'll be back soon with a much larger order."

Timmy was almost drooling at the thought of the money to be made, and that made him reckless. Playboy Hat . . . no, *Braydon*—Seamus resented having to waste valuable neurons on remembering the man's name—was eyeing Seamus suspiciously, but that slap hadn't left him too inclined to give his boss any more good advice.

"Buy a sample? C'mon, man, we're gonna do business. I'll give you a taste for free, and you can tell me if it's not the best thing since cash and ass."

Seamus smiled and inclined his head. "That sounds even better."

Timmy handed Seamus five of the vials, then raised a finger in warning. "You come back with an order, yeah?"

"I'm sure I will, if this Platinum's as good as you say . . ."

"It is. We're gonna cut those vials, make five, ten doses out of each. Each one of those is two hundred, street price."

Seamus nodded. "Don't cut them all. Two hundred dollars a hit—I can make that happen."

"Sure, sure," said Timmy, as his men moved to replace the box in the safe. "And if you move enough, I can come down on the price some. You have to understand, though, manufacture ain't easy."

Seamus raised a vial to the dim fluorescent light, squinting into the cloudy vial of pinkish fluid.

"I believe you."

Back in the noise of the club, Seamus bought a bottle of Hennessy for Timmy's friends, to general acclaim. He'd happily have bought them the whole bar—he had his lead, and Ruby's fifty grand was in sight. Braydon had followed with a fake smile and joined the crowd of faceless frat boys. Seamus kept his attention on them for any potential threats, only barely noticing the crowd that moved past. From the corner of his eye he saw a herd of goths, two lovers enjoying their foreplay on the dance floor, a man on what must have been his seventh martini and likely his second liver. Seamus only let his attention dance over them, though—he needed to stick the landing and get out with his evidence.

Three of Timmy's men had managed to gather some disturbingly young-looking girls off the dance floor, who alternated between giggling and glancing around like captive deer. One girl with almond eyes and a cherry-red skirt seemed to have caught the particular attention of Braydon.

He was grabbing at the girl's wrists and now he held them for just long enough to let panic rush into her eyes. Braydon's eyes glittered darkly with lust and violence—each was fine on its own, in Seamus's opinion, but they curdled when mixed. The man had had the same look in his eyes when he'd been getting ready to beat Maxwell last night—likely this girl was going to be his consolation prize. Timmy's men cheered and laughed and offered her a shot.

Seamus's drink, which he'd twice emptied quietly onto the floor, tasted acrid in his mouth. He cleared his throat and moved closer to her. Timmy grinned and waved his man back, letting his new customer get close enough to whisper in the frightened girl's ear: "I'd advise against staying long enough for them to get another drink down. Follow me out."

In a loud voice, Seamus confessed that he'd better be going home, but that he wouldn't mind a bit of company—this with a glance at the cherry-skirted girl. Timmy's boys all hooted, and Timmy waved them out, ignoring Braydon's disappointment. That was good—Braydon was the only one who seemed to have his wits about him, and him being angry with Timmy could only be an advantage to Seamus. Seamus kept the act up, one arm around the girl's shoulders, until they were out in the cold. She shivered, and her head pivoted from side to side, looking for a direction to bolt. When they'd made it a few steps onto the street he drew his hand back politely and leaned against a graffiti-scarred wall.

"Go home, kid."

She blinked at him. Then she ran.

He rubbed his arms as he walked—it was a bitter night, and too cold for a flimsy silk suit. When he was sure he was alone, he pulled out a bar napkin and wiped off the makeup. It was theatre-grade, slick and clinging and damnably uncomfortable. The latex scar went last, coming off with a rubbery squeak. It was just past 2 a.m. and the streets were deserted, the only sound the soft transformer hum of the streetlights and the salt blowing down the road. All he passed was a lone figure on a street bench, bent double against the cold. Seamus started past her, but there was something familiar about the dress the hunched woman wore. He drew closer to her.

"Mariah Lopez?"

She looked up and gave a feeble smile. "Ah, you're the young man with the police, aren't you?"

"Are you alright? It's late for you to be out on your own."

"Ah, fine, fine." Unsteadily, she got to her feet. In the first cold hours of the morning, the streetlights shone down on a woman who barely managed to stand to greet Seamus. Out of her house, it was like her supports had been removed, leaving her crumbling.

"What are you doing here?"

"Ah, visiting. When my son died, it wasn't far from here. Some nights I can't sleep, I come to visit."

"You should get home," said Seamus. "Wait here, and I'll find a cab."

She was too cold and tired to protest, even when Seamus hung his jacket over her shoulders—it wasn't much better than tissue paper, but it'd do her more good than it did him. Seamus found an orange cab, waiting to pick up stragglers from the Montmorency, and shepherded it down the street to where Mariah waited, got it as close to where she was standing as possible. Carefully, with a trembling hand, Mariah gripped the door and lowered herself into the seat beside Seamus.

The two rode in silence for a time. Mariah was trying to hide that she was shivering. As Seamus watched, her eyes drifted closed and snapped back open again, but it didn't seem like an old woman nodding so much as someone teetering on the edge of a coma.

"On second thought, maybe we should get you to the hospital."

She opened her mouth to protest, then shut it tight as she pressed her side as if wracked by some internal pain. It took her several breaths to speak again. "Maybe—for the best."

Seamus gave new instructions to the driver, who agreed with that strange alien cheerfulness you sometimes see in people who work the nightshift. They turned north, onto quieter streets. Mariah was now more obviously struggling to stay awake and aware, and Seamus cast about for something to hold her focus—pain might work. It always had in his case.

"How did your son die, Mariah?"

She flinched slightly but didn't turn away. Seamus, who'd seen plenty of men die, occasionally at his own hands, didn't see the point in being squeamish about mortality or grief.

"He kept bad company," she said. "He was a good boy. The best. But . . . bad friends. They said it was an overdose."

"A painless death, at least," observed Seamus. Having heard the phrase very often when he was a child, he never said, *I'm sorry for your loss*. Not unless it really was *his* fault.

"I don't believe it," she said sharply. "Tony was a good boy, he didn't smoke, never drank much alcohol even. I remember: always only one drink, so he wouldn't do anything foolish. He was happy, he wouldn't have—" Mariah took a breath. Her eyes had regained some of their sharpness. "He was a good man, my little Tony. Someone did it to him, poisoned him."

Seamus said nothing—he wasn't that cruel. Denial wasn't a vice if it was what let you get out of bed in the morning.

"I went to the police," she continued, her voice quiet and distant. "But you see it when they look—just a crazy old woman." She looked at Seamus, a hint of challenge in her eyes. "And you, you don't believe me either, do you, young man?"

"I never met your son, Mrs. Lopez. But a mother knows her children," said Seamus. "You said he was a good boy, and I believe that. He'd want you somewhere safe and warm, not out past midnight when you might get sick."

"Ah, young man, I'm already sick."

"Still. He'd want you to rest, to heal up."

"You're right, maybe," she said, with a strange tone—almost regretful. The cab was nearly to the hospital now, and bright windows shone out of the dark, the harsh flash of ambulance lights ahead. "But you know, detective, there are things you only do at night. Thank you for bringing me—I'll be fine from here. I know the doctors very well."

Nonetheless, Seamus helped her inside and made sure she got to the front desk. The receptionist recognized her, of course, and two nurses came to her side looking worried. They'd be more help to her now than Seamus could be, and in any case he didn't need any more witnesses to remember that a strange man dressed too lightly for the winter had come with Mariah to the hospital. He retreated to the entrance.

"Take care, Mariah."

"Make sure you go home, too, yes? You young people, staying up late, bad for your health."

Seamus laughed. "Don't worry, Mrs. Lopez. I'll be going straight to bed. Good night."

The cab dropped him off by his office, and Seamus handed the smiling driver a fat tip. He hurried up the stairs, dumped the vials of Platinum onto his desk, threw the blanket down, and fell asleep in his cheap silk jacket.

CHAPTER SIX

Maxwell arrived the next morning and was promptly deployed in search of breakfast. Seamus didn't fall back asleep, but he needed an empty office for a half hour to clear his head and stop his heart racing before the day began.

By the time she got back with iced coffee and fried breadsticks from Minnie's, Seamus had changed into his work clothes and managed to rotate into a more productive frame of mind.

"So," she said, setting down the coffees. "That half-assed plan of yours work?"

"Like all my plans, it worked perfectly. Wheels turning within wheels within buttered clockwork."

"*Buttered clockwork*?"

"Timmy seems to be moving on his own—he's importing some new drug to the city, and Olexa doesn't move narcotics. Looks like both Williams and Ryba were involved. I'd say a rival pusher is our most likely suspect here."

"What about Olexa? Wouldn't she be pissed that Timmy's doing this?"

"Oh, very. When she finds out she'll come down on him like a hammer—the fact that Timmy's alive at all means she doesn't know.

I don't know how Timmy's managed to avoid realizing what's going to happen to him when that changes, but it's a neat trick—he ought to write a book on positive thinking."

Maxwell shivered. "She's really scary, boss. Can't imagine what'd be like being her husband."

"She doesn't have one. I've heard that she had a lover, once, till she found out he was dealing with the Algerians on the side. Poor bastard died of a broken heart."

"Really?"

"Yep. Six of her men took ball-peen hammers and broke it, along with the rest of his chest cavity. Now for some breakfast."

Seamus ripped right through the plastic bag to get at the breadsticks—Maxwell took one and watched as the rest of the golden fried dough fell to him one after another like a doomed garrison. Maxwell stirred her coffee pensively for a few minutes before she asked her next question.

"You know boss, I've been wondering. How did you and Sandra meet?"

"Trick-or-treating."

Seamus continued on with his breadsticks.

"You're just gonna leave me with that, huh?"

"Her parents didn't want her to go," said Seamus. "But she snuck out anyway and ran into me. We would've been—what, seven? The memory's blurry. I pulled a fast one on her, convinced her to trade her Pocky for a jawbreaker."

"Damn, sneaking out at seven? Bet her parents were freaking out."

Seamus sipped his coffee. "Her mother didn't hurt her too badly. She always was careful not to leave marks—imagine the risk to the family reputation."

"Oh."

He gave Maxwell a warning look. "I'd avoid bringing it up with Sandra, if I were you. She spent ten odd years getting out of that house—she doesn't like it when people put her back inside."

Maxwell looked as if she wanted to sink down into her boots.

Seamus could call the image to his mind as sharp as if it had been burned in silver nitrate, clearer than the memory of his own childhood house. Red bricks and pink tulips—Sandra's mother won prizes for her tulips, and more than once Sandra'd had to water them when she was cut off from water herself for coming home late. The night that they'd left for Toronto, she and Seamus had taken baseball bats to every last one of those terracotta planters.

"Sorry, boss," she said at length.

"It's fine," said Seamus, neatly folding up a wax paper wrapper. "The two of us have different policies when it comes to the past. But enough history—there's work to be done."

One thing was still bothering him—and he had five vials of it in his jacket. If this Platinum were going to hit the streets, it'd be worth knowing more about it.

"We need to look into rivals who would've wanted to target Ryba, but first I'm going to the coroner's, try to figure out what Timmy's selling. You want to come?"

Maxwell shrugged. "Never done anything science-y before. Sounds dope."

At 1 p.m. Seamus looked up and noticed that Maxwell was face down on the lab bench.

"Can I just drink some of these chemical bottles and get it over with?"

"These tests take time," he said, looking back to his work.

Maxwell sat up and fiddled with a centrifuge. "Have you found anything besides it's a little pink?"

"I've got lots of results, but not many answers," he said, his voice distracted but patient. Lab work always put him in a bit of a trance. "There's a trace amount of the compound that was in that briefcase, but just a trace. If whatever that hacker kid took was the pure form, this has been diluted tens of thousands of times over."

"Makes sense. I mean, that stuff did put him in a coma."

"Not many substances are psychoactive at such small dosages—we're talking about micrograms here. Whatever this stuff is, it's either powerful as all hell, or just one part of the mix."

"You think there's other sauce in there too?" asked Maxwell.

"Looks like it. There are at least two distinct drugs, chemically similar to ecstasy, but with some differences, going by spectroscopy results. Plus a stabilizer, and a few other things I can't pin down."

Maxwell was giving the vials a very interested look. Seamus looked up to glare at her, and she glanced away quickly.

"Anyway," she said, "this all sounds a bit mastermind-y for the dude who sells shitty coke at his club."

"You're right—this is way above Timmy's pay grade. My guess? It's a neurosis."

"I'm a music major, Sherlock. What's a neurosis?"

"A hang-up—someone like Timmy, floundering, feeling out of place when he's sober enough to feel anything. This is his big play—one big number to bring the house down. That's the only reason I can think of he'd take so many risks. You'll notice, Maxwell, that you never see a successful man go all in like this. But a loser with something to prove—they want a quick, spectacular success."

As he spoke, drops of diluted Platinum crept through tiny channels in the plastic chip he'd laid out in front of him. This was from the sample Timmy had given him—the concentrated powder he'd found on Baldwin was carefully stashed away. If it was that strong, he'd need to take some extra precautions before he unsealed that vial again. A biosafety cabinet, maybe. Maxwell watched the minuscule paths the drops traced through the channels.

"You think he could really sell this stuff?" she asked at last.

"Depends. He was asking for two hundred a shot."

Maxwell choked at that. Seamus couldn't blame her—you'd never move numbers with prices like that, not for something new. But what interested him was why Timmy expected it to sell.

"He'll have to come down on the price—but if this is as good as Timmy seems to think? He'll have a market. Club scene, mostly, and it looks like he's already got a presence there."

"Seems to me, boss, that this all might be easier if you had a test subject."

Seamus's fingers tightened on the remaining sample in his hand. But there was a rule for this too: "If you're that eager—I'd never stop someone from gambling. Here." He handed her the vial, forcing himself to be careless, with an attempt at a smile that came out more of a sneer.

Maxwell considered, seemed a little less enthusiastic. "Or maybe not, boss. Let me hang onto it?"

"As you like. I already have all the samples I need, after all."

Seamus turned back to his work again. After a moment, Maxwell cleared her throat.

"So Olexa," she said, "is gonna throw him out a window when she finds out. What's his angle *there*?"

"Not a clue. I can only imagine," said Seamus, leaning back on the battered lab chair, "that he doesn't actually have one. Unless he thinks he can get big enough to compete with her selling this stuff. Which would be insane. Greene's one of the biggest importers in the city—weapons, ivory, Pokémon cards. And her men are loyal to the point of death. Timmy could never buy them off. I give him a week breathing once she knows about this."

"And then Rei's safe."

"Sure," said Seamus. "But there's one problem."

Maxwell waited, expectant, and Seamus just looked back at her. At length, she sighed. "Alright, genius, what's the problem?"

"So glad you asked, protégé. The problem is who's behind Timmy."

Seamus saw as the light went on in her head. Timmy was about as quick as a train on the green line—he'd never have invented a new drug, and a big distribution scheme, on his own. And whoever was pulling his strings might not be happy when their frontman came crashing down. That one guy, Braydon, had clearly been coordinating a sale last night. Perhaps he was orchestrating things and hoping Timmy would take the fall when everyone else in the city moved to crush the operation. The sort of plan a stupid person would think was clever.

Maxwell wandered out at some point with a promise to come in early the next day. Perhaps it was cruel to let her keep that vial. But that too was a test—someone who was willing to take a stupid risk like that for a quick high was a liability, and Seamus would have to cut her loose, preferably before she got her commission. If Maxwell came in tomorrow with her eyes drawn wide, talking about the new concerto she'd written and the new instrument she'd invented to play it on, he'd know. And while a first-hand account of the effects *would* be useful, Seamus found himself hoping it wouldn't come to that.

In his line of work, contacts were money, and Seamus's greatest professional weakness had always been his inability to play nice with pushers. He could grin and grovel through a few meetings, but sooner or later the cracks would show and he'd throw his new "friend" through a window. Which was unfortunate, because right now he needed to know who'd be willing to kill to shut Timmy's operation down. That meant other pushers, and, more specifically, other pushers who knew about Platinum.

Most of the men he called either hung up on him or called him a motherfucker *then* hung up on him. People were braver on the phone—not one of them would have looked at him sideways if he were standing in arm's reach. Five failures in, Seamus stopped and rubbed his eyes, feeling the strain of the previous two nights. Then he dialled a sixth number. The voice that answered was dry, rasping with scar tissue from a thousand pulls on a glass stem.

"Who is this?"

"A buyer."

"Don't meet with anyone, they don't give me a name."

Seamus could hear the hunger in his voice—pushers would snap at any opportunity to make money, something Seamus could use to his advantage.

"Seamus. You remember me."

A pause. "I remember what happened to the last guy you did business with."

"Maybe I've got enough cash on me to make you forget, huh?" Seamus said nothing else—he let the line play, let the hook sink deep.

"Tomorrow at lunch. The Harvey's."

The next day, Maxwell came in looking her usual sullen self. Just to be sure, Seamus light-fingered her jacket while she was looking away and found the vial was still there, not a drop missing. Smiling to himself, Seamus sent her hunting toxicology reports at the university archives. He figured she'd run into a cute co-ed and he'd have the rest of the day free for his meeting—he'd need to get that out of the way before he went to Sandra's for dinner. He set out to his meeting, facing into the wind.

On the corner of Broadview and Queen stood the Harvey's: an opium den, bordello, and low-rent hostel that also occasionally sold burgers. Seamus stomped his way through slush all the way there—it had warmed up that morning, fresh-fallen snow gone from glittering winter silver to the usual grey Toronto sludge. He arrived on time, and waited, as was customary, for Ricky. Ricky was the owner of the Harvey's, a position he had maintained by gutting all challengers.

Ricky was a midrange pusher who'd held an uneasy truce with Olexa and the other powers in the city for a few years. It was possible that he'd caught wind of Timmy's distribution plans and wanted to send a message by killing Ryba. It was a long shot—there were plenty of people in the city who would've wanted to shut down the competition before it got started—but one thing was definite: Ricky was immersed in the flow of drugs and information that kept the Toronto underworld functioning. If there was something worth knowing about the Ryba murder, Ricky would know it.

The only problem would be extracting that information from him.

While he waited, Seamus went out of his way to fidget with the table—his hair was too short to look really unkempt, but he ordered fries and deliberately smudged some grease and ketchup on his shirt, trying to ignore the faint smell of urine that hung beneath the ethyl tang of antiseptic. He chatted up a regular who sat beside him; the man offered a number of interesting opinions on the nature of quantum chromodynamics and how it related to geopolitics.

At last Ricky arrived in a brown coat the same shade as the grubby linoleum floors, only slightly greasier—a thin, shrewd man with cracking skin. The theoretician Seamus had been talking to recognized the new arrival and quickly hustled out of the way, back into a darker corner of the restaurant. Ricky nodded briskly to Seamus, and one of his employees rushed over just as he sat down, setting a milkshake on the table in front of him like a sacrificial offering. Seamus stood and shook Ricky's hand, clapping him on the back and discreetly running a hand over his jacket. No gun—that was excellent news. Ricky smiled at Seamus, showing a mouthful of yellowed but straight teeth, and sat down.

"Hey there, Seamus. Never thought I'd see the day you wanted help from me."

"Yeah, well, shit happens. That's how your business keeps running, right?"

"Sure, everyone needs a friend sometimes. But 'the Surgeon'? Didn't see it coming."

Seamus hadn't heard that name in a while, but it had been hard-earned.

He'd worked for quite a few grey-area businesses and lenders, but he'd made the most money under Little Dan, the financier of East Chinatown, who gave him ten percent of any money he was able to recover, no questions asked. Seamus had managed to survive that way for some time, living in the little gaps of the city's economy, which were plugged with cash and an abundance of discretion. He'd been out on a standard job, intimidating a man in his fifties who'd gone in deep to finance his mistress's taste in purebreds. Seamus had done the job—nothing serious, just a cheerful reminder and a broken nose for the debtor. Hadn't even taken the dogs. The man had overreacted and called in five younger friends to jump Seamus. That was fine—all in good fun—but one of them had pulled a knife.

Seamus didn't kill any of those young men, but he didn't restrain himself either. Two of them were still in wheelchairs and weren't going to get out of them in this lifetime. The nickname had been given to him by the youngest and most intelligent of the five men. He'd stood there shaking, barely able to stay on his feet, while Seamus walked slowly towards him, wiping his friends' blood off his hands. Seamus had looked at him, that old ice in his blood, and while he couldn't remember exactly what he said, the story on the street was that he'd smiled with about a thousand teeth and thanked the kid for donating his body to science. That kid had run before Seamus got within reach, and he'd called him the Surgeon whenever he told the story.

"Maybe we'd better talk in the back," said Ricky, and he stood and moved to the back of the restaurant, towards a grey door marked *private*. Seamus followed him through.

Inside that back office was a cracked television screen flickering with security camera footage of the restaurant, some porno calendars that seemed to have been put up out of grim obligation rather than any actual interest, and, inexplicably, a gritty collection of snow globes. The desk was encrusted with the inevitable layers of oil and spread with papers, but what held Seamus's attention was the other door, just behind the desk. It was a potential escape route, but also where Ricky's reinforcements would be coming from.

Ricky clearly wasn't buying Seamus's cover, but Seamus wasn't going to give it up just yet. Asking about Timmy directly would raise an alarm, but there was a more oblique angle of attack: the Platinum. Seamus jammed a fidgeting hand in his pocket.

"Sorry," he said, "mind if I take the edge off?"

"Hey, be my guest," said Ricky as Seamus put a bullet-shaped dispenser to his nose, clicked at it, and inhaled greedily. It was the sort of dispenser you normally used for cocaine in the club—Seamus kept an empty one in his jacket to throw people off. He watched Ricky relax as Seamus exaggerated sniffing and rubbing his nose. Seamus smiled internally—every con worked by making the mark feel secure.

"So, tell me what you need," said Ricky.

"It's a tough job I've got," said Seamus, "and even I have to relax sometimes. I've been into this new stuff—enjoying it. But I'm getting kind of low. You have any Platinum?"

Pushers could smell desperation—it was blood in the water to them. And deceit under any circumstances followed the principle of stage magic—the trick was always showing people what they wanted to see.

Ricky tapped a hand over the surface of his desk.

"That slang, Seamus? You mean H?"

"No, something new. Comes in these little vials," said Seamus, adding a tinge of desperation to his voice. "Before, I bought it from Timmy Greene."

Ricky's eyes narrowed. "Then what the hell are you coming to me for?"

Seamus spread his hands wide, his shoulders relaxed. "C'mon, Ricky, Timmy's a shitspoon. I want to deal with a businessman."

"Look," said Ricky, obviously impatient to get back to separating addicts from their rent money, "I can get you H, coke, pills, but I don't know what new-type shit you're talking about. You'd better go back to the shitspoon."

Seamus smiled and leaned back in his chair, letting the pretense of nervousness fall away from him. It was just as well—he was more comfortable with the second option.

As with most mid-level criminals, Ricky was mildly intelligent but thought he was Einstein born again. If he or one of his friends had killed Ryba, he wouldn't be stupid enough to admit that to Seamus. But Seamus could layer his deceits: he'd pretend that he was after Timmy Greene himself and see how Ricky responded. If Ricky was trying to sabotage Timmy, he'd be all too happy to feed Seamus information about his rival, true or false. And his guard would be down, thinking he'd seen through Seamus's game already.

Seamus slipped a fast hand into his jacket and took a moment's pleasure in watching Ricky twitch and grab for the gun Seamus had made sure he wasn't carrying.

"How about now, Ricky?" he said, slapping a roll of hundred-dollar bills down onto the greasy table. "Anything you want to tell me about Timmy Greene and his import business?"

Ricky's eyes popped open, then immediately narrowed again. "I knew something was off. You'd never buy an Advil from me."

Seamus just kept grinning and said nothing. He'd laid out three thousand dollars—a risk, to be sure, but a calculated one, when you weighed it against the fifty grand he stood to gain.

"If you give me a couple days," said Ricky, "I can find whatever you're looking for."

"I'll be honest," said Seamus. "I'm interested in the supply chain. Who's running it, who's for, and who's against."

"How much bread did you just put on the table?"

"Three thousand. You're welcome to count it—I won't take offence."

"Fuck that, Caron. You're going to get me six thousand."

Seamus suppressed the urge to curl his lip and offered an overly friendly smile instead. "I've got what you need, Ricky."

He laid another three thousand on the table, careful to hide the fact that he still had plenty of bribe money hidden in his coat. Always wise to split your rolls between several pockets.

"That's more like it," said Ricky with a cracked-lip grin. He reached for the money, but Seamus put a single hand out over it. It was the hand with the knife scars—he wanted Ricky to see those, think about all the other men Seamus had survived. Ricky drew back. "I'll tell you what I know, Caron. I haven't heard much about this new shit . . ."

"Platinum. Might go by other names. Comes in liquid form."

"Right. No fucking clue. But I can give you one of *my* suppliers, the man who's best connected. Let me tell you, if Timmy's trying to get in on the game, my guy's not going to be happy about it. I'll set up an appointment for you, huh?"

Seamus nodded, forcing his thoughts to speed up. It looked like Ricky wasn't all that interested in Timmy. And offering Seamus one of his suppliers was an obvious ploy on Ricky's part—he was either feeding Seamus a rival or a problematic business partner he wanted out of the picture. Still, it was better than *no* lead, and if he was going to find a man with enough reach and foresight to see Timmy and Ryba as a threat to be dealt with, he'd need a connection higher up the supply chain than Ricky. And if Ricky was sending him on a wild goose chase, well, Seamus could always come back by and fracture his skull as he locked up for the night.

Ricky pocketed the six thousand, then scribbled out a name and number on an old promotional flyer. "You get in touch with this guy—I'll tell him you're calling."

"Don't give him my name—just an interested customer, right?"

"Right. He's not dangerous, but he spooks easy. The best supplier I have in pills—if anyone knows, it'll be him."

Seamus took the flyer and went slightly stiff when his eye caught the name.

Alister Carleton

If Seamus had been a few years younger, he'd have flinched. Instead, he kept his face neutral as he searched for an angle to work. "You said he's in the pill business?" asked Seamus.

"Yeah, mostly prescription, but he moves bulk too. Pure stuff. And he does wholesale. If anyone knows about something new hitting the streets, it'll be him."

Seamus nodded. "How about you sell me one of his prescriptions too?" More leverage was always better.

Ricky smiled his bloody-lipped smile. "'Nother three hundred."

"Done." Seamus laid out a few more bills, turned on his heel, pushed his way out the door, and walked out into the cold.

Alister Carleton. Doctor at East General—he'd been on call when Ryba was murdered, and suddenly that fact seemed much more significant. Sandra's instincts were rarely wrong, a lesson it seemed he still hadn't finished learning. If Carleton was a rival drug runner, it would make perfect sense for him to target Timmy Greene. All that squared away with his wanting Seamus's advice.

Sandra'd been spot-on when she said to give Carleton a call, and it was past time Seamus did. He suspected she'd be eager to pay the old doctor a visit, once she saw Seamus's prize.

Seamus got on the road and walked towards Logan, where there were still a few old, embattled payphones. He didn't use the number Ricky had given him—that was probably a burner, and it wouldn't do for him to call Carleton on it anyway. Instead, he dialled the number Sandra had given him.

"Hi there, I'd like to speak to Dr. Carleton?"

The voice that answered had an upper layer of forced cheerfulness and an undercurrent of tension and fatigue. "Speaking. Who's this?"

"Seamus Caron. You'll remember me, I think—"

"Thomas's boy! Well, I was hoping you'd call. I ran into that old friend of yours at work. Sasha was her name, I think?"

"Sandra, yes. She told me you had some questions for me."

"That's right. I've gotten into—well, better we'd discuss it in person. Will you be able to come up to the farm?"

"Sounds delightful," said Seamus, and he was grateful you couldn't see expressions over landline. "Let's say two days from now. I could bring something—"

"Lorraine would be furious with me if she didn't get a chance to feed you. Come on up—bring a friend! Let's have a family dinner together, just like old times."

"An excellent suggestion." Seamus was looking forward to the look on Alister's face when his friend turned out to be the chief of homicide and they brought along some very solid evidence of Carleton's involvement in a murder. "See you soon, Alister."

With the more pleasant task for the day finished, Seamus walked back to the office and dressed for dinner. He'd told Sandra he'd come before he'd found out Michael was a stack of human shit wearing a beanie, but a promise was a promise. On went a ragged cotton blazer under the oilskin.

There was a chance this dinner would be less tense than the one he'd scheduled to blackmail the doctor, but Seamus didn't get his hopes up. He spent his walk to Sandra's apartment trying to decide how many teeth Michael strictly needed—fewer than he happened to have, to be sure.

Winter had set its jaw, and every step crunched with frost, even under the cloudless sunlight. Sandra's apartment was small but comfortable, a ground-floor flat with a little postage-stamp patio that looked out onto a quiet residential street, up the road from an excellent ice cream parlour.

Sandra had an abiding hatred of putting on appearances, a product of her mother's unhinged obsession with them. When they'd gone to school together, Sandra'd always had her skirt exactly regulation length, hair perfectly neat, and red stripes on her wrist marking out how many transgressions she'd been guilty of the previous night. She usually had a fair number of those, since she'd insist on returning home with branches jammed through her hair and her uniform dredged in mud. You couldn't intimidate Sandra with pain, then or ever.

Any concessions to aesthetics in her apartment were concessions to Michael—the bits of art that he collected had aggregated on the empty surfaces. Sandra's plain wood and granite had slowly been covered by imported knick-knacks and rag carpets in far too many colours. On the wall hung a Picasso sketch of a horse, which Seamus recognized as Michael's last birthday present from Sandra. Seamus glared at it.

His eyes caught on something else—a framed, faded photo. It had been taken at a school event, some bake sale or raffle—Sandra, with her hair tied back, looking completely miserable, and Seamus grinning next to her in an already-too-small suit. As Seamus remembered,

Sandra's parents had been in that photo, starched through and with their rigor mortis smiles. They'd been cropped out of the frame, but she'd left in Ma and Seamus's father, and a smiling teenage girl, half-embarrassed, holding a candy apple. Lauren Carres. Seamus looked away and busied himself getting a glass of water from the sink.

Sandra was busy with a colleague on the phone. "Listen, I don't care what you have to do, I need him in court," she yelled into the phone. "You tell him if he doesn't cough up some fucking testimony—hi, Seamus, beer's in the fridge—I'm gonna put him in gen pop. He'll last four days there if he's lucky. He's worried about his friends? Tell him to worry about the shiv he's gonna find in his skull if he doesn't testify!" She slammed the phone down on the counter and took a deep breath. Then she glanced over to Seamus and laughed. "Hell. Stressful job, huh? Michael's out for parsley—says it's a disaster we don't have any. Something 'bout a symphony of flavours or some shit. You have a good day?"

"I have a lead. Remember Carleton?"

"'Course I do. You finally give him a call?"

"That I did, but there's more than that. I've got a contact who says he's slinging pills," said Seamus. "A possible motive for attacking the Greenes—killing Ryba could have been a message."

"Since when has Olexa cared about the pill business?"

"Anonymous source says Timmy Greene may have dipped his toes into the market without her knowing. But one thing at a time—Carleton had a solid motive for killing Ryba."

Sandra gave him a serious look.

"Do you have enough evidence to move on? I can call down a team on him."

"Not yet. But I figure he might crack when we show up for dinner in a couple of nights. Come armed. But that's enough incriminating myself, anything fresh on your end?"

Sandra nodded. "Lab results came back. The knife's American, technically illegal but not hard to buy if you know where to look. Nothing strange about that, but those carvings—you were right.

Amateur work, probably done with hand tools, not the sort of thing you'd expect the user to leave behind. I'm digging into evidence, gonna see if it matches anything we've picked up before. But that's enough of that, what else's been happening?"

Seamus gave her a puzzled look. "Like I said, Carleton's looking good. Don't know how he'd match up with the knife, though—"

"No, dumbass, in real life."

Seamus continued to stare at her. "You know I don't have one of those."

"Well, *I've* been reading. Grabbed some poetry shit at the bookstore."

"You're reading something that doesn't have a gunfighter on the cover? Never thought I'd see the day."

"Yeah, well, I'm regretting it."

"That bad?"

"I read five pages a day. Any more than that, and I think I might get a seizure. The lady who wrote it's got a whole dictionary of words she likes using but they all mean *sad*, and why the lines don't go all the way across the page is a mystery. Waste of perfectly good paper, if you ask me. If they formatted it right, they could fit all the poems on a napkin, and you could blow your nose with it too."

"You should write the publisher with that suggestion," said Seamus. "But why poetry?"

"I promised Michael I'd give it a try," said Sandra, her face resolute, like someone who'd sworn an oath of vengeance.

Seamus rolled his eyes. "I know it won't do any good telling you this," he said, "but you don't have to do *everything* you say you will. Remember the marble incident?"

Back in third grade, Sandra's friend had made her promise to watch some marbles and make sure no one took them. This would've been fine, except for the fact that said marbles were lost somewhere on an acre of land, in the middle of winter, during a record-making blizzard. The alleged friend had then gone home and forgotten all about the affair, leaving Sandra standing in an empty field as the sun went down.

It was an old joke now, but there were even odds Sandra would've died of exposure on that field if Seamus hadn't gone looking for her.

"I told Sally I'd watch her marbles, and that's what I did."

"It's not *Sally's* marbles I'd have worried about."

Sandra laughed at that—her real laugh was different than the bluff one she used in front of strangers, and Seamus only heard it rarely. It was soft and called to mind the few pleasant memories he had of his childhood—skipping rocks down the creek, trying to roll hay bales into forts.

Looking at Sandra's smile in the fading sunlight, Seamus felt an itch in the back of his skull. It was the same one that told him when the kid behind him was about to pull a gun—it meant danger. He wanted to tell her, right now, that Michael was a bastard, tell her all about Evey.

The front door clicked open, and Michael walked in carrying a bag of parsley.

"Oh, Seamus," he said, wearing the stretched smile of someone receiving a particularly hideous Christmas sweater. "How nice of you to come."

"Thank you for the invitation," Seamus said, his voice perfectly flat. He found, to his surprise and dismay, he couldn't put any false joviality in his expression at all.

Michael walked across the small, cluttered apartment and kissed Sandra, then started cutting the parsley.

"Thanks for making dinner," she said.

Michael gave her a melting look. "Anything for you, darling."

Seamus heard the glass in his hand crack—luckily, no one else did. He forced his fingers to relax and snuck the glass into the trash, his eye catching on the glitter of red where he'd pricked his finger against a freshly broken edge. The *correct* course of action, which was usually as obvious to him as a path bordered in fire, was suddenly unclear. Seamus felt strangely off-balance and had none of the clarity that anger was supposed to bring.

Dinner was not off to a good start.

There was a momentary break in the tension when the other guests arrived carrying a mountainous carrot cake. Seamus liked Lydia and Kyle well enough: their conversation was a bit drier than what Seamus was used to, but it was a nice change not to have to check for people sneaking up behind him while they chatted.

Michael laid his roast on the table with a magician's flourish. It was delicious, with whorls of fat and soft muscle, but Seamus had to choke it down.

Once they'd exhausted complimenting the chef and the usual topics of weather, employment, and the routinely abysmal performance of the Leafs, Michael, to Seamus's genuine amazement, began lecturing the table on a love poem he was writing.

"The inner mechanics of the metaphor were difficult to sort out," he was saying, chest puffed. "I at last set upon the image of a pomegranate, over-ripe, and the fine line between desire and revulsion—"

"Is it such a fine line?" asked Seamus. He wanted to idly spin his knife in his hand, but that would've been too obvious. "When I like something, I'd say I'm usually fairly sure about it."

The table turned to face him, and Michael chuckled indulgently. "I'm not talking about some petty like–dislike dichotomy," he said. "We're talking intense passion, when you're truly run away with feeling, plunging headfirst into desire."

"I see a lot of that sort of thing at work," said Seamus evenly. His heart pulsed in his chest, moved by a certain cold rage he felt only rarely when he fought. "But I've found that people who do all their thinking with their heart and none with their head tend to end up with holes in one or the other." He ignored the glare he was getting from Sandra and continued: "In any case, I'm afraid I don't see the connection to love."

Michael rolled his eyes. "You don't see what desire has to do with love?"

"Oh, it plays a part, I think. But there are more important things."

"Please, enlighten us," said Michael.

Seamus at least had the satisfaction of seeing him nettled. "Loyalty," he said, keeping his eyes on Michael. "Constancy. You can't always be wanting someone, I don't think. It's not how your heart—or the rest of your biology—works. But you love them just the same. If you understand the meaning of the word."

Michael had blanched, but he answered with a rising voice: "Right, and when was the last time you were with someone, Seamus? You live alone, in that little office. Never having to do anything actually difficult, or make any kind of sacrifice—"

"Couple days ago I broke a man's nose with my knee," Seamus said, and grinned, showing too many teeth. Lydia gagged slightly and put her napkin to her mouth. "A discussion with him and his colleagues got out of hand—it was as difficult as writing poetry, I assure you. And I've *sacrificed* plenty of ribs, in my line of business."

The table was silent at this. Seamus, after a moment, shrugged and returned to his dinner. No sense in letting it go to waste, especially seeing as this would probably be the last time he was invited. Lydia and Kyle said little else and excused themselves to leave early, their dessert uneaten on the table. Michael was seeing them out when Sandra rounded on him.

"You can leave now."

"I was right, Sandra."

She pinched the bridge of her nose. "Christ, you think that matters? You picked a stupid fight over dinner, and who do you think has to deal with Michael being pissy for the next two weeks? Who has to fight to get you invited to our wedding?"

I'd just as soon miss it. The words nearly made it out, and Seamus startled slightly, realizing how badly his mask had slipped.

Sandra took a sharp breath and leaned back on the counter. "Listen," she said, her voice taking on the forced control her mother had beaten into her and she'd never quite managed to lose. "This place is mine. This little apartment and Michael—I worked hard to get them, both of 'em. You can stay out there on the edge, if that's where you've gotta be. I won't say shit about the cuts on your hands or the black eyes or the nights I wonder whether I'm going to be the one who has to zip the bag up over your head in the end—" the control wavered there, wavered but didn't break "—but you will not come into my house ready to break shit. You see Michael, you play nice, and you don't fucking embarrass me in front of my friends."

Seamus nodded briskly. The correct path was clear once again, and even if it stung, the clarity was worth any temporary pain. Sandra wanted her life, and Seamus would leave her to it and live the way he'd learned to. If there were any emotions that made that difficult for him, well, he was plenty used to fighting: he'd strangle them.

"I understand, Sandra. I'm sorry for ruining your party."

With that, Seamus grabbed his jacket and strode out, careful to go the opposite way Michael had. Sandra didn't say anything, likely stunned into silence—Seamus couldn't remember any other time he'd agreed with her immediately in an argument. But she was right—that had been the deal when they started speaking again. Seamus had his way of dealing with memories: he grinned his bloody-toothed grin at them, fought and kept on fighting till someone mean enough to put him down for good finally came along. Sandra fought, too, in her own way, but she was fighting away from that crumbling old town and that past, fighting for a career and a life and calm and peace. Peace—that was what she was really after, Seamus figured, and she'd never once had it. Even laughing, even sleeping, some part of Sandra Blair was bracing to take a punch. Seamus was the same way, of course—the difference was that she believed there was another way to live. That she wanted that.

They'd made their deal, three years ago—they could be friends again, so long as they didn't get in the way of the other person's fight.

The wind blew hard outside, and Seamus flicked his collar up against it. His best friend was getting married, and Michael's indiscretion was history. Hopefully Evey would loosen a few of Michael's fillings, and that would have to be enough.

For once in his life, Seamus wasn't going to break everything.

CHAPTER SEVEN

The next morning was a light daze of struggling to read toxicology reports. It was dry work but required enough attention to keep him from thinking about the previous night, which Seamus was grateful for. Most likely the visit to Carleton would crack open the murder case, and he had time to kill, so he turned his attention back to Platinum. Funnily enough, after about an hour of work, Seamus found he couldn't stop thinking about it—there was always one more citation to check, another pile of clinical data to scan. An unpleasant urgency pricked at his attention whenever it drifted, like a bit of metal caught under the skin.

Maxwell wandered in and said little—Seamus suspected he wasn't giving off a very kindly feeling. She hung in the corner, playing with her phone and occasionally pulling up a reference for him, which suited him fine.

There wasn't much that looked promising, just references to a private pharmaceutical study. As far as he could find from the abstracts, there had been a battery of tests done on the one organic compound he'd managed to identify, a drug the inventors had thought would inhibit plaque formation in the brains of Alzheimer patients. The problem was that once the damage was done, preventing new plaques from forming didn't seem to improve symptoms, and the side effects from long-term use were severe.

Seamus had found traces of the compound in both samples—the one he'd taken from Williams's briefcase and the Platinum he'd gotten off Timmy, although it was heavily diluted in the second. The uppers in the mix were less mysterious—but what was that protein he couldn't identify, and why was there an Alzheimer drug, of all things, mixed into Timmy's shit?

Finally exhausted by the endless circling trail of endnotes and citations, Seamus pushed up from his desk. No sense wasting more time on it, even if he couldn't help spending a few days and nights thinking about it.

"Come on, Maxwell. I think I owe you lunch."

She followed him down onto the street, still watching him warily. She needn't have worried—Seamus rarely acted when he was angry. The morning's clouds had blown away, and the sun blazed down on the cold pavement. Seamus rolled the puzzle over in his mind as he walked, talking half to himself.

"What I can't crack is exactly what that drug *is*. The active ingredient, the stimulant, is chemically similar to ecstasy, but that's not what Williams was smuggling in. That briefcase was full of a protein I've got no leads on, and some failed Alzheimer drug. Expensive and pointless."

Maxwell shrugged. "What about the case we're actually getting paid for, boss?"

"All but solved," said Seamus, brightening a bit. "Tomorrow we'll go visit Dr. Carleton, he'll confess to killing Ryba to shut down Timmy as competition, and we'll collect on Ruby Ryba's reward. That reminds me—be up and ready to go at a reasonable time tomorrow. Sandra and I are picking you up at eleven to run a couple errands before we drive out."

Maxwell wailed her discontent with that, likely having anticipated a proper Saturday night out—maybe even a day off that weekend—but Seamus just kept walking.

He was up early the next morning, before the sun came up, and the wind slashed at his jacket as he stepped out of his office. A woman who owed Seamus a favour worked at the Planet Fitness, and she let him in—a workout cleared his head from sleep, though it didn't do much for his mood.

As he returned to his office, it was late morning and time to start thinking about the logistics of the trip. He hadn't heard from Sandra yet, and after leaving things the way he did on Friday night, Seamus might have to see about renting a car after all, hit the road with Maxwell alone. He started up the steps to his apartment, but something made him stop. As Seamus stood there in the early morning dark, an ancient, road-salt-crusted car pulled round the corner. It was a good five minutes before the time Sandra'd agreed to meet him, before the unpleasantness of dinner, but there she was. The engine guttered to a stop, and Sandra swung out of the driver's door to face Seamus, arms crossed over her chest and eyes steady on his. She didn't say anything, but after watching her for a moment he walked over to the passenger's side.

They drove out together. Not straight to Maxwell's—she pulled around on a side street and killed the engine. Some winter sunlight glinted off the dash and caught silver on the scar on her nose. The first break—her mother had done that, the night she left for good.

"Hey."

"Hey, Sandra."

"Michael's pissed at you."

Seamus gave a weary laugh. "What else is new?"

Sandra didn't say anything, just kept her eyes forward.

Seamus inclined his head slightly. "Sorry for the trouble."

"Mm-hm. You're always trouble. I'm used to it." After a moment, she drew a sharp breath. "Listen, are we good?"

"Like you said: You've got your life. I've got mine, such as it is. Doesn't mean we can't have a beer at Jackson's at the end of the day."

Sandra turned to him then, and though she was smiling, there was a certain sadness in her eyes. Might've been that Seamus just imagined it, though, because she shook her head and then he saw nothing but her usual brash smile. "Alright! Enough of this serious shit. In the past, right? And Michael—he'll get over it. He'll be inviting you over for drinks before you know it."

Seamus felt like he was swallowing a paper clip, but he nodded. You didn't go changing your mind once it was set. He offered her his hand. "I'd shake on that, Steady."

Sandra shook his hand, still grinning. "Alright, Trouble. Let's go see if Carleton's our man."

Maxwell was, predictably, twenty minutes late getting ready, and stumbled out the door only once Seamus had threatened to kick it down.

"Christ, boss, untwist your panties, what's the rush?"

"You don't see the urgency in earning your five thousand dollar commission?"

Maxwell blinked, then pushed past him to the stairs. "Okay, quit standing around! We've got to move."

Leaving Maxwell's apartment, Seamus drove—if Sandra brought the car, he had to drive, and she was pressed firmly back into the passenger seat, partially by the lead in his foot and partially to keep the seat from sliding out of place. Seamus was wrestling with a steering wheel that tended to jump to the left when the mood struck it.

Sandra's car, an '89 Geo Metro, was lovingly referred to as the Widowmaker. Once, it had been blue. Seamus's abortive attempt to repaint it ten years ago had left it blue-with-red-areas. The upholstery had an unfortunate habit of coming out in clumps. While the heaters still worked, actually turning them on was only marginally safer than starting a fire on the dash, so all three riders were wrapped tightly in their jackets. It was the car Sandra and Seamus had first driven to the city in, and she'd sworn she'd drive it into the ground before giving it up.

"I gave Carleton a call," said Seamus over the noise of the engine. "We've got the all-clear to come up. One stop at the farmers' market first."

"Good call," said Sandra, "don't want to show up empty-handed. And I've got to pick up a few things myself."

Maxwell called out from the backseat: "Where'd you buy this car? Value Village?"

Seamus smiled, though he kept his eyes forward—driving the Widowmaker required absolute concentration. "Take a nap on the way there," said Seamus, "and either you'll wake up with it all over, or you'll die in your sleep. Win-win."

Sandra blew out a breath that fogged and hung around her head.

"If we're going to the farmers' market," Sandra said, "you're buying me hot chocolate."

"That goes without saying."

The St. Lawrence Market had two faces. There was the Instagram-friendly side, housed in antique masonry and ivy, with heavy oak doors and twenty-somethings hawking power crystals at the entrance. The chocolatier and the cheese boutique were worth a visit there, but most of the market had been overrun by gourmet sandwich-makers and organic juiceries. If you knew where to look, though, you could still find the old, grim-faced butchers arguing over the price of chicken liver, and the bacon at Carnicero's was hot and greasy as ever.

Sandra and Seamus went picking through the market and left Maxwell to nurse a hot chocolate and her hatred for road trips in rundown cars. Sandra picked through the vegetables—not much to see in November.

"All they've got is fucking rutabaga."

"What are you looking for?"

"A couple spices I can't pronounce and this one type of fish broth. Comes in a can, he says, and the man tells me you need it to make

French seafood soup. Michael's gotta start doing some of the shopping himself. I love it when he cooks, but damn if he doesn't give me the weirdest shopping lists."

Seamus didn't have anything pleasant to say about her fiancé, so he said nothing. Instead, he stole a small handful of chocolate-covered almonds as they passed the candy store and held them out to her.

"You tryin' to bribe me, Trouble?"

"You'd rather I try to poison you with the triple-salted licorice?"

They wound their way through St. Lawrence Market, picking up a few odd items. Seamus contemplated the sheep heads, Sandra sprang for a roasted-bacon sandwich, and they finally made it back to Maxwell, who'd sucked down her hot chocolate and three coffees and was looking more like someone who'd survived a war and less like someone who'd died in one. Sandra leaned close as if to inspect her.

"Good secretary you got here. Usually, the cracks start to show at this point."

"It's not too bad," said Maxwell, slightly defensive. "The job's kinda fun. And the boss beat the shit out of some dudes who really deserved it."

"Seamus is good at that. Hey, looks like our hot chocolate's ready," said Sandra.

Seamus's eyes lit up as he and Sandra took their oversize Styrofoam cups from Maxwell. "Marshmallows!" Maxwell had a slightly bemused expression on her face. Seamus frowned at her—after he'd had a sip of his hot chocolate, of course. "What?"

"You two are like the most threatening people I know. It's weird seeing you do normal-human things."

"Well, we try not to make a habit of it," Seamus said, and sipped his drink contentedly, sucking back pink mini-marshmallows.

"Tough-as-nails private eye," said Sandra with a grin.

"I take issue with your tone," said Seamus. "I'm as tough as they come. You may have heard that revenge is sweet? These marshmallows—they're the marshmallows of revenge."

"All I'm saying is, you'd have a hard time threatening mobsters if they knew what you did in your downtime."

Maxwell managed to wedge herself into the backseat with their market haul, though she complained a bit when one of the window rollers came off in her hand. Sandra and Seamus rode in the front, Seamus fiddling with the stereo system.

"We've got some cassettes," said Seamus. "Any requests?"

"Why the fuck do you still have tapes, boss?"

"The Widowmaker doesn't take anything else."

"Well, have you got any early Kim Petras?"

"Never heard of her."

"Any deadmau5?" asked Maxwell, desperation edging into her voice.

"Sure," said Seamus, "there's probably a few in the dash."

"Hey, I keep the Widowmaker clean," said Sandra. "It's just the loose wires rattling around in there."

"What *do* you have?"

"Early Taylor Swift. And the glam-rock highlights of the eighties. Got the tapes at a yard sale."

"You have any cyanide I can borrow in that jacket, boss?"

Carleton's farm was fenced in by tall pines—as they came up the driveway, the trees suddenly broke, revealing acres of grass gone white and rigid with frost. As they pulled alongside the house, Mrs. Alister stuck her head out the door of the farmhouse and waved from the porch—at least, Seamus assumed it was her. It'd been almost twenty years since he last saw Lorraine, and he'd filed her as something of a non-entity at the time. She was slightly rounded and friendly looking, but Seamus kept his guard up and one hand in his coat pocket, where his pistol was. The old lady didn't move to draw, though—probably safe to pull up.

As Seamus parked, Maxwell jostled the seatbelt open and threw herself out of the car before it had completely stopped moving, her hands over her ears. Say what you wanted about the Widowmaker, she had a hell of a stereo system.

Lorraine's husband came out and stood beside her, and even Seamus had to admit it was a picturesque scene. He looked like your classic country doctor, the kind of guy who'd always have lollipops on hand to give out to his patients. Carleton turned a little green on seeing their party begin to unload from the car, and his eyes lingered on Sandra—she was a cop, after all. Seamus had neglected to mention that she'd be coming, and it was too late for Carleton to complain now.

On the whitewashed porch, Carleton offered everyone a hot coffee and Seamus declined with the certain stiff politeness that he tended to get stuck in when he was angry.

"Mind if we go for a little walk before we come in?" Seamus asked. "Stretch our legs?"

"Not at all. The best view's to the northeast, near the edge of the farm. You'll know it when you see it. When I retire, I think I'll spend all my time watching the trees change colour out there."

"Thanks, Carleton. Why don't you come along? We've got some catching up to do."

The doctor laughed, just slightly too quick and too loud. "We sure do," he said. "I'll be out in half an hour. Just need to set some files in order. Make sure Lorraine's all set up in the kitchen."

The three of them headed along a rough path that curved north. Seamus and Sandra walked slightly ahead, and he waited till Maxwell seemed distracted by the view to turn to Sandra.

"Let me have a crack at him," said Seamus. "I can't get him, we can work out another plan. He seems jittery—I might get a confession if we're alone."

Sandra looked at him through narrowed eyes. "You brought me here to scare him, didn't you? So he'd be nice and desperate once you got to him."

Seamus just gave her a cold smile, which Sandra returned.

"Smart."

Between the hot chocolate and the morning drive out, Seamus had been enjoying himself. He wasn't looking forward to dealing with the good doctor—it wasn't that he felt badly about feeding him to the piranhas on the prosecutor's bench, or the twenty-five years to life that'd follow his conviction. Carleton deserved worse, and there was a sort of dark glee that came with meting out punishment. But looking at the old doctor sickened him slightly. It was like flipping over a rotten log: you could steel yourself, but the sight of all the white wriggling things would still turn your stomach.

When he saw the doctor coming up the path, hobbling slightly, Seamus nodded to Sandra, who put a hand on Maxwell's shoulder. Maxwell tried to shrug it off and failed.

"C'mon, kid. Let's walk over this way."

"I think—wow, your hand is *really* strong—I want to stay."

"I appreciate the loyalty," said Seamus, "but there're some very interesting trees just down that path. Sandra can show you."

"What are you gonna do to that old guy, boss?"

Seamus's smile got a little chillier. "Oh, nothing he won't recover from."

Sandra steered a reluctant Maxwell into the woods, and Seamus turned to watch Carleton approach. It was winter-silent, with snow on the ground—that was convenient. Sound wouldn't travel far. In the worst case, a scream would barely be louder than the wind once it reached the house.

"Seamus," said the doctor, "it's good to see you again. When did I last have the chance?"

"Years ago. At my mother's house, I think."

"That's right," said Carleton, affecting a nostalgic look that was about as convincing as a dollar-store engagement ring. "Is she doing well?"

"I wouldn't know," said Seamus, "but she's still alive. I'd get a call if that changed."

"Ah."

That put a crimp in the conversation, but after a moment Carleton blundered forward: "Well, you know, I understand you're a private eye, now? I've gotten into a bit of trouble, and I was hoping I could ask you for some advice."

"Of course," said Seamus, grinning, showing his canines. Carleton flinched. "But first, I found something of yours in the city," he said, reaching into his coat. "I wanted to return it."

The doctor's face went first red, then white, as he recognized the battered prescription Seamus was holding. When he spoke, his words came out with the sound a man makes when you punch him in the diaphragm. That, at least, was satisfying. "Where did you get that?"

"A burger place on Queen," said Seamus blithely. "General practice isn't all it's cracked up to be, hmm? But set that aside for a moment—I want to know about what happened at the hospital." Seamus got in close, right up to Carleton's face. "Listen to me. You're in a pretty tight spot here—medical licence gone, and a nice long retirement in a jail cell. I've even got my friend Sandra here—I say the word, show her this scrip, and she'll have narcotics on you like flies on shit. But that doesn't have to happen. You see, I do freelance—so you and I, we can work something out."

Seamus, of course, didn't actually intend to take any money from Carleton. He was set for the next few months once he caught him, and in any case covering up a murder wouldn't be worth the risk. But he had to feed Carleton a little bit of hope, give him a way out. There was an art to interrogation, jostling people's emotions up and down until you got what you needed out of them.

With the initial shock fading from him, Carleton had the gall to look indignant. "You're here for my money, Seamus? I never thought Thomas's son would wind up as a common thug—"

"Your hypocrisy is charming," said Seamus, letting some of the coldness in his chest creep into his voice. "The way I see it, you can either take my help or go it alone. Don't see that second one ending well for you."

Carleton was shivering, all the blood having drained from his face. "How much do you want?"

"Eighty thousand," said Seamus. Relief flared in Carleton's eyes, and Seamus knew he'd hit the mark. It was a price that would sting, but that he could scrape together or borrow. Nothing blurred rational thought like the promise of relief. "But if I'm going to protect you," he continued, "I need to know what I'm dealing with."

Carleton nodded rapidly, and Seamus knew he had him. He'd fed him hope like a poison, and it had gone to the doctor's heart.

He told Seamus a story of a taste for Texas Hold 'em and high roller tables that wasn't matched by skill at cards, mounting debts to card sharks, of a tortured conscience as he went dipping into his hospital's stock of opioids and barbiturates. Bargains made and alliances with Ricky, Carleton shivering as he said the name. Seamus got it all easily, a whole web of contacts and deals he could hand over to Sandra on a silver platter, Carleton sure even as he spilled his guts over that Seamus's greed would protect him. Seamus just waited for him to get to the part about Timmy, and Ryba, and this new rival he had to eliminate for his own safety. But that never came, and finally Carleton stopped his confession, looking at Seamus with wet, wide pleading eyes.

"That's it, Seamus. Can you get me out of it?"

"I thought I said I had to know *all* the details, Alister. That's the only way this is going to work."

Carleton gave him a blank look, or a simulacrum of one.

Seamus narrowed his eyes. "Timmy Greene. And a patient on your floor—John Ryba."

Carleton blinked. "Ryba? Something happened at the hospital, but the police haven't given me any details."

Seamus gave him a reproachful look. "If you're not going to trust me, maybe I'd better look for another job—"

"No!" Carleton caught his arm with a surprisingly firm grip, and Seamus saw the raw desperation glinting in his eyes. "I can't—I can't go to jail. I can't do that to Lorraine. I'll tell you anything you need to know, but I swear I've got nothing to do with what happened to Ryba. Timmy Greene—I heard whispers. I just want to get out, Seamus, I didn't pay too much attention. But I heard he was working for someone."

"Timmy was working for someone?"

Carleton nodded and drew closer to Seamus, glancing around as if afraid the pines were listening. His breath smelled of Fisherman's Friend and stale coffee.

"I heard a name—the Angelmaker. And I heard they're dangerous. Christ, Seamus, I need to get out of this."

Seamus regarded him for a long moment. The sun was starting to go down, and the old man's wet eyes flashed with reflected fire from the sunset. Finally, he nodded—Carleton was a bust. There was no reason for him to lie to Seamus about Ryba since he'd already given him everything else.

"Well, if you say so. I'll make sure you stay clear," said Seamus, with a smile to himself. "But right now, I think we're due for some dinner. We can arrange my payment at a later date," he said generously. Better if he never actually received any money from Carleton—it would complicate things legally. Seamus started back towards the house, and Carleton came behind him, walking hunched, like something deep in his internal architecture had snapped.

"Seamus, you know I never wanted to get all tied up in this."

"I know, Carleton. My father always spoke highly of you."

"Just feels like I ran out of options," said the doctor, half to himself. "The money just kept going, like I was bleeding out. But I haven't played a hand in a year," he said with some pride. "Quit the game."

Seamus marvelled at him but said nothing.

After a moment, Carleton continued: "You know, sometimes I wish your father were still here. He'd have kept me out of trouble, always did. He was a good man, a strong man."

"Not strong enough," said Seamus before he could help himself. Carleton looked disturbed.

"Well—if you see it that way. But he kept to what was right. You know, he came to me when he was treating Lauren. I don't know if you ever heard this, but she refused treatment—"

"I heard," said Seamus, his voice perfectly flat.

"Well, Thomas wasn't sure what to do. But in the end, he knew to stick to regulation. I helped him with that, told him it was the right thing to do."

That aggrieved pride again. Insufferable.

"You're a regular paragon, Alister. Such a firm grasp of medical ethics. You know, I found someone who overdosed in their apartment the other day—but I'm sure you've seen plenty of those deaths at the hospital. Not a pleasant sight, is it? All that fluid in the body just comes out. Wonder how many of those you've caused over the years, huh?"

Carleton's eyes were wide at Seamus's tone, his sudden anger. It didn't fit the part he was supposed to be playing, the greedy operator who was going to cover up Carleton's little mistakes. Seamus didn't care. Carleton had already given him everything he needed.

"Seamus, your father's death—"

"Is not why I'm here," Seamus suppressed the flinch that came with the memory. "I need information, Carleton. You need to protect your pathetic life." Seamus smiled. "And we worked out a little arrangement. Everyone's happy."

Carleton stared at him, and Seamus saw the realization hit him—he'd given Seamus everything, his guilt and all the specifics needed for a clean prosecution, and received no guarantees in return. Desperate men could be dangerous, but Seamus found his mind going back to something his mother used to say—*never be afraid of a weak man.*

Seamus turned and walked back along the path, leaving Carleton to return alone, tail between his legs.

Seamus wasn't about to let the tension from their conversation get in the way of a good meal. Carleton hardly spoke, and Maxwell was looking at Seamus with more suspicion than normal. But he tried to keep the ball rolling, chatting with Lorraine.

"Delicious horseradish, where did you get it?"

"Oh, dear, there's a tiny little farmers' market down the road—I'll give you directions so you can stop there next time you visit."

Carleton made a slight gurgling sound at this, but Seamus nodded pleasantly.

"I'd love that. And the meat's perfectly done—don't you think, Sandra?"

Sandra found it difficult to answer, seeing as she had about a half of the prime rib roast on her plate and another quarter of it in her mouth, but she nodded appreciatively. Lorraine was absolutely delighted at her and Seamus's enthusiasm for eating and cast only the occasional angry, fretful glance at her husband, who was on his fifth glass of wine and staring hard at Seamus, no doubt trying to think his way out of the hole he'd dug himself into. Seamus, who'd kept to water, found his red-eyed glare quite amusing.

While they waited for dessert, Seamus asked for the washroom and was directed upstairs. He walked up, but went to the primary bedroom instead and was hit by a wave of mingled candle scents as he pushed the door open. He crouched by the huge, carefully made bed and started feeling around underneath its frame. It was a gamble but worth a shot. The first thing his hand hit was a zip-lock bag, which he pulled out, revealing a carefully curated selection of neon vibrators and bondage gear. He just shrugged, replaced the bag under the bed, and resumed his search—spend enough time rummaging through people's private lives, and you get to the point where very little surprises you. At least shopping at the farmers' market wasn't Lorraine's only occupation.

Seamus kept digging until he hit a long case made of cast resin, textured and cool to the touch. He recognized it by feel—the carrying case for a shotgun or rifle. He drew it out—this was what he'd been looking for. Carleton might have a gun safe in the shed, but odds were he wouldn't make it there. Instead, he'd use the weapon he kept close at hand, the one he kept to defend his home. If he decided he had to undo his confession in the woods, this was what he'd use.

Seamus pulled two special cartridges from his jacket pocket and snapped the breach open, replacing the bright red live rounds with his yellow-marked shells. He always carried a couple of them—good for dry fire training, or sabotage. Then he shoved the case back under the bed and got to his feet.

Seamus went straight to the washroom, closing each door he passed through softly behind him. He flushed the toilet and washed his hands.

When he came downstairs, there was a meringue pie on the table. Seamus and Sandra inhaled most of it, to Lorraine's delight. Carleton looked like he'd come to a decision during his sixth glass of wine—Seamus noticed that and hurried to finish his pie, make his apologies, and shove Sandra and Maxwell out the door as Carleton stumbled up the stairs, towards his bedroom.

As the three of them stepped out onto the porch, Seamus turned to Sandra. "You two get in the car," he said. "I've got business to close out with Carleton."

"Yeah, I saw him sweating. You need backup?"

"I can handle one old man," said Seamus. "Take the secretary."

Sandra nodded and put a hand on Maxwell's shoulder. She shook it off with an annoyed look.

"I'm staying."

Sandra said nothing. She was well trained, Sandra Blair—she couldn't match Seamus's viciousness in a fight, but her technique was at least as good as his. She could have knocked Maxwell out with one hand and dragged her back to the car with the other. But Sandra didn't grab for her, just cocked her head at Seamus, who gave a low laugh.

"Shouldn't be too dangerous. Let her stay."

Sandra nodded and walked out into the dusk, where snow had just started to fall. Seamus stood on the porch, waiting for the old man.

"Boss, are you fucking with this poor guy?"

"What gave you that idea, Maxwell?"

"He's been shitting himself ever since you came in for dinner. You gotta blackmail someone everywhere you go?"

"It's what puts food on the table, Maxwell. Don't forget about that payday once we find out who killed Ryba."

"Listen, I like getting paid as much as the next girl, but you don't have to scare a nice old man like—"

The words died in her throat as she found herself staring down the end of a double-barrelled shotgun. Alister stood in the doorway, shivering slightly, with a bead drawn on her.

Seamus laughed. Alister flicked the shotgun over to his chest, and Seamus met his eyes.

"This is because Sandra and I ate all of your pie, isn't it?" said Seamus.

"You're going to sell me out. I saw it—I know. If the people I work with find out I've told you, I'm going to die. Slowly. And Lorraine will too." His voice hitched. Seemed the old man had been crying.

Seamus inspected himself for sympathy, found none, and returned to the task at hand. "Seems you shouldn't have told me in the first place," he said. "But it's so easy to talk when you want something off your chest, isn't it? When there's finally someone there to help you?"

Maxwell found her voice, though she could only manage a whisper: "Boss, shut the fuck up."

He gave her a slight smile and kept talking. Seamus didn't have many vices, in his own estimation, but one of them was absolute contempt for weakness.

"Why are we playing games here, Alister? You've got the drop on me—if you're going to do it, do it. Don't want to kill Thomas's son out here in the snow? You going to let us go? And when your life burns down around you, you'll tell yourself you had no choice, that you did everything you could? You've done it once already."

Maxwell had turned to stare at him. He wasn't afraid—it was cold fury that shone on his face, like he'd been injected with steel.

"It seems to me, Alister," said Seamus, hard and mocking, "you haven't got any balls."

Alister's face contorted in helpless rage, and he pulled the trigger.

The sound of the hammer falling was distinct, even as Maxwell threw herself to the side, crashing through a planter box and covering her head with her hands. What followed was an eloquent winter silence, not even the sound of the wind to interrupt it. Seamus just went on grinning that cold, cold grin.

"Of course," he said, "it's possible what you're really lacking is live ammunition."

He closed the gap faster than Alister could twitch, pulled the gun out of his hands and raised it to strike as Alister fell back, skittering over the frozen porch.

"Boss! Stop, don't—"

Seamus brought the butt of the shotgun down, an inch shy of Alister's shivering head.

"You're lucky my secretary's here, Carleton."

Seamus tossed the gun into a pile of leaves by the porch, then strode away. Maxwell hurried after him, a step behind. The sound of Lorraine's voice came through, high and worried, asking what had happened.

Seamus called over his shoulder: "Stay where you are, Doctor. You try to run, you'll only hurt yourself."

Once they were out of sight of the house, Maxwell knelt by the driveway and threw up most of her dinner.

Seamus stood beside her and absently patted her on the back. "It's alright."

She spat out a mouthful of mucus and turned to look at him, the edges of her face just visible in the moonlight, black eyes made silver. She looked, as usual, angry.

"Keeping nice old men safe from the likes of me, Maxwell? I admire the conviction."

"How did you do that? Make his gun jam?"

"An astounding series of logical deductions—or I'd say that if I wanted to fuck with you. I switched out his bullets for practice rounds when I used the washroom. Old man was too drunk to check his ammunition."

She looked out into the night.

"You enjoy living like this, boss?"

"I do what's necessary, Maxwell. Now come on, we're going home."

Sandra was waiting for them and said nothing as Seamus slipped into the driver's seat. She handed him a small foil package, and they pulled away from the old farmhouse.

Seamus said nothing as he drove, and Sandra didn't ask, as per their usual policy. She just made an observation: "You're angry."

"Yes."

Seamus steadied his breathing and forced himself to loosen his grip on the steering wheel. He looked at the package she'd given him: green tea–flavoured Pocky. He popped one in his mouth and felt his heartbeat slow as he did.

"Thanks, Sandra."

She nodded and leaned back in her seat.

"No worries. So, what've you got?"

"Carleton's been sneaking OxyContin and Xanax out of hospital supply for years—started getting more heavily involved in the black market recently. I'll give you the specifics, but I think you'll have no trouble getting a confession out of him. The man's ready to crack. Send some uniforms down tomorrow with a warrant."

"What about Ryba?"

Seamus shook his head.

"He's not our man. No motive, as far as I can see—Carleton didn't know Timmy was getting into the drug business until after Ryba's death, and he wanted to get out anyway."

Sandra snorted.

"Well, he'll get his wish. Nice and peaceful down at Toronto South. Now let's saddle up and get the fuck out of here."

Seamus managed a smile. "If the Widowmaker were a horse, the only place I'd be riding her is the glue factory."

"Careful. She'll throw you."

Snow continued to fall, which made driving a delicate proposition at best—Seamus turned on the windshield wipers, but the Widowmaker's defrost had stopped working a decade ago. Sandra periodically reached out the window and scraped snow off with an ice scraper.

Maxwell seemed to have crashed in the back, and by the time they hit the onramp Sandra's eyes were slipping closed, bundled as she was in her winter coat. Seamus pulled onto the freeway as Sandra fell asleep, her hands crossed tight over her chest against the cold. Once he'd made sure his friend was asleep, he undid his seatbelt and shrugged off his oilskin, laying it over her.

Muted pop, high and tinny, whispered through the speakers as he drove into the winter night.

CHAPTER EIGHT

Sandra and Maxwell started waking up once they hit the noise and stop-start traffic of the city. A few minutes before she'd blinked her eyes open, Seamus had deftly pulled his jacket back around his own shoulders. Not that there was anything untoward about it—it wasn't a crime to want your friend to be comfortable, was it?

After dropping Maxwell off, Seamus pulled to a stop in front of his office and waved goodnight to Sandra, who waved back and took the driver's seat. The Widowmaker pulled away from the curb with a groan, leaving him on the cracked sidewalk outside his office. Seamus took in a breath of the cold night air and picked out one of the few stars bright enough to see through the glow of the city, then headed up the stairs to his office. The hallway was dark, and Seamus hurried up, eager for a chance to lie down and order his thoughts with his eyes closed.

If he'd noticed it about two seconds sooner, he could've retreated onto the street, drawn a weapon, or at least have come in with his fists up. As it was, Seamus froze as he opened his door, realizing that he was too far into the ambush to draw back. There was nothing visibly wrong, but the air smelled of Black Russian cigarettes and a cologne Seamus didn't wear. Silently counting his fingers, he assessed his advantages, which were few enough—picklocks and gloves in his jacket, a half-packet of Pocky in his breast pocket.

"Nice of you to visit," said Seamus, "Cup of tea?"

Trelly stepped out of the dark, wearing his scowl. He towered close to the ceiling of the office and was about as wide as he was tall. "You are sharp man, Seamus. Olexa wants you."

"I'd be delighted. My office hours are nine to six—"

Trelly stepped forward and grabbed Seamus's forearm, pressing with huge, blunt fingertips. There weren't many other men in the city who could move that quickly and none at all who were that size.

A left cross followed by a hard elbow to the face might buy him a few seconds. Seamus might not have been able to beat the old wrestling champion, but he'd seen his grating bone-on-bone limp, and Seamus could certainly run faster.

Of course, since it was Olexa who'd sent him, they'd have armed men waiting outside. Better to wait till he knew what was going on—Olexa never killed a man before she explained what he'd done wrong. And that would be an opening.

Seamus glanced coolly at the gigantic hand on his arm. "No need for that. You can tell your boss I'm coming."

Mollified, Trelly let Seamus set his bag down, though he blocked the doorway. The window was four stories up, and Seamus wasn't desperate enough to attempt an escape along that avenue.

"Let's go, then," said Seamus.

He walked beside Trelly, who hung back far enough that Seamus could have bolted away. That was a bad sign—it meant he had backup at every possible exit. Seamus was acting like a damned amateur—he should have seen the signs before he'd stepped into the building.

Seamus kept his pace steady, his face impassive, every step measured. A car idled on the street, two more men waiting in it, both large and muscle-bound and each at least half the size of Trelly. It was a soccer-mom minivan, the bumper plastered with stickers that lauded the academic, athletic, and spiritual merits of the driver's children, but it had tinted windows.

Olexa Greene had a knack for camouflage.

The men nodded as Seamus got in, and two other cars on the street peeled off just as they did. They clearly weren't heading downtown to her office.

"A man takes a day off and everything falls to pieces," said Seamus. "Any chance you'll tell me where I'm being taken?"

"To see Ms. Greene. At the Freezer."

The Freezer—an abandoned ice cream factory on the outskirts of Brampton. Seamus had never gone in person, but he'd heard the stories. Apparently, Olexa had found other uses for those industrial freezers and stainless-steel vats. Seamus kept his breathing steady. Trelly hadn't shot him from a dark window, which meant they needed him alive, which meant he'd have a chance to counterattack.

"How's business been, Trelly?"

"Same as always, Caron."

Trelly squinted hard as he drove, occasionally rubbing his temples. Seamus watched him—any weakness, no matter how slight, was an opportunity he needed to capitalize on.

"Headache?"

"Always headaches. An American, Olympic semifinals. He break two bones in my neck. Always headaches after that. But I win that match," said Trelly, with a look of warning. "And I win finals too. With broken neck. Headache does not stop me."

Seamus said nothing more.

Trelly stayed off the highways, moving along mostly empty city streets at a leisurely pace. After about an hour of driving in silence, the engine guttered out in front of the dilapidated factory, faded cartoon children still smiling from the facade. Seamus knew people had disappeared here, but not how many exactly. Olexa Greene's casualties usually deserved it—and Seamus had always known that if he got too curious about the disappearances, he'd find himself deserving it as well.

There were no additional guards at the door—if he could take Trelly out first and get his hands on a hostage, Seamus *might* fight his way out. But Olexa kept her men sharp—one chance in ten, optimistically.

Ice spread through Seamus's chest, and a hard grin spread over his face.

Trelly marched him through the tangle of tubing and compressors to a card table at the centre of the factory floor. Seamus, hand in his jacket pocket, was directed to sit on a folding chair there, opposite an ornate wooden armchair. Trelly took position behind him, motionless and silent. The lights were bright, near-blinding white halogen. Everything was scrubbed clean, even the concrete floor. Freezers that should have long since been decommissioned hummed softly on either side of them.

After a few breaths, Seamus heard a door he hadn't noticed slide open, and he turned to see Olexa walking towards him, flanked by two armed guards. Seamus smiled at her, genuinely enough—she'd gotten within his reach, a stupid mistake. If the need arose, he'd use her as a shield.

"Can I have a hot chocolate before you shoot me?"

Olexa took her seat, utterly impassive. The guards had their pistols at their sides, but Seamus could take her hostage before they'd be able to raise their guns. He'd have to move fast.

"I'm sorry if you were roughly handled, Detective. I mean you no harm. Tonight. But I needed you immediately and could not tell you why by messenger. So I sent Trelly—I knew you would not be stupid enough to fight him, however much you enjoy the pastime."

Seamus let out a breath and leaned back. He glanced over at Trelly's forearms, each one about the girth of his head. "Well, I wouldn't pick on a little guy."

That got a low cement-mixer chuckle out of Trelly.

Olexa laid her palms on the table, and Seamus started to look at her more closely, now that he could take his attention off the guards. Her composure was, as always, immaculate, but Seamus saw the slightly crumpled vest and the bloodshot eyes. He wasn't sure if the woman slept at all, but if she did, it appeared she'd been doing it less than normal. Interesting—and potentially dangerous.

"I have a job for you, Detective."

Seamus raised an eyebrow. "Why aren't we discussing this at your office?"

"The materials you will require are here." Olexa nodded to her men, who walked over to a massive chest freezer. They came back rolling a collapsible stretcher, and Seamus stood to look at its occupant. There, wearing a designer T-shirt and fresh freezer burns, was the body of Timmy Greene.

"Well," said Seamus, "isn't that interesting."

"We want to know how he died."

"And you don't want the police to."

"I have forty thousand dollars in a paper bag, for when you complete the autopsy. You have some medical experience, yes?"

"Some. I wouldn't operate on a living body, but I think my skills will suit a corpse."

Trelly was busy laying out surgical tools, his hands surprisingly deft. The scalpel and the bone saw, though both equipped with fresh blades, were worn with use.

"You must do a lot of surgery out here, Olexa," said Seamus.

"Yes."

Seamus balanced a scalpel in his hand, contemplated Timmy Greene's frost-etched body laid out before him. If Seamus had heard that Timmy dropped dead in his club, his first thought would've been that Olexa found out about his little distribution plan and decided to nip it in the bud. But if that were true, she wouldn't be paying Seamus to perform his autopsy.

"I want to know who did this, Detective. Ryba, then Timmy—this is the beginning of an attack on the Company itself, however . . . inconsequential the first targets."

"There's a chance it was someone moving against Timmy alone," said Seamus. "He's been importing something new to the city, without, I presume, the knowledge of the Company. Called it Platinum."

Olexa narrowed her eyes. "Timmy was going behind my back? Who told you this?"

"For me to know."

Olexa's lip quirked up slightly. "Ah. Perhaps this informant lost a briefcase—a shipment of this Platinum?"

"You're not going to waste time going after Timmy's patsies when you have treason to deal with, are you?"

"So protective of your clients. But you're right, there are much larger concerns. Platinum, was it?"

Seamus nodded, and she whispered a word to one of her men, who moved quickly to the door. If Seamus had to guess, every Company man would be asking where he could buy Platinum tomorrow, and anyone willing to sell it to them would be dead the day after. Not that Seamus minded, particularly.

"Do you still want this autopsy done?"

"Of course," said Olexa. "I must know who did me this... favour."

As Seamus set to work, grateful for the chill that kept him from sweating, Olexa recounted the circumstances of Timmy's death. It had happened a night after Seamus visited the Montmorency, but Seamus thought it would be prudent not to mention he'd likely been one of the last people to meet with Timmy.

He'd died at the bar, disoriented, his last words choked by vomit. The paramedics arrived long after his heart had stopped and had been unable to coax it into starting again—the Company having the body now was nothing to wonder about. Olexa had at least one man on the take in every police district, and she could move in and out of the morgue almost as freely as Seamus could.

The autopsy itself was messy, as autopsies in abandoned ice cream factories tended to be, but Seamus had done the basic cadaver dissection and knew his way around. The abdominal cavity didn't show much of interest, and some liver scarring was more or less to be expected—but that would have killed him in thirty years, not last week. No other organs bore a distinguishing mark, although Seamus reserved the liver to test for toxins—Trelly helpfully provided a cookie tin when Seamus asked for a container. The work wasn't too hard. Seamus didn't mind blood on his hands, and the tools were very sharp, the same crisp disposable steel they'd have used in a hospital. Still, it took hours before the abdomen was hollowed out, doll-like. And it wouldn't do to look as though he wasn't being thorough.

"Nothing so far."

Olexa, who'd been watching, sipping a cup of tea, walked over and peered into her nephew's open chest.

"Can't you test for poison?"

"Depends on the poison," said Seamus, closing his eyes to think. If he could get those liver samples back to the morgue, maybe. What else could he try—where else would traces linger on the body?

"Hair," he muttered.

"Excuse me, Detective?"

"Don't suppose you've got a microscope around here, do you?"

Olexa nodded to Trelly, who lumbered off and returned carrying a high school–grade dissection microscope.

"I had the men bring this while we waited for you," she said, as Trelly set the microscope in front of Seamus.

It was a piece of crap, of course, but after about twenty minutes of fiddling with mirrors Seamus got it focused well enough to see what he was looking for. A single hair, pulled from Timmy's scalp, and a dark line that ran along the base. The symptoms coalesced with the evidence, and Seamus snapped his fingers at the picture they formed—which he regretted immediately as a bit of gore spattered his coat.

"Thallium. Do you have much experience with poisoning, Olexa?"

She curled her lip. "An honest woman works with her own hands."

"Fair enough," said Seamus. His attention was still tight on the sample, but he could multitask. "Now, if I were poisoning someone, I would use nicotine. Easy to get out of vape juice, fast acting . . . Also easy to identify, though, and you'd have to inject it, which complicates the murder if you're not confident in being able to overpower the victim. There's americium poisoning, but it'd take so long—"

"Detective."

"Right, sorry. Thallium used to be found in rat poison, but they discontinued it as an ingredient in off-the-shelf pesticides. Odourless, tasteless . . . Folks kept using it to kill their spouses."

As Seamus spoke, he frowned slightly. Thallium was an excellent assassination weapon—in the early 1920s. Nowadays, thallium purchases were tracked, and it would be one of the first things any coroner tested against in a suspected poisoning case.

"You're certain?"

"Of course not. Other compounds have similar effects. But for nonspecific symptoms and a relatively quick death, thallium's a good bet."

Seamus peeled off his bloody gloves, then flopped back onto the folding chair and rubbed his eyes.

"Past my bedtime. Have any bourbon?"

Olexa gestured for what was left of Timmy to be taken away. The corpse was promptly replaced by a gilded bar cart, and Trelly himself handed Seamus four fingers of Willett Family Estate. Seamus tried to savour it—he'd never had the money to buy it himself, although it looked as though that was about to change—but the ferrous scent of blood lingered in his nose, and he couldn't taste anything but the raw alcohol when he drank. Olexa watched him take a sip—if she blinked at any point, Seamus didn't see it.

"I knew Timmy was doing something foolish," she said at last, "but I did not know what. A new drug—I had not expected this. He came to me drunk, one night, and told me he was going to poison many people. Some hostage game, I thought. I cracked him about the ears, told him to stop talking nonsense."

Seamus set his glass down. "I suppose that's the business pushers are in, although I'm surprised he was smart enough to say it in so many words. There's a kid dying in the hospital who took a hefty dose of what Timmy was selling—of one of the ingredients, anyway. Still haven't cracked what it is," Seamus said, trailing off. "In any case, I'll take my forty thousand now. And a ride back to my office, if you don't mind. Might as well try to sleep tonight. I assume I can leave whatever's left of this drug ring to you? I don't want this Platinum on the streets."

"You have a soft heart, Detective. There's nothing worse for business."

"I'm not in your business, Greene," said Seamus, exhaustion finally creeping into his voice. "And everyone's got a soft heart. That's why you aim for it. Now send me home."

Olexa watched him. In the unnatural fluorescent glow of the Freezer, her expression might have been mistaken for concern. Seamus knew better.

"Good night, Detective. Trelly will return you."

The drive homewards was just as quiet, though slightly more convivial. Seamus's eye was caught again by the little crucifix Trelly wore round his neck—there was the cross, but also an odd lump of dark metal that hung against his skin.

"Didn't peg you for a religious man, Trelly."

He grunted agreement, eyes still fixed on the road ahead. "If there was a god, I would not pray to him. But this was a gift."

"A gift?"

"Funeral gift," said Trelly, putting a firm end to the conversation.

CHAPTER NINE

You didn't dream properly in the first few hours of sleep. That was when your body demanded quiet, and sleep, for the most part, was black and absolute. Seamus had taken advantage of that when he was younger, sleeping three or four hours a night to keep dreams pressed back to a few spare images, a few smudges of emotion. As the sunlight woke him, Seamus rubbed his eyes and remembered those years, feeling the nightmares that meant to come while he slept shivering through his mind, without enough time to form properly. Then he sat up, and remembered why he'd stopped using that particular trick—his eyes burned, and when he shook his head, it felt like someone was trepanning him with a screwdriver. Seamus just clenched his jaw and shook his head harder—no excuse not to get to work.

Parsimony suggested that Timmy and Ryba had been killed by the same person, or at least that the motive had been the same. Assume further that the motive tied to Platinum, the only clear link between the two men. That meant there were two possibilities.

First: That one of Timmy's rivals wanted him dead and planned to wipe out the whole operation by cutting off its head and right hand. Seamus had been working off that assumption in going after Carleton, but there was a problem with it that the visit to Carleton had made clear—Timmy hadn't started to sell at scale. He wouldn't have had the time to find many rivals in the drug business, let alone rivals determined enough to risk a war with the Company. Whoever wanted Ryba and Timmy dead must've known about Platinum and stood to gain from their deaths.

Which led to the second theory: It was an inside job. The boss died, along with his most loyal subordinate—that sounded like the work of a jealous underling.

This Angelmaker Carleton had whispered to him about was another problem, but Seamus didn't think that mattered much to him. Probably just a name Timmy's supplier used, and a supplier wasn't likely to kill their employees. Seamus tried to put it out of his mind, but something about the name wouldn't let his attention fully shift. It was a distant memory he couldn't quite call up. The Angelmaker—he'd heard it before, a long time ago, and the only association he recalled was death.

Still, all this speculation was just so much spun sugar without evidence behind it. Seamus needed more information, but he didn't have any leads to follow besides the drug itself. If he understood what it was, that might give him information on where the manufacturers were hiding, who else would know about it and have been willing to kill Timmy and Ryba for it . . .

Maxwell broke in on his thinking, knocking the door against the wall with a crack. "Morning, boss. Someone gonna point a gun at us again today?"

"We don't get excitement every day, I'm afraid. We're going to the hospital."

"Why?"

"Because Platinum's the key to the Ryba case," said Seamus, shouldering his coat, "and I still don't know what it is, who the supplier is, what level distribution works at . . . If I can figure that out, I'll have a better picture of who might be killing people over it."

It was a better plan than sitting in his office twiddling his thumbs, at least.

Maxwell followed close at his heels, a determined look in her eyes, boots skidding on sidewalks coated in ice after the overnight rain and a cold snap. They gathered themselves for a moment just outside the hospital doors, watching the streams of people flow in and out.

"Alright, Maxwell," said Seamus, turning to squint at his secretary, "think of something sad."

"What?"

Seamus strode into the hospital and leaned over the front desk with a worried look. "I'm here to see my cousin. Sam Ewe."

"ID?"

Seamus produced one of the five fake driver's licences he usually carried with him, the one that matched the name he'd snuck into the visitor list while the attendant's back was turned last time. In any case, he was too busy to do more than glance at the ID before he waved Seamus through. "Go on ahead. Visiting hours end at six."

"Thank you so much."

He slipped Maxwell in, too, while the clerk dealt with a wailing woman who was clearly in need of the psych ward.

Seamus made a beeline down the hall for the ICU, where he'd seen the hacker kid last, but came to a sudden stop in a doorway.

"What is it, boss?"

"I think I recognize someone."

He knocked softly on the open door, then pushed it wide. Lying in bed, wearing the unmoored look that came with strong painkillers, was Mariah Lopez.

"Mrs. Lopez? I didn't know you were still in the hospital."

With a visible effort, she focused her eyes on Seamus. "Ah, you're the detective. You helped me here."

"Yes." Seamus looked her over. Pale, yellowed skin, and already thinner than when he'd last seen her. At a glance, it might seem like a sudden collapse, but Seamus could see it wasn't really a great change: she'd just let go. When Seamus had brought her to the hospital, there'd been a certain steely determination in her eyes, something stronger than the pain. That kind of determination can keep you standing, but it hurts to maintain, like holding tight to a knife's blade. That determination was gone now.

"You're a kind young man. You help me, now you visit me. Remind me of my son. A good boy . . ." her voice trailed off, and her eyes lost what clarity they'd had.

"I'm sure he was," said Seamus gently.

"You know, when he died, I could see it in the people at the hospital, the police. They all thought he was just a criminal. But he was a good boy. The people that did that to him—"

Seamus moved to her bedside without quite knowing why—maybe a hand over hers would be some small comfort. But he was surprised when instead she propped herself up on one arm and grabbed his sleeve with the other. Maxwell hurried to her side in alarm.

"Hey, lie back down—shit, boss, what's wrong?"

"Detective," she said, her voice a strained whisper, "forgive me, but please look at his case one time more. Antonio Lopez . . ."

Seamus nodded. It was bad form to lie to someone on their deathbed, but right now it seemed better than telling the truth. "I'll check on it for you," he said, easing her back down.

"Please—" she whispered.

"Just rest, Mariah. You don't have to worry."

"—just make sure—it's finished." She gasped out these words, like a person wracked by fever. Psychosis, Seamus figured. It was a sad way to go, but the mind went as the body did. Still, there was something about her deathbed raving that didn't seem quite right to him. Her eyes were clear, locked on his, not dancing about the way a psychotic person's usually did. And there was an old pain in her voice, like the thing she really wanted to say was something she couldn't quite get out.

At last, he managed to calm her, and she relaxed her grip on his sleeve. Maxwell nervously patted her shoulder—she wasn't any better than him at being comforting.

"I'll be back to visit, Mariah. Save your strength—you've got a fight to win."

That got a smile out of her, but she was too tired to say anything.

When Seamus pushed his way into the sterile light of the hacker's room, the bed was empty, a dangling IV waiting for a fresh vein. He stared—no chart, clean sheets. Seamus ground his teeth slightly. "It'll be a pain for us if he died," he said. "We need some hint of what Platinum actually is, and symptoms would help with that."

"Plus, you know, the value of a human life," said Maxwell.

"Right." Seamus ducked out the door and saw a nurse wrestling with a young woman who'd pulled off her hospital gown and was wielding her IV pole like a glaive. "My cousin was in this room," Seamus called, during a brief pause in the action. "Do you know where he's gotten to?"

"Sam?" said the nurse, dodging a swing from the pole. "He's—come now, Felicity, you'll feel much better once the Thorazine kicks in—he's in the recovery ward."

"Thank you," said Seamus. "Need a hand?"

"Oh, no," said the nurse, deftly catching the IV pole as Felicity staggered back. "This young woman's a bit confused, but I imagine the antipsychotics and the sedative will kick in any second now." On cue, Felicity stumbled into the nurse's arms. "There we go, we'll get you back in bed. Things'll look better in the morning."

Doubtful, but at least by then she'd be fully restrained.

Seamus turned to Maxwell. "If they moved him, that means he stabilized. Excellent news for the case."

"Human life, boss. Let's try to pretend we're worried about it, huh?"

After a few inquiries, they managed to find the hacker's room on the second floor of the recovery wing. It was more comfortable than the last, with a wooden bedside table and a large west-facing window. In the neighbouring bed, separated by a small blue curtain, a woman was cheerfully knitting a very small sweater. The weasel doctor who had given Seamus attitude over the floor plans was standing by the bedside, wearing a deeply self-satisfied grin. Seamus recognized the expression—it was the smile of a mark who hadn't yet realized the deal was too good to be true.

With the sun still rising, the room was painted in pale light; even the grey medical hardware looked soft and inviting. A card on the hacker's bedside table caught Seamus's eye for a moment before the patient pulled his attention away. The boy on the bed was thin and unconscious, but he seemed to have a bit more colour to him than the last time Seamus saw him. The doctor looked up and lost some of his smile when he recognized the visitors.

"You're that detective, aren't you?"

"Good to see you, too, Doctor. You decided to move him out of intensive care?"

"Yes. His condition has improved rapidly, and thanks to quite a stroke of inspiration, if I do say so myself. I expect him to regain consciousness within days."

The kid stirred and moaned softly—if Seamus could get a more precise explanation of the drug's effects, the payoff could be huge. "What did you find?" he asked.

"A prion disease. Similar to mad cow, but it showed a few key differences. Nothing that I'd expect a layman to notice, of course. The proteins involved were different and accreted much faster. We've kept samples, of course." Here he visibly inflated with pride. "But I have developed an effective treatment, which I'm formalizing as a protocol for any future outbreaks. An entirely unexpected treatment course proved effective."

Seamus nodded appreciatively. "What might that have been, Doctor?"

The doctor gave a little smile of condescension. "I think I will *not* be disclosing the treatment details. I can't imagine how it might be important to your work as a policeman."

Seamus didn't bother correcting him on that point. "Doctor, it may be more important than you realize. Once we can identify the substance this young man took, we'll know where to start looking—"

"You have no authority to view those records without a warrant—it's a matter of patient confidentiality. You and your associate may leave now."

Seamus stared at the doctor. Violence wasn't likely to be helpful here, which was unfortunate, since it was clearly deserved.

"You're right, Doctor," said Maxwell. Seamus gave her a warning glance, but she kept looking right ahead, stepping forward to lay a hand on the doctor's arm. "We really want to apologize for overstepping. I hope you won't hold it against us—just trying to do our job."

The weaselly doctor hemmed and hawed, but clearly wasn't averse to having a pretty twenty-something hanging off his arm. Maxwell kept talking, saying that she was very impressed with his clinical skills, and as she did it pointed discreetly with her other hand to show Seamus what he himself had missed—the doctor's keycard and lanyard, laying on the bedside table.

Seamus quickly blocked the doctor's line of sight and slipped the keycard into his jacket pocket—Maxwell seemed to be talking about her interest in a career in medicine, asking if they could meet for coffee sometime. The weaselly doctor was actually blushing at this, and Seamus decided it was time for a speedy exit. He nodded to Maxwell.

"Let's move, Moscovitz. Sorry for any inconvenience, Doctor."

They left the room at a quick pace, certainly not running. Seamus gave Maxwell an appreciative look. "Quick thinking."

"Yeah, well, I'll need to take about a dozen showers tonight to wash the ick off, but we had to do something. Guy's got a stick up his ass."

He and Maxwell cut through the hospital, towards the room number on the lanyard he'd swiped. Seamus sped up without quite noticing it, only pausing when Maxwell started swearing at him to slow down.

Prion disease—that was a wrinkle Seamus hadn't been expecting. A pre-existing condition, brought to a head by an overdose? It was possible, but it seemed unlikely to Seamus. It wasn't all that common for young college students in Toronto to be coming down with prion diseases—not a demographic that ate many cow brains.

The coast was clear—a pleasant second-floor office, empty when Seamus glanced in through the door lite. He looked to Maxwell—she was out of breath, but she grinned and gave him a thumbs-up.

"Get after it, boss. I'll stand guard."

An excellent secretary. Seamus swiped the stolen keycard in the lock and pushed inside. Met with a square of ten desks, he quickly scanned them. His eyes fell on a stack of business cards that matched the name on the weasel doctor's lanyard. Seamus pocketed one, then bent to search the desk. It was a mess, strewn with paperwork and rubber bands. Good—that meant he wouldn't have to cover his tracks. With professional quickness, he picked the lock on the desk drawer and rummaged through it, finding the hacker's file. But just as he flipped it open, he heard footsteps on the other side of the door.

Freezing was for amateurs—there was no time to waste. Seamus set the folder down and dug into his coat pocket. The footsteps were brisk, getting louder, till they stopped just short of the door. He pulled a nylon over his face—wouldn't do much good if they had security camera footage of him entering, but it was better than nothing. He didn't want to have to hurt hospital staff, but there'd be guards at the door—maybe he could burst past them and break free. There'd be hell to pay for it when complaints got back to Sandra's department, but no time to think of that now. Seamus was crouched to run when he heard Maxwell's voice from beyond the door.

"Listen, ma'am, you can't go in there."

"Why not?" asked a different, pinched female voice.

"Uh—construction. You know asbestos? There was a bunch of it in the pipes. The guys are in there right now, taking it out. Can't go in without protective shit. Masks."

"That's ridiculous," said the pinched voice. "I was in here an hour ago, and there wasn't even a work crew."

"Yeah, well, uh—Caron Construction works fast. We pride ourselves on it." And then, in a lower, almost sultry tone: "Did anyone ever tell you you've got the most amazing nails?"

"Who let you in here?"

There was a stretching silence on the other side of the door. Then came a thump, and a pinched voice calling out: "What do you think you're doing? That's my latte!"

"It's my latte now, bitch!" Then the clunking sound of someone running in combat boots. Exit Maxwell, with a second, rapid set of footsteps following her. After waiting a moment, Seamus pulled the nylon off his face and bent to scan the file. When he recognized the name of the drug they were using for treatment, he puzzled for a moment—another Alzheimer drug? It didn't add up.

It was a risk—a stupid one, perhaps—but Seamus kept digging, ripping through the doctor's files. His eyes fell on a scribbled note: a list of suspected similar cases from the hospital records.

There were a handful, all dead or comatose, but only one name there mattered: *Antonio Lopez.* It took a moment, but when the realization did hit him, it was like an aluminum baseball bat to the skull. He stuffed the files back in the desk in a haze, only just remembering to re-lock the cabinet before he left. Seamus peeked out the door, but the hallway was empty, only a few loose papers and a splash of milky coffee on the ground.

After slipping out of the hospital, he found Maxwell hiding in a holly bush a block south of the hospital gates. She was sipping at half of what smelled like a vanilla latte—the other half had soaked her jacket and pants. Normally, Seamus would have grinned, but even he couldn't manage to be blithe just then.

"That was excellent work, Moscovitz. I owe you one."

"Nope. We're even now. Did you find what you needed?"

"That I did. He's being treated with Aducanumab—a commercial antibody therapy that's used to treat Alzheimer's." Seamus pulled Maxwell to her feet. "The vials Timmy gave us contained three stimulants, an Alzheimer drug that's just like what our friend the doctor used, and a tiny speck of some unknown protein. What Arya Williams was shipping in that briefcase was the protein in a pure form—pure enough that a single dose nearly killed that kid in the hospital. How does it fit together?"

"You're the detective."

"I'll give you a hint," said Seamus, walking briskly in the direction of his office. "That particular mixture of stimulants is difficult to synthesize. There's no way Timmy'd turn a profit on it. He'd lose money on every dose he sells."

She frowned, looking thoughtful, and rubbed her chin. Seamus glared at her.

"You're trying to look like you're thinking while you wait for me to tell you the answer."

"Yeah. Is it working?"

"One last hint—I wasn't sure until I saw this in the doctor's case notes. Mariah Lopez's son's name is on a preliminary list of suspected similar cases. His symptoms were similar to what the hacker presented. See the connection?"

Maxwell rubbed her temples. "Your hints suck balls."

"It all fits together," said Seamus, impatience catching in his voice. His fingers were twitching again. Here was the usual sense of urgency and none of the usual satisfaction of solving a case. "The kid had a prion disease, something unusually fast-acting. Like mad cow, but more aggressive. You can catch it off a minuscule amount of infectious material. And it's spread by a protein—which can remain viable for long periods at room temperature, unlike a virus or a bacterium.

Mariah's son—those bad men he hung around were Timmy's crew. He was one of the test subjects, and they must have shot him up before they got the dosages right. Or before their supplier did."

Maxwell stumbled to a stop. "You mean there's this mad cow shit *in the drugs*? Why?"

"Why are drugs a good business to get into, Maxwell?"

She shrugged. "They sell well."

"Right. Basically, you're selling both a sickness and the cure—a temporary cure. That's the essence of it. This Platinum is the same old philosophy on a whole new level." Even the name was appropriate—it was the highest possible form of dealing. Seamus would have to congratulate the Angelmaker, before he killed them.

"So, you're saying the prion thingy, that spreads the disease—"

"—is mixed in with a drug that suppresses the symptoms. The hacker there just took it pure, before it had been mixed with the blocker—that's why his brains leaked out his ears, medically speaking."

"But why the stimulants? How's Timmy thinking he's gonna make money off this?"

"Oh, it's how *was* Timmy going to make money..." Seamus had quite forgotten to tell Maxwell about Timmy. His death would probably be good news to her, but there wasn't time for that now. Maxwell spluttered, and Seamus waved her new questions aside. "Timmy had deep pockets," he continued. "His plan must've been to sell Platinum at a loss, get everyone to try it once. He might go into the hole at first, but then he'd have a city full of people who now needed to buy his drug every week to keep their brains from turning to aspic. Eventually, he'd be able to cut the stimulants out completely, sell the treatment alone, and name his price."

"Smart. Too smart for him, though. And when you used the past tense—"

"You're absolutely right," said Seamus, ignoring the second half of her statement and dodging some traffic. "Timmy couldn't have pulled this off on his own if you gave him a lifetime to plan. My bet is it's one of his men—staying out of the spotlight, pulling the strings. Maybe they're the Angelmaker." As he said the name, Seamus drew his jacket tighter about his shoulders before he even realized he was doing it. Where had he heard it last?

He and Maxwell retreated to Jackson's for the rest of the day—Seamus needed to figure out how to use the knowledge of what Platinum was to guess who was willing to kill over it. At length, Maxwell managed to extract the news of Timmy's demise—though Seamus didn't go into the details of his visit to the Freezer—and was so pleased by the news that she bought everyone a round. Boomtown, who'd wandered in and grabbed a seat nearby without anyone quite noticing, somehow wound up with three bottles in front of him.

Seamus couldn't share her exultation. The Platinum problem was cracked, but what really would've made Seamus happy was any hint as to who was killing people connected to it—and whether they'd soon decide a certain Seamus Caron was asking too many questions about their work. He hadn't exactly been subtle in his investigations back when he thought he was chasing a one-off killer.

If he followed the theory that it was one of Timmy's subordinates who'd killed him and Ryba, maybe hoping to cut a deal with the Angelmaker directly, then the only option he had left was to try to organize a meeting with Timmy's men and get more information. But that would be a desperate move, even for Seamus.

Maxwell left early in the evening, probably headed somewhere to continue her celebration. Seamus sat at the bar, the same glass of bourbon he'd nursed for the last hour held loosely in one hand, thinking. He should have been pondering angles of attack, but one image kept pulling at his attention, dragging it off target—the hacker resting in his cot, that single card at his bedside. Seamus tried to shake the image off—it wasn't important. It looped in his head, though, and his thoughts were moving like molasses.

Finally, he shook his head clear and tossed back the last watered-down swallow of whisky. With any luck, Sam Ewe would wake up, and Seamus could push his way in to ask some questions, confirm his guesses. It would take time, but Sandra could lean on the drug task force and look for anyone buying supplies to grow prions in the lab—what those supplies might've looked like was a matter for actual scientists, not a lone private eye. For now, there was nothing to do but head home and try to make up on lost sleep—Seamus felt, as he pushed himself up from the bar, how badly blurred his thoughts were by fatigue. The problem would yield to a night's rest.

CHAPTER TEN

Seamus jerked awake in his blankets. A glance at the grey of the window confirmed the sun was rising, and he bit out a curse as he jumped to his feet, heart already pounding. That, at least, was good. He'd need to run shortly.

The kid in the hospital was a living evidence cache, the prion still eating away at his brain. If he ever woke up, his testimony and his labs would be the first key in spotting future cases.

Sometime before he woke up, Seamus's mind had dredged up a grisly bit of historical trivia from a forensics course a half-lifetime ago—the Angel Makers of Nagyrév. Whoever was behind Platinum clearly looked up to them, if they wanted to borrow the name—Seamus should have seen it as soon as he realized just what the drug was. Prion diseases? That wasn't the work of some jumped up pusher, but someone with resources, dark labs, and an almost gleeful willingness to kill hundreds of people. Someone who admired the most prolific poisoner in history. Whoever that sick fuck was, Sam Ewe had stolen from them, disrupting their supply chain, and might be a liability if he recovered. He was sitting unguarded in a hospital bed—if Seamus could get in, so could an assassin hoping to slip something into his IV. He should've seen it sooner—while he'd been putting the pieces together, he'd given the Angelmaker all the time in the world to make their move.

He found the weaselly doctor's business card in his jacket pocket and called on the landline as he pulled on fresh clothes.

"Who is this?" crackled a sleepy voice on the other end of the receiver.

"I'm working with the police," said Seamus. "We have reason to believe one of your patients is being targeted. We'll arrive shortly, but I want you and several nurses in his room right now, monitoring. No unauthorized visitors."

"Wait—are you the detective I saw yesterday? You can call me during working hours."

"A man's in danger—" said Seamus, his voice rising, but the line was already dead. He could've crushed the phone, but that would've helped no one. Instead, he called Sandra—at least there was one person in this damn city he could count on—and told her in a calm voice to get in her squad car, put the siren on, and drive straight for the hospital. Then he threw himself out the door, jacket over his shoulders, and ran down the stairs, grabbing the railings to make faster turns. He hailed a taxi—even at a sprint, he'd be too slow, was *already* too slow.

The fact the hacker had looked safe in his bed meant exactly nothing, and it wasn't exactly a good sign how easily he and Maxwell had managed to get into the hospital: if they could, so could anyone else. And that card he'd seen by the bedside indicated the possibility that someone already had.

Seamus ran all the way to the recovery wing, dodging nurses and security guards, pushing himself so hard he was panting.

He stopped dead when he saw the blood. His eyes went cold, all the urgency gone out of them, and he stepped into the hospital room, carefully avoiding the droplets on the floor.

The weaselly doctor stood in the centre of the devastation, his lab coat soaked, red. The kid was curled into a ball on the bed, blood still trickling from his mouth and eyes. Other doctors were still rushing about, shouting for anticoagulants, but this wasn't even flatlining—he was beyond saving. No wounds on his body—he'd been dissolved from the inside out. Bloody vomit covered the once-sterile surfaces of the hospital room, and even Seamus wrinkled his nose at the stink of iron and stomach acid. The woman in the neighbouring bed seemed to be slipping into shock, even though she only had a few specks of blood on her. She was rocking back and forth, ignored amidst the bustle of doctors, frantically knitting with her empty needles. Seamus stepped over to block her view of the carnage, bending down at her bedside. All the urgency was gone—the kid was dead. Might as well deal with the casualties.

"Hello. My name's Seamus Caron. How can I help?"

She stared at him with huge, rheumy eyes. Seamus laid a hand over one bony wrist—she didn't have an IV in, wasn't connected to any monitoring devices.

"Can you stand? Let's get you to another room."

"I want to go home."

"That's probably for the best," said Seamus, helping her to her feet. He walked her to the door, had her sit in a chair in the hallway, then strode back to the charnel house to grab the weaselly doctor by the collar. He was gibbering—almost incoherent. Pathetic.

"You. That woman in the neighbouring bed—is she ready to be released?"

"He—he just started convulsing," babbled the doctor. "Blood everywhere—"

"Thank you," said Seamus through gritted teeth, "I gathered that much. You should've been here a half hour ago, when I called you."

Likely there wasn't anything the doctor could've done at that point, but the man's uselessness, and the fact he'd forgotten about the woman he *could* help, inclined Seamus towards cruelty. Seamus took a breath and looked at the doctor with clear eyes. "The woman: When's she due to be discharged?"

"Her—her son will be here in a few hours to take her home."

That was when Sandra came pushing through the crowd with her uniformed officers, roaring curses and yelling at the doctors *get back, poor fucker's got all his insides squeezed out like a juicebox, how the hell did this happen . . .*

Seamus turned to her. "There's a lady outside."

"Saw her when I came in. Witness?"

"Right, though I doubt you'll get much out of her now. Get your nicest uniformed officer to take her for a coffee and wait with her till her son gets here."

Sandra nodded briskly.

"On it. Can you tell me what happened here, Seamus? I can't get a straight answer out of the docs."

Seamus pulled on some nitrile gloves and steadied himself. The nurses and doctors had started to pull back—the kid hadn't had a heartbeat for at least five minutes, if there was even anything left in his chest to pump. Seamus recognized the old veteran nurse who'd been helping Felicity the day before, and even she'd gone pale with the sheer horror of the kid's death. Seamus walked into the centre of the room, ignoring the tacky slickness under his shoes.

That lone card was still on the bedside table, and then, as fast as Seamus's gloved hand flickered out, it wasn't, it was safely stashed in an evidence bag and hidden in his coat instead.

"I can't tell you much yet," he said as he walked back by Sandra on his way out. "But don't touch that blood, and have the doctors wash immediately. You're dealing with a poisoning."

Seamus could recognize the moment to retreat, and he took it. Sandra would be busy with damage control for the next hour, and he didn't want to be around to jog memories when her colleagues started asking if any suspicious people had been hanging around the hospital. Jackson's would do, though Seamus would be drinking water—you don't take a dull sword to the battlefield.

Some sort of enzymatic poison, taken orally or put in his IV. After thinking it over for a moment, Seamus pulled out the card he'd found on the kid's bedside—wearing a fresh pair of gloves, just in case. He'd had enough of being careless.

The edges were crisp, the stock thick cotton, hand pressed. The script inside was light and loopy, printed in black ink that bled to purple at the edge of each letter.

> *So the old woman lay on her belly on the bank and sucked up all the water in the pond. The princess was now inside the body of the witch. She assumed her former shape and sliced open the belly with the sword she had borrowed from the prince, leaving the witch lying there, dead.*
>
> *You shouldn't touch other people's things. It's easy to hurt yourself.*
>
> *With love, the Angelmaker.*

Seamus stared a moment, then pressed his eyelids closed.

So, this new player, the Angelmaker, had had enough of their men being killed and decided to retaliate. Poisoning the kid—who, after all, had stolen a shipment of prion and promptly snorted it—was a rational choice, but it wouldn't be the end of the killing. Timmy and Ryba were dead, and Seamus suspected that if the bodies kept piling up, the Angelmaker would be more than happy to go after the Company, or whoever they thought was the most likely culprit.

He had to find the man who killed Ryba and poisoned Timmy, and he had to do it fast.

"Life's a shit sandwich, Seamus."

Seamus had walked to the station to find Sandra buried under a mountain of paperwork, trying to ignore the low sobbing coming from the holding cell. He followed her as she carted an armful of paperwork along.

"I wouldn't normally agree with you, but the last few days prove your point."

"Forensics says there was some shit in the IV—collagenase? Figured you'd know what that meant."

Seamus rubbed his eyes, wincing.

"That checks out. Collagenase is used to treat open wounds sometimes—wouldn't even be that hard getting your hands on it. There'd be a delay between the bag draining and the first symptoms showing up, and it'd be too late to do anything by then anyways."

"It turned that kid into soup, Seamus. You're saying they use it for medicine?"

"Externally. I think they usually use collagenase as an ointment—it helps break down damaged tissue, so your body can get in there and do the repair work. But if you injected a high dose of it right into a vein..."

Neither of them spoke for a moment, remembering the blood, the skin like a loose bag lying in the hospital bed. Sandra swallowed once and bared her teeth slightly.

It wasn't just the killing. Both of them were used to the casual horror of violence—it was their living, after all. But to use that particular poison—there were more efficient ways, easier ways of killing. Putting collagenase in an IV wasn't an act of desperation, or even of malice, but curiosity; the same curiosity that tells a child to put a stick through an earthworm and see how long it takes to die.

Sandra shook her head in a quick motion, almost a shudder.

"We grilled the nurses, but they've got nothing. Best guess is someone snuck in while he was alone."

"It's a good guess. Listen, I took something from the crime scene."

Seamus handed her the get-well card—well, perhaps that wasn't quite the right word for it—out of his jacket.

"Found this on the kid's bedside table."

Sandra's eyes flickered over the card, her mouth opening and closing but not producing any sound. She waved some uniformed officers over to take her manilla burden, then sat down hard on a spare chair. At last, she asked: "Why'd they sign as *the Angelmaker*?"

"There's a story behind the pseudonym," said Seamus, taking a seat by her side, wincing at the fact he'd remembered this story just slightly too late. "During the First World War, all the men in this small village in Hungary had gone off to fight, and the women took lovers, not to mention got a taste of having control of the village. Nagyrév. Turns out there was some discontent when the war ended and the men came home all PTSD-ridden and went back to beating their wives."

"Can't imagine how this could go wrong . . ." muttered Sandra. Seamus gestured his agreement.

"There was this midwife in town—she'd boil down fly paper and sell a little vial of arsenic to any woman who was having marriage trouble.

"Absolute power, as the saying goes. Those women in Nagyrév—the Angel Makers, as they came to be known—finished off their abusive husbands, then they got to work on the unpleasant ones, then those pesky parents and children. Tough to feed all those mouths back in postwar Hungary, I suppose."

"Christ."

"Their picking that name," said Seamus drily, "doesn't indicate to me the Angelmaker is going to be an especially reasonable person."

"So, we've got the Ryba murder, and now we have to deal with the Angelmaker too?"

"That reminds me. Timmy's dead—poisoning."

Sandra almost fell out of her chair.

"Nice of you to remember to tell me, Trouble. How long've you known?"

"It's been a busy few days."

"So, you figure that was the Angelmaker? But why would—"

"No. See, the commonality between Ryba and Timmy is they were both smuggling Platinum into the city. The Angelmaker's either their supplier or their boss outright. As far as I can see, someone kills Ryba, then Timmy. The Angelmaker retaliates and kills the kid in the hospital."

Sandra nodded, frowning.

"Which means we've got *two* psychos running around the city. Great."

"There are a lot more than two," said Seamus. "But there are two we have to worry about at the moment."

"Well, with the Ryba murder—I got some good news there, but I'm not sure how it fits with all this new shit." She pulled up a file on her desk and flipped it open, fanning pictures of carved knives across her desk. "I went digging in evidence," she said. "We've confiscated another knife with similar carvings, and forensics says they were probably done by the same person. Picked it up on a drunk and disorderly charge in the east end—the name Braydon Fraser ring any bells?"

Seamus narrowed his eyes. Playboy Hat. "Wouldn't happen to be as far east as the Montmorency, would it?"

"Just a block south. Guy got picked up for kicking garbage cans at three in the morning. We pulled the knife when we searched him."

"I know Braydon. He was working under Timmy—seemed like a piece of shit, but he had a little more behind the eyes than the rest of his friends. If the knife was his—let's run with the hypothesis. Say he killed Ryba, and Timmy too. Why would he kill his own friends?"

Sandra shrugged. "Same reason anyone does—'cause they're in the way."

Suddenly it snapped into place. The glares Braydon had been giving Timmy. Timmy was the head of the operation, Ryba was the right hand, but Braydon was the brains, the administration, the person who did the work and got nothing for it. Stuck in that position, Braydon had found himself thinking how convenient it would be should his superiors happen to disappear.

Add the Angelmaker to the mix—a supplier, who Braydon knows will retaliate if Timmy dies. The Angelmaker's response is predictable, and Braydon can use it. If Timmy and Ryba both die, the Angelmaker would assume—like Seamus had at first—it's some rival who's killed them. Or that Greene found him out and came down hard, in which case the Angelmaker would attack the Company. Either way, it would mean a whole lot of bloodshed but no one's eyes on Braydon himself, not to mention a nice power vacuum for him to crawl his way into.

An excellent plan, if you didn't take issue with the killings and the inevitable innocent casualties.

"You've got that face on."

"Hmm?"

"It's your should-I-tell-Sandra-what-I'm-thinking face."

"I have no idea what you're talking about."

"Trust me, it's your expression about half the time we're together. I don't know why you worry about it so much, the answer's always yes."

Seamus glanced round the station, then moved closer and lowered his voice. "Let's take a walk. Make sure we aren't overheard."

Sandra followed Seamus onto the roof—he'd swiped the keys ages ago, and it was one of the few of Seamus's crimes Sandra was willing to benefit from. Sandra did a quick sweep, finding a crowd of very cold pigeons but no other eavesdroppers. Seamus crossed his arms against the cold and told her about his guess at Braydon's motive, Sandra's look growing graver with each word. When Seamus finished, she sucked in her breath with a hiss.

"Braydon—you figure he's masterminding this whole thing?"

"That's my best guess. It seems likely it was his knife that killed Ryba, after all, and he's hanging around Timmy every night—all the time in the world to slip some poison into his beer."

"Seems pretty damn complicated for a guy who got picked up for kicking over green bins."

"Malice makes people resourceful."

"Can't argue with that," said Sandra. "So now we've got an angle. A few weeks to gather evidence, we'll set up a sting—"

"There isn't time for that. If my guess is right, Braydon's trying to start a war. If we wait a few weeks, he'll have finished the job, and shutting him down then won't do any good."

"What do you want me to do? I can't get clearance any faster—"

"I'll call him myself," said Seamus, speaking as the words formed in his mind. "Set up a meeting. I've already made contact once, and I'll go undercover—confirm the hunch, get more evidence that Braydon's the murderer. If we get lucky, maybe I can even record a confession."

The most expedient thing of all would be if Seamus managed to shoot Braydon in the head, but he didn't mention that option to Sandra. She was frowning.

"It'll still take at least two weeks to get a support team together—"

"I need to go alone, Sandra. These aren't people to take lightly—you send in a team, and your men will be going home in bags."

His mouth was set in a hard line. Hers popped open slightly, as if she couldn't quite comprehend how annoying he was being. That, at least, was familiar.

"Are you trying to get yourself killed?" she demanded.

"Not actively."

"You're not going in alone, Seamus. If I have to break your legs, I will."

"I'll crawl," he said. "Sandra, look at the big picture here. Braydon's eliminated any opposition to his control of Platinum, and it looks like he has plans to start importing wholesale. If there's fighting in the streets, all your budget and manpower goes into that, and he poisons the city in the meantime. Your men can't move fast enough. If even a small shipment hits the streets, we're talking about casualties in the hundreds, maybe thousands. If I can shut this down now, we avoid a lot of needless death."

"*Now* you're worried about civilians? You've finally snapped on me."

Seamus was pretty surprised himself. He hadn't meant to care about anything much besides getting his money from Ruby, but that was what he got for speaking without thinking. He grinned weakly.

"Eh, it's been a good run—"

Sandra grabbed his collar in a tight fist, her eyes burning. Seamus had never seen her cry, not even when they were children, and he didn't now, but he recognized the shine in her eyes.

He answered by leaning forward and putting one hand on her cheek. That, too, he hadn't done since they were very young, on the nights when she'd come to his mother's house to wash the blood out of her mouth and eat a proper dinner. After a moment, she let her grip loosen and her head fall against his chest. He felt an urge to pull her close, smell the cedarwood in her hair—she wasn't wrong, after all. Even odds he was going to his death. Couldn't some small indiscretion be forgiven? A rush of longing, as well as something darker and more insistent, ran through him . . .

And Seamus denied it, wiped it from his mind. More advice from his mother: *right is right, whether you're laughing or dying.* Thinking like this? He'd been letting the stress get to him more than he ought to. He took his hand off her cheek and laid it on her shoulder, kind but resolute.

"Dammit, Seamus," she said at last.

"I'm sorry, Sandra. Truly. I'll make it back."

"Yeah," she said, raising her eyes to meet his, "and I'll be there to make sure of it. The two of us—just like old times. When's the meeting?"

"I'll set it for Saturday—don't want to come in too hot on the heels of Timmy's death."

He and Sandra fleshed out the details—rendezvous points, a floor plan he sketched out from his last visit, a plan to drive away from the scene. Sandra was soon smiling, nodding to herself. "We can pull this off. You go in, get enough evidence for a warrant—it'll work."

Seamus nodded, and he left for his office promising her to make the call and set up a meeting with Braydon.

Back home, he locked the door and drew the blinds, leaned back at his desk in the dusty half-light. He hadn't mentioned to her that there was a more expedient solution than evidence and a warrant—the whole situation tied itself up nicely if Braydon happened to wind up dead behind the Montmorency. He took three breaths, then dialled Timmy's business number.

"Who the fuck is this?"

"Dominic Terrazzo," said Seamus, slipping easily into a tone of oily confidence. "I hear Timmy ate something that didn't agree with him. But I've got business for you. My customers liked your samples—liked them a great deal. I need more."

"Who says Timmy's dead?"

"I'm well informed. How soon can we meet?"

There was a silence. Then: "I've got what you need, Dominic. When can you bring the money?"

"I need a few days to gather cash," said Seamus. "How's Friday night?"

Seamus had every intention of taking the expedient solution, which meant he couldn't have Sandra with him. Besides, her wedding was coming up. Bullet wounds would steal attention from the dress.

CHAPTER ELEVEN

Seamus had three days.

Three days was basically worthless. Not enough time to build a stronger position, just enough time that the sleeplessness of anticipation would start to dull the edge. Luckily, though, his mother had taught him what to do in this sort of situation.

Seamus trained.

It wasn't possible to get meaningfully stronger in three days. Or three months. With three years, you might start making progress. But training was better than doing nothing. And as Seamus had discovered when he was twelve, collapsing from exhaustion at the end of the day helped you sleep.

The first day he went out to the spit of rock that ran into the lake. Tommy Thompson Park was a popular place for biking in the summer, and a windswept hellscape in the dead of winter. He wouldn't likely see anyone out there, but, just in case, Seamus jumped the chain-link fence that blocked off the bridge to the small island at the end and continued onward till he stood on the outcropping of stone at the water's edge, where jagged, cubelike chunks of discarded concrete were crusted with ice and battered by the low waves that broke against them.

It was snowing, and his coat whipped in the wind when he took it off and laid it down in the soft powder that coated the stone. Seamus stood there in the cold and waited. In a fight, you didn't have the luxury of waiting. You had to respond, had to move as fast as you could think. But when he was training, it could be perfect.

It was Ma who'd trained him first—Muay Thai she'd learned from one of her innumerable uncles back home, enough to make money helping out at a gym once his father died. She'd trained him up the old-fashioned way, with a ten-mile run and a hundred kicks before the sun came up and he had to drag himself to school. But she'd never had much technique to teach him, beyond a good straight punch and a clean low kick—he'd picked up the rest he knew over the years, along with his scars. It was a workable way to learn to fight, so long as you were extremely lucky and extremely durable.

Times like this, he could feel every one of those scars, remember their stories. Other thoughts ran past—Sandra, Carleton. Seamus let them drift away with the falling flakes. He waited. His mind had to be steady. He let his eyes close.

Three steps behind him was an enemy. Seamus shifted his weight, dodged their first attack, answered with a fist to the chest. He opened his eyes, saw the expanse of whiteness and ice. That punch would have landed too low, where the muscles of the stomach could absorb it—you needed to aim for the floating ribs, which a fist could crack. His eyes closed again.

Five steps away. Two men. Seamus danced back, feigning uncertainty, then kicked the first one's legs out. Broke the man's tibia—Seamus's low kick was his strongest, he could break most of a man's leg bones with it if he hit at the right angle. The second man rushed him, grabbed at his throat—Seamus crushed his nose with an open palm, threw him over his shoulder. He opened his eyes.

The wind screamed through the gaps in the concrete refuse, and Seamus turned to see where his imagined opponent would have fallen. Then he took his stance on the ice-slicked rock again and closed his eyes.

After five hours, it wasn't *perfect*, but it was better. He wiped the sweat off his face, hung his jacket from his shoulders, and went down to the lake, jumping from rock to rock. The ice was thin over it—a well-placed kick broke it, and Seamus knelt where the water was exposed.

If he were still in the forest, kneeling by a stream, he'd have drunk from it. Generally, you didn't drink from Lake Ontario unless you were trying to lose weight with a quick bout of E. coli. But Seamus washed his face and wet his hair, letting the icy water drip down his back, over his burning shoulders and the wind-cut skin of his knuckles. He counted his fingers once, then turned back homeward.

It was enough to help him sleep that night.

On the second day, as he moved to leave—time to get to the range and work on his aim—Maxwell blocked his way with a hand across the door. Seamus looked at her in surprise—he hadn't realized she'd come in that day.

"Aren't you supposed to be doing research on postwar Hungary?"

Maxwell pointed to a loose stack of papers on the desk.

"Done."

"Excellent. Now, go and find everything you can on protease poisoning—start with collagenase, maybe . . ."

Maxwell fixed him with a glare.

"You know, I can tell when you're trying to get rid of me."

"Clearly it's not working."

She just rolled her eyes at him.

"You've been acting weird all week. Something's up. Tell me."

"Just a small problem I need to deal with," said Seamus affably, bag of guns slung over his shoulder. "Nothing you need to worry about."

"Well, wherever you're off to again, you're taking me with you. I'm sick of sitting around here."

"Entertain yourself. Can't you find someone to flirt with on your phone?"

"First: rude. Second: yes, but not at ten on a Thursday morning. Third: There's only so many women in the GTA. I don't want to run through them all before I turn thirty. I'd get bored."

Seamus chuckled slightly at that. "Alright, come. I'm working, though. Keep up, or you're getting left behind."

She armoured up with her coat and gloves, then they headed south and east, along the frozen waterfront. Seamus didn't say anything as they walked, just moved forward at a steady pace.

They arrived at an abandoned condo complex with rotting plywood screwed over the lower windows. Seamus moved down the steps, gesturing for Maxwell to follow as he peeled open a taped-over door that looked like it should've been locked. Inside, it smelled of mould and the long absence of human life.

"Listen, Maxwell. Since you're here, you might as well help out. Once we get inside, I might need you to create a distraction. The signal is *peculiar*."

"What kinda distraction?"

"I leave that in your capable hands, Maxwell."

Once they got through the door, they found themselves in a surprisingly clean lobby, with a shag carpet and a single stool pushed back against the far wall. Trelly was sitting there, staring at his phone in the corner, perched on the lone barstool like an elephant on a beach ball. His hand went to his jacket pocket, clearly waiting to shoot down an unwelcome visitor, but withdrew it empty when he saw Seamus.

"Caron. You come to train?"

"Always. You can never get enough training."

That got a rare grin out of Trelly—a thin cut in a large grey potato. "You bring secretary? She also train?"

Seamus glanced at Maxwell, who seemed to be doing her best to keep out of view behind him. She cleared her throat and stepped forward, though she kept a clear path to the door. Smart woman.

"Yeah. Wanted to see what the boss was up to."

"He knows where range is." Trelly frowned. "Better to learn to fight with your hands, first. Guns are too easy, no discipline. I should teach you?"

Maxwell edged for the door, and Seamus gave a loud laugh. "She's not quite in your weight class, Trelly. How's the morning treating you?"

Trelly frowned deeper than usual and rubbed his head as if in pain. "Fine. Always fine."

"Glad to hear it. We'll be on our way. But tell me something—I saw a tape of one of your matches the other day—Olympic, I think—and I was very impressed by the arm drag you used against—was it the Dominican . . . ?"

"The Cuban," said Trelly, a sparkle in those deep-set eyes as he raised himself from his seat. "Demonstrate?"

"Of course."

Now for the delicate part. Trelly might've been a great fighter, but he wasn't a thief. He wouldn't notice Seamus slipping the wallet out of his jacket—hopefully. If he did, he'd likely keep hold of Seamus's arm and beat him to a fine paste against the cinderblocks. The first bit went smoothly: He let Trelly grab his arm, obligingly slow for the sake of demonstration. With Trelly's view blocked by Seamus's arm, Seamus slipped Trelly's wallet out with the other hand. Trelly whipped Seamus's arm back just as Seamus hid the wallet in his sleeve. It felt like Seamus's shoulder was mostly still in place, which was a victory in and of itself.

"Understand now?"

"I think so. There's something *peculiar* about the way you block the hip."

For a moment, nothing happened. Seamus felt the weight of the leather wallet pressed against his wrist and resolved that, if he made it out of Olexa's bootleg shooting gallery alive, he'd be feeding his secretary to the pigeons at Yonge and Dundas. Then he heard Maxwell's voice: "Oh! Oh, uh, shit. I think I'm falling down."

Trelly and Seamus turned to stare, the former with confusion and the latter with naked disbelief, as Maxwell wobbled backwards, forwards, and finally fell smack to the ground without any provocation besides the breeze through the door. He *had* asked for a distraction, and here it was—watching Maxwell flail, Seamus almost forgot to sneak a glance at Trelly's driver's licence before he slipped the wallet back in his pocket, but he got what he needed.

"Caron," said Trelly solemnly. "It is very kind of you to give employment to this poor, simple woman."

"What can I say, Trelly? I'm a charitable man."

Trelly finished his demonstration, and Maxwell and Seamus made it down the stairs, Trelly resuming his post staring holes into the phone in his lap and massaging his temples. The big guy was strong as ever, but Seamus had felt a tremble in his wrist. Nerve damage from an old injury?

"My nose hurts," said Maxwell. "I think it hit the concrete."

"Good work. Although maybe next time you try a distraction that doesn't make you look like an extra on *Just for Laughs*."

"Go piss up a flagpole, boss."

Seamus liked Trelly. He was the closest thing Seamus had to a friend in the Company. But you didn't get away with breaking into Seamus's office without retaliation. Seamus wouldn't do anything—unless he was provoked. But now that Seamus knew Trelly's home address, the next time Trelly broke into his office he would repay the visit with a small calibre pistol and a reminder that Trelly wasn't the only one who could force a lock.

Down the stairs, the corridors were lined with soundproofing foam fitted against the walls. As they turned a corner, the hallway opened into a low, wide room, all concrete.

"The building's condemned," said Seamus. "But it'll be a few years before it's torn down. In the meantime, Olexa cut a deal with the developer—" Seamus gestured to the crude steel targets lined up in front of them.

He wanted to train, but Seamus forced himself to spend a half hour teaching Maxwell the basics of trigger discipline. He also gave her a friendly warning: "If you shoot me, I'll shoot back, and I guarantee I've got better aim." Then they both put on earmuffs from out of the canvas bag and took their places along the faded orange line spray-painted along the floor. Maxwell futzed with her aim, but Seamus had finished the instructional portion of the day: he emptied his clip downrange, then surveyed the results—close patterns, but not close enough. He'd always been a stronger fighter than marksman. He sucked his teeth in frustration and loaded another magazine.

They spent the rest of the day shredding paper targets taped over steel plates—Maxwell just managed to start hitting the paper by the end of it. Seamus visualized his targets—men coming at him, moving fast. Men who hadn't seen him yet, off their guard, slouching. He dropped them all, bullets sparking white on the steel as they struck true.

When they finally emerged, Trelly was hunched over his phone with the same unblinking intensity. Maxwell whispered to Seamus as they passed: "Buddy's job is to sit here watching porn all day? Grim."

Trelly looked up to glare at her. At least one of his crushed ears still worked, it seemed. "Dostoevsky. *Demons*—best novel ever written. You should try to read."

That got a laugh out of Seamus and a muttered apology out of Maxwell, who flushed down to her collar.

"People will surprise you, Maxwell," said Seamus, as they stepped into the dim cold of early twilight. "And Olexa encourages her men to improve themselves."

"Encourages, huh?"

"With pliers, if necessary."

The sun was down, which didn't bode well for the walk home. As they pushed through the whipping wind, Maxwell turned to Seamus. "So, when are you gonna teach me to fight, boss?"

"That's what I've been doing all day. Aim for centre mass. A quick draw is flashy, but it can be useful in certain—"

"Not that shit. It's so military-industrial. I want to learn how you fight, throwing punches and stuff." Maxwell showed off her fighting stance—it looked like she'd taken it from the least probable kung fu movie she'd ever seen—and threw a couple haymakers into the air.

Seamus squinted at her. Then he pointed to a park they were passing, emptied by the cold and falling darkness. The afternoon sun had melted some of the ground, and the grass was a muddy brown. "I'll teach you to fight."

Seamus slung his bag onto the ground, and Maxwell took that ridiculous stance, both fists up by her face where they'd snap back and break her nose if she tried to use them to block. Seamus sat down in the mud. "Alright, come at me," he said. "I won't use my legs, or my left arm. Hit as hard as you like, use whatever technique you want."

"Seriously? Even you can't fight with one arm."

"Secretary, you're too young to tell me what I can and can't do."

Maxwell scowled and started forward.

She stumbled to a stop when Seamus's hand flickered to his jacket and reappeared with a pistol. It was different than the one he'd trained with—always carry a spare. He didn't point it at her, just gave her a warning look, then replaced it in his jacket. Then he reached into a different pocket and pulled out a switchblade. He flicked it open and closed, still sitting on the ground.

"Here's how to fight, Maxwell: Run. And if you can't run, shoot them in the chest. If you can't manage that, pick up a knife. Or a chair." His voice was quiet, and deadly serious.

"That's not how *you* fight."

"You might notice how many scars I have," said Seamus drily. "And when I was learning, my mother had me kick trees till I bled."

He'd been eleven at the time. It had started in the year before his father died, when everything was shaking apart—Ma hadn't been all there. But he hadn't complained. It was good to have something that could be controlled, even if it was the flow of your own blood, and that basic training was why now it was the other man's shin that would break when he threw his low kick, not his own.

"You know, boss, you always talk about your mom, not your dad. With all these detecting skills I've picked up, I figure that—"

"My father was a doctor," said Seamus with an even look. He refused to flinch. He refused to look down. Seamus Caron would never yield to pain. "One of his patients was a family friend. Lauren Carres. Religious—same church as those fuckers who call themselves Sandra's parents. Lauren was close to my parents, growing up. My father'd taken care of her ever since she was ten. Sometimes she'd come to watch me and Sandra—that was just about the only time her parents would let her out of the house, if Lauren was babysitting. She always burned the pancakes, but she liked Monopoly and would play with us for hours.

"Lauren had a heart defect—that's how my family got to know her so well, from all the visits and checkups. Her health got worse around when she was eighteen, just finishing up high school—bad enough that she needed surgery. Thing about heart surgery is, artificial valves can't grow with the heart, so it's better to wait if you can till the patient's finished growing."

Seamus's eyes were fixed in the distance, on the ice and mud and darkening sky. The only person he might've talked about this sort of thing with was Sandra, but of course she already knew the story, had lived it, and he wasn't going to force her to endure it again. Still, Seamus found it hard to stop speaking once he'd started. Not impossible—he could have been silent, he always had that control. But here, with Maxwell, he couldn't see the harm in telling Lauren's tale.

"Now, the church her family was in took a dim view of medical practice in general and blood transfusions in particular. But you need to be able to supply blood during heart surgery. My father managed to convince her to take the blood—like I said, she was a good kid. She wanted to keep her family happy, but she had a brain—you can't do heart surgery without a transfusion ready.

"The day before the surgery, three old men in suits came to her hospital room and told her that if she took the transfusion, her parents would never speak to her again. That she'd be an outcast—before she got the chance to roast in hell, of course." Seamus's eyes burned. His voice was steady. He'd never seen any one of those old men again, which was just as well—if he had, he'd have beaten them to death with his bare hands. "She retracted her consent, and without a transfusion, it was too dangerous to operate. Thomas—my father—didn't operate. She died in her hospital bed about two months later, when her heart had finished sputtering out."

Her eyes had been quick, right up till the end. Her skin had gone pale and her lips whitened as her blood oxygen ticked down, day by day, week by week, but her eyes had been the same quick blue. Seamus had gone to see her right up till the end—he'd known what death was at that age, and he'd seen the fear in those quick eyes. Sandra's parents hadn't let her visit, but Seamus had brought Sandra's crudely drawn get-well cards and lined them up on Lauren's dresser, one for every week.

He hadn't known, at the time, how simple it would have been to fudge a few informed consent forms and convince a sympathetic anaesthetist to put her under. Might've cost some jail time, in the end, but that wasn't an argument for letting a girl die. Even then, Seamus had known it was wrong to let her die. Thomas Caron had known it too—he'd started prescribing himself Dilaudid, the day she finally flatlined. It weighs on your conscience, letting a girl you've known since she was ten die.

Ma hadn't exactly been supportive back then—she hadn't spoken to his father when he came back from the hospital, after Lauren died, she'd just taken Seamus and gone out to train. She never showed Thomas a hint of forgiveness, and in that she'd been right, in Seamus's assessment. Like she'd told Seamus that first night, it might be hard to do the right thing, but knowing what it was was easy. You didn't let a kid die because some fuckers had scared her into thinking it was a good idea.

Seamus cleared his throat.

"Anyway, things went predictably from there. He missed the funeral—recreational opiates will put you in bed, alright. I didn't see him much, and when I did I don't think he saw me."

Seamus fixed Maxwell, who'd gone so pale she was almost transparent, with a hard look.

"He wasn't in pain. That was what killed him. Pain—you want to be strong, you want to survive, you've got to take a bite out of pain, chew it up, swallow it, ask for seconds. If pain's all there is to feel, then you damn well better feel it. He wasn't willing to, and he had the pharmacology for that, but numbness'll kill you in the end. It got worse for a few months . . . he'd have lost his medical licence eventually, but an overdose got him first."

An overdose, an accident—that was what it said on his medical certificate. Seamus looked at his hands, traced his fingers over the scars.

"Overdose." Seamus shook his head. "He killed himself with Dilaudid and cognac. I tried to get him help, but he'd been dead overnight. Not much you can do for that."

The whole affair had been utterly pointless. Ma'd gone out before sunrise that morning as she always did, and Thomas must have been dead some hours when Seamus found him in his office chair, eyes blind and cloudy and staring, endlessly staring. Seamus had slung his body onto his shoulders—he could still remember the rigid weight of it, if he let himself. Thomas Caron had gotten very thin in the last few months of his life, and Seamus had been able to cross his father's wrists over his throat and get to his feet. That was a common nightmare, the weight on his back and neck making it hard to breathe, the swollen-blue fingers. But Seamus hadn't felt particularly afraid, or sad, in the moment. There was something he needed to do and no one else to do it—fear didn't enter into it.

He'd managed to carry the body a few blocks before neighbours found him, walking towards the hospital. Seamus had been strong, even then.

Seamus's chest felt colder than the winter air, but it softened when he saw Maxwell's horrified look.

"Don't worry about it," he said. "'People can stand the truth, for they are already enduring it.'"

That was a lie, but it shouldn't have been.

After a pause, Seamus sighed and stood, brushing himself off.

"Ma never said it in so many words, but she was angry—that Thomas Caron had left her alone to feed me. Not to mention Sandra, on those weeks when her parents decided she needed some extra discipline." Seamus grinned slightly. "Ma was all alone in this damned country, where the bananas don't taste right. She trained me up—she thought my father was weak, to break like that. Didn't want her son to follow his example, and to be fair to her, I certainly didn't."

Seamus rocked back on his heels.

"The point is, Maxwell, people who are really good at fighting are usually a little fucked in the head. Don't try to imitate us."

There were, of course, advantages to being able to tear through five men like paper. Seamus had spent most of his life on the battlefield, and he liked it out there. It was only tiring sometimes.

"Anyway. If you absolutely have to fight with your hands—I'll show you a choke."

She was wary, but she came over in the end, and Seamus showed her a basic rear naked choke, pressing it just tight enough that she'd get the feel. Doing something so familiar steadied him.

"You're not going be the strongest in any fight you wind up in," he said, "and it takes years to actually build a base. If you can't run, if you don't have a weapon—don't bother trying for a knockout. You'll need to cut off the brain's blood supply. Give it a try."

He let her get the choke on him—wasn't often he let his guard down enough for that—and adjusted her grip till he could feel the pressure on his carotid. She was a fast learner.

"That'll do. Keep practising," he said, standing and turning to leave.

"What's going on, boss? You're strung tight. Well, tighter than normal."

Seamus sighed. "I'm meeting with Braydon tomorrow. If you don't see me after that, I'm afraid you'll have to consider your contract terminated."

Maxwell froze for a moment. Then her jaw took a hard set. "Right. When are we leaving? Got all the guns we need?"

"Don't be stupid, Maxwell."

"You can't go alone, boss!"

"Maxwell, look at me."

She glared at him in the twilight. Seamus noted with some surprise the tears glittering in the corners of her eyes.

"There's a fairly good chance I'll survive this," he said. "If you come, it's almost guaranteed you'll die, and that you'll get me killed too."

She looked like she wanted to argue, but in the end she held it down and turned away. The last of the day's light had gone out and the wind had picked up, whistling through the bare trees. Seamus shook some of the dust off his jacket and stood. He walked west with his jacket pulled tight against the cold, but he kept his head up. Maxwell said nothing.

CHAPTER TWELVE

Seamus Caron stood alone in the evening desolation of the east end, watching the pale glow of the streetlights. His last day had come and gone slowly as days usually do when you spend them watching the minute hand tick around the clock face, and there was just an hour between him and his meeting with Braydon. The twilight sparkled with frost that caught flashes of light as the shadows grew in amongst the few trees and many squat buildings. He chewed on the last of the Pocky Sandra had given him and blew a white breath up at the moon, which was full and pale in the darkening sky. Frozen puddles crackled underfoot as he walked, about twenty pounds heavier than normal. His suit jacket only just fit over the holster, and the straps on his armour dug into his shoulders. He was grateful it was too cold to sweat—greasepaint wouldn't run, but it clung to wet skin like a coat of lard.

He only had his one pistol. It was his emotional-support pistol—just there for comfort. The way Seamus figured it, he wouldn't use the gun if he didn't need it, and if he did need a gun, he'd need more firepower than he could carry anyway. But with luck, it wouldn't come to that.

He also had his rifle armour. That'd been pricey, not least because it was still in its test phase when he bought it, and Seamus had had to pull some strings to get his hands on one. The armour shifted as he walked, hexagons of ceramic moving against his chest.

The club appeared to be deserted—unusual. A murder or two shouldn't have been enough to shut down the Montmorency. Perhaps it made a difference when the victim was the proprietor. He pushed the door closed behind him, moonlight trickling in pale through the dust, and walked towards the bar, which looked like it hadn't been cleaned since he was there last. There were still bits of napkins, spilled drinks, and what might have been vomit staining the floor.

Two men emerged from the shadows. Seamus took three steps to the left and glanced pointedly to his right. Sure enough, a glint of silver on a man's ear caught his eye—there was someone sidling up quietly behind him, who looked slightly embarrassed when Seamus saw him. Classic mob tactic—draw the attention in front while the third man circles behind. Usually, they used it to intimidate, but it could also be used in an ambush. The third man's hands were empty, but Seamus had no doubt all of them were armed.

The smart thing to do now would be to run. But the only way this was going to end quietly was if Braydon gave Seamus enough evidence that Sandra could lock up him and the rest of Timmy's men, or if Seamus managed to separate him from his men and give him a quick, quiet death by asphyxiation—there'd be too much blood and noise if he used his emotional support pistol. Options, options. Seamus put a big smile on his face and stepped forward, as if he hadn't even noticed the aborted ambush.

"Evening, gentlemen. I believe Braydon is expecting me."

The three unsmiling men said nothing, but they guided Seamus to the back. Earring showed Seamus to his seat, just as three more men joined them.

At the centre of the room was a small desk, empty except for what looked disturbingly like dentistry tools, gleaming chrome. Better and better—Seamus should've ignored Jackson and opened a hotdog stand two years ago instead.

Seamus glanced around, taking in the situation: None of the men looked like they'd be trouble barehanded, but they all had pistols at their side. All were carefully watching Seamus.

A seventh man came in through the door, swaggering with a confidence belied by the bandages covering his nose. Braydon. As Seamus watched, he pulled a knife from his jacket and toyed with it, in that special way of men who prefer *Guns & Ammo* to *Playboy*. Seamus gave him a professional smile.

"Dominic Terrazzo, at your service. There's been a hiccup in the supply chain, I understand, but I'm eager to get things back on track."

Braydon smiled, showing off silvery crowns on each of his teeth. He levelled the knife at Seamus's face. "You're one dumb fuck, walking in here after you killed Timmy."

Seamus shook his head still smiling calmly. His mind turned rapidly through a few possibilities. Braydon was trying to pin Timmy's murder on him—why? For the benefit of his men? The former frat boys who surrounded him didn't seem terribly loyal, and if they suspected Braydon, why had he brought them here in the first place? "That wasn't me. I'd been working with Mr. Greene—"

Braydon slapped him, and Seamus tasted the bright ferrous bloom of blood in his mouth. "Timmy's dead, and you're the first person to call, to try and replace him? Even the cops don't know what happened to him yet, must be his fucking aunt keeping him in a fridge somewhere. And you buying him drinks the very night before he died. You think we're stupid?"

Seamus thought it best to keep his opinions on the matter to himself. Braydon nodded to the man behind him, who brought out a tattered plastic bag.

"My boys found this outside the bar the night that you came to talk. Got a little careless, huh?"

Braydon spread the contents of the bag out on the table. There were two glass ampules, both empty, but Seamus could read the labels and hazard warnings. They'd held thallium samples.

There was more—a Montmorency napkin, carefully pressed and folded. A half-crushed cigarette butt, of all things. And a gold chain. Braydon held it up to Seamus's face.

"Ryba always wore his chain—you like your trophies, huh? Guess you forgot this here when you did Timmy."

There was an edge of fear in Braydon's voice, under the bravado. Seamus kept his face controlled, but he blinked and saw that he'd been an idiot—Braydon had no reason to lie here, he genuinely believed Dominic Terrazzo had killed his boss. Braydon wasn't the killer, and assuming this had been a gambit to play the Angelmaker off the rest of the city had been a wild overestimation of his abilities—he was just a low-rent thug who was trying to avoid winding up the way his boss did.

Killing him wouldn't solve anything—whoever had killed Timmy and Ryba would still be running loose, and Seamus didn't have even a long shot guess who that was at this point.

In a flash of annoyance, he bit the inside of his cheek hard enough to draw blood. He'd moved too quickly—panicked by the poisoning at the hospital, he hadn't even thought about how suspicious that call would look. Stupid amateur.

The men around him stood with their arms crossed—more experienced in looking intimidating than actually dishing out violence, he suspected. Seamus spoke as the words came to him, trying to spin a story that didn't end with him hacked into a dozen pieces and tossed in the Montmorency dumpster.

"Fine. I did what had to be done—there was no doing business with those two, you must have known it. Ryba—I approached him first, he turned me down. A mistake you only get to make once. And Timmy—surely, he was deadweight to you? I think you'll find me a good business partner, if you're more intelligent than that shitspoon."

"Quiet, dumb fuck. You killed Timmy, and you think you're gonna walk out of here?"

Seamus gave him a bored look and dropped the accent. Throw them off, buy some time. "What'll it be? Torture? Pliers and razor blades? You mobsters are never very original. Most of you, anyway. My one regret will be that I won't live to see what Olexa Greene does to *you*."

Braydon's smile slid off.

An angle, a finger hold— "That's right: We're partners," improvised Seamus. "Olexa and I work very closely together. She's the one who wanted Timmy dead—you think she was happy about your little distribution scheme? One time, you know, she extracted a man's eyes with a melon baller and made him eat them out of a sundae glass." Bluffing was dangerous, and hiding behind Olexa Greene's name without her permission was a few inches short of suicide, but it was the only move he had left.

Braydon snarled and grabbed the knife off the table. "You're bluffing. And I'm not afraid of Olexa Greene."

Seamus raised an eyebrow at that. "If that's true, you're more stupid than you look."

Braydon glared back but said nothing. Instead, he held the blade in his hand so it caught the light, flashing a hair's breadth from Seamus's eyes. Seamus knew what Braydon was looking for: a shudder of terror. He kept still, his face impassive. Then he yawned.

"Tiresome. Is this really how you do business?"

Braydon pulled the knife over Seamus's cheek, leaving a shallow cut. His breathing grew heavier as he traced it down his neck, but he didn't cut deep enough to hit anything worth worrying about. Blood ran down, staining his collar, beading as it ran over the makeup. Seamus didn't flinch—no one had drawn on him yet. That was good. All he needed now was an opening. It would be bloody work, and pointless—the man he needed to find wasn't here. But survival would have to do as a motive for tonight's work.

He had enough bullets for them all. So long as he didn't miss. So long as he could drop all of them before they could draw. Seamus stretched the fingers of his right hand, felt the tendons pull taut under his skin.

"You know," he said, "I'm not an unreasonable man. Surrender now, and I might let you go."

"Let's see how well you talk without your tongue, hmm?"

That was it, get him riled. Don't let him see the hand in the jacket. "Enjoy your work, do you?" asked Seamus.

Braydon gave him a twisted grin, a strange urgency in his eyes. It was a lucky break—a decent man would've just shot him. Braydon's eyes were glassy, unfocused: here was Seamus's opening.

The rivulet of blood reached his lips. Seamus tasted the salt and iron and grabbed for his pistol. The six men surrounding him all reached to draw, and Seamus jumped left. The folding chair he'd been sitting on exploded into a spray of torn aluminum as their bullets hit the spot he'd been one breath ago.

Seamus ran for the door—he was pinned down, had to get clear and pick them off one at a time. His thoughts went clear as ice, and each lurched step to the door seemed to have an eternity surrounding it.

Bang.

Poor shots.

Bang.

Olexa's men would've put him down already.

Bang.

Seamus's fingers met the door frame and he grabbed on to spin himself around the corner. Almost to cover.

The first bullet to hit him got his back. Seamus felt a ceramic plate under his jacket shatter; he staggered under the blow but kept moving.

With the second bullet, he wasn't so lucky. As he rounded the corner, he felt a burst of pain in his leg and saw blood spatter the wall opposite. He put his weight on the leg as he ran anyway—either he'd die because his leg gave out, or he'd die because he couldn't run. No sense worrying about which.

The leg held, but Seamus could feel its unwillingness to move, the way he had to drag it as he ran for the bar, shouts of Timmy's men at his back. Bad—his bloodstream was half adrenalin now, and the injury was fresh. Things would only get worse from here. He'd have to finish this quick, before the leg froze on him.

Seamus made it back to the abandoned bar and threw himself over it just as the bottles began exploding above him. Seamus crouched under the counter, a gout of gin and broken glass rushing over his jacket. The men stopped firing, fanned out opposite him. One of them crept towards the bar—Seamus heard his uncertain footsteps, attempting a stealth he couldn't achieve. The man jumped around the corner of the bar, tried to raise his gun, which he was carrying low like an action hero. Seamus shot him three times before he fell.

He heard a raspy voice as the echoes of the gunshots died down: "Fuck. Did he get Rico?"

"Yeah. But he's still trapped. We've just got to keep him pinned down."

Seamus hated to agree with morons, but it was true. He contemplated his situation—he had seven bullets left in the gun, one more magazine in his breast pocket. To his left an exploded tap was gushing Coors Light over the bar top. Seamus considered that—the Montmorency specialized in cheap grain alcohol. Its clientele wasn't particularly interested in something you'd have to drink several glasses of before the floor started moving under you. Seamus pulled open the cabinet beneath the taps, and a rush of cold air hit him—they were keeping the kegs up here, along with CO_2 cylinders.

While Timmy's men tried to coordinate themselves, Seamus got to work. He grabbed a cylinder, disconnected it from the feed line, a spurt of beer wetting his hands. He hefted the tank in his hands—it weighed about ten pounds—and let it hit the wet floor behind the bar with a gritty thud. Braydon's voice rang out from the other side of the bar.

"Alright, ready?"

Seamus set his back and heaved the pressure cylinder into the air, then took his aim as it reached the peak of its arc. Could be a waste of ammo, but this was his best chance at a distraction.

His first shot missed. The cylinder was falling now, almost out of view. Timmy's henchmen shouted to each other, the noise indistinct, distant. Seamus fired again—this one struck true.

It wasn't a massive explosion, but it did the job. In the closed room, the boom set Seamus's ears ringing and shrapnel skittering across the floor. Seamus sprang to his feet, surveyed his six surviving enemies. They were crouched down, staggered by the blast—one seemed to have been hit with a stray piece of metal, and was clutching a spot where red bloomed on his arm.

Excellent.

Seamus started firing, and the men dove for cover. He dropped two before they got to the booths at the far side of the room. The others started returning fire, and he had to duck back down behind the bar.

Four left. Seamus's leg throbbed. He'd done a fair bit of damage, but he was out of tricks. They'd moved out of range of another explosion, and if Seamus raised his head again it would get perforated.

A burst of gunfire rang out, and Seamus gasped as a bullet punched his shoulder and knocked the breath out of him. His armour stopped it, but how had they hit him?

He went to his belly and glanced back—the bullet had punched clear through the plywood bar. They were firing blind, but the bar itself wasn't bulletproof. Seamus crawled away on his elbows as another volley tore through the bar. They'd finally thought of something smart to do, and he was pinned down. They had enough ammunition to keep sweeping the bar with gunfire till they took him out.

Seamus lay on his belly, trying to steady his breathing. The pain in his leg made that difficult, and his hit shoulder pinched with every exhale. Another volley burst through the air, and the glass cabinet behind him shattered. There was a gaping hole in the bar now—they'd be able to see him soon enough, and Seamus doubted he'd manage to crawl out of the way in time. He set his jaw—he'd die on his feet, if it came to that. Seamus laid one hand on the ground, snapped a fresh magazine into his pistol, and got ready to spring. Damned if he didn't bring down at least two more of them before they killed him.

Seamus had spent enough time close to death that he wasn't especially afraid of it, but he felt oddly sad as he took a few deep breaths before the last stand. There was a fleeting intrusion of an old memory, of cedarwood oil and a crooked smile.

Sandra. Goodbye.

"You hear something?"

Quite suddenly, the lights went out. A high voice came in through the speakers: "Hope you're ready for a show, boys and girls. We've got a really special night planned for you. Hey, boss! Quit screwing around and kill these shitspoons!"

It took Seamus a second to realize who was speaking, but when he did, he couldn't help smiling. He'd have to wonder about how Maxwell got here, or whether he was hallucinating her voice, distorted by the cheap speaker system, as he bled out under the bar, later. The hiss of a smoke machine filled the air, and a grey fog spread over the dance floor. Spotlights flicked on, and blinding beams of light lit Braydon's and his men's positions across the room.

Seamus heard shouts of panic and grinned to himself. You'd have a clear view of the whole club from the DJ booth.

When you were outnumbered, you needed an edge. Total concealment and spotlights on your enemies would do. Seamus came out from behind the bar—it was almost pitch black in the smoke, but he could see two men raising their hands against the light, blinking and cursing. Not thinking—they were easy targets now, and Seamus dropped them both with a bullet each. Another man rushed at him, blinking against the smoke, and Seamus dropped him from his position in the shadows. Only one left, now—Seamus glanced from side to side, waiting for the spotlights to paint a halo around his next target. Instead, there was the screech of a microphone getting hit, and a cry of pain as the audio cut out.

Seamus ran for the DJ booth.

Braydon had kicked down one of the glass partitions—so he was the last one. He had his pistol in one hand, trained on the back of Maxwell's head. Seamus regarded him. Maxwell, her hands splayed out on the lighting panel, murmured slightly. "H-hey, boss. I'm gonna be really pissed if you let this guy shoot me."

Braydon couldn't quite manage a sneer—he stared at Seamus with wild eyes and a blood-streaked look of partial shock, and he attempted to sound cool when he spoke.

"Alright, fuckhead. Here's what's gonna happen. I'll take the girl, stop by the vault, and we'll go our separate ways."

He was teetering on the edge of panic. Normally, that would be a good thing—fear made your enemy reckless—but you didn't exactly want an itchy trigger finger when they had a hostage.

Seamus kept his gun down, loose at his side. "How do you think this is going to go for you? You kill her, you think you're going to walk out of here alive? I've already killed all your men—what's one more to me?"

"I'll fucking kill you too." The gun twitched. "You've got no idea what you've done. If I don't—if we don't start moving product soon—you think *this* is the worst that'll happen to me?" He gave a desperate laugh.

Apparently the Angelmaker was a more demanding employer than Seamus had thought. Seamus held very still, showed him nothing but cool scorn. "I know it: I'm the worst thing that can happen to anyone. Now, I don't know who's been threatening you, but I do know they can't kill you any better than I can."

Braydon's eyes rolled, wild, whites showing. Then he turned his gun on Seamus. "Yeah. Good point."

The first shot rang out, and Seamus rushed him. That was it—keep his aim on centre mass, and away from Maxwell. Standard nine millimetre—his armour would stop the bullets. A second shot hit, and Seamus felt a rib break in his side, then a third—Braydon was emptying his clip, screaming. He got five shots off before Seamus reached him, knocked the barrel of his gun aside. Seamus's chest burned like someone had stomped on it, but he'd have to hold out until he'd finished the job. Seamus dropped his own gun—unfortunate, but he needed both hands to keep Braydon from shooting Maxwell.

They fought over the weapon—Seamus was stronger, but he was struggling to breathe right. Braydon kicked at his bad leg, and Seamus dropped to one knee but didn't let go of the gun and countered with a headbutt that sent them both to the ground. Braydon managed to pull the trigger once, and the stray shot sparked off a bank of speakers. Seamus felt his head go light, fought to control his hands as they started to loosen. The pistol inched closer to his face. Not yet. Don't black out yet. Just a little bit more—

Bang.

Braydon's head snapped back and to the side, and he went limp under Seamus's hands. Seamus glanced up. Maxwell, shivering, slowly lowered his gun.

"Nice shot."

"He . . . he was pretty close—are those brains?"

"Probably. Don't look. Let's get out of here—did you bring a getaway car?"

Seamus hurried her out the door, but not before he grabbed that tattered bag and all the evidence from the backroom. Seamus would find answers in there when he was capable of thinking again.

It wasn't generally advisable for someone with multiple gunshot wounds to drive, but Maxwell was trembling so badly she could barely hand him the keys. They couldn't afford to rest—there was a distant wail of sirens as they left through the backdoor. Seamus hadn't exactly worked quietly.

"Didn't he shoot you, like, a lot of times, boss?"

"I'm invulnerable," said Seamus, breathing very carefully so his broken ribs didn't shift any more than they already had. "Also—bulletproof vest. Could've used a little more bulletproofing, though, I think."

Seamus crept homeward along the backroads, finally pulling onto the highway alongside a trickle of traffic he could disappear into. He got Maxwell, still pale, into her apartment, and told her she had the morning off. The fresh cuts on his face that had just stopped bleeding were starting to swell, and they complained when he moved his lips to speak. Before she turned to climb her stairs, the ghost of a smile crossed Maxwell's face.

"Weren't expecting me, were you, boss?"

"I wasn't. You'll get yourself killed pulling stunts like that."

She hung her head—a mark of just how hard the night had hit her.

Seamus smiled and softened his voice. "That doesn't mean I'm not grateful for the help. Try to rest and eat something with sugar in it. Sugar's good for recovery."

Seamus took the car with the promise she could pick it up tomorrow—Maxwell had borrowed it from one of her friends. He did his best not to bleed on the seat.

His right foot wasn't working the way it was supposed to, but Seamus managed to get to Jackson's by stomping on pedals with his heel and ignoring the bursts of pain from his calf.

Going to the bar wasn't a strategic move—Seamus had used up his capacity for strategy for that night. Some old, quiet corner of his mind knew that Jackson's meant safety, meant a chance to rest and dress his injuries. The front door was locked—closed for the night—so Seamus limped around the back. He found Jackson locking up.

"Slow evening, Jackson?"

"Late for you, Seamus," said the barkeeper, his back still turned. Seamus mumbled an indistinct reply. His hands tingled as the sensation left his fingers. A clear stream—he was a clear stream, the pain washing away, no more real than he allowed it to be. There was so much of it, though.

Jackson, who'd turned around, started moving towards him, his face lit only by the dim security light. For some reason, he wasn't smiling.

Seamus didn't see anything or feel the impact with the ground, but he heard the dull thud as he fell, just slightly too fast for Jackson to catch him.

CHAPTER THIRTEEN

Seamus opened his eyes to see Sandra's profile, her face drawn with exhaustion and worry.

"Hey there . . . Steady. You know . . . the men in this town . . . can't aim for shit."

His voice rasped like a knife on stone. Sandra blinked as it registered, and a rush of expressions Seamus couldn't make out ran over her face.

"Seamus! You're awake! Just rest—you don't have to talk."

"But that's . . . what I'm good at." With a great effort, Seamus managed to focus his eyes on his surroundings. He was in Jackson's bolt-hole under the bar, on a rough cot with a few winter jackets stacked over him. "How did you get here?"

"Jackson called me."

"How bad was it?"

She leaned forward over her knees. "Just bad enough to give me and Jackson a couple heart attacks. You got hit five times—busted rib, and bruises on your chest. That armour you were wearing's shot to shit, but it held up well. The one slug punched through your leg. I think you'll be alright—you didn't lose that much blood."

"That's good. Don't have . . . that much to spare."

"Braydon do this to you?"

"They attacked me . . . I defended myself. Sorry . . . I lied about the meeting. Didn't want you . . . hurt."

Sandra pursed her lips, but she didn't ask any other questions. Instead, she handed Seamus a glass of water, which he accepted gratefully. His throat felt like he'd been eating road salt.

"Thanks for not taking me to the hospital—I'd be . . . handcuffed to the bed."

"Jail's better than the morgue," said Sandra. "I wanted to take you. Got my phone out for the ambulance. But Jackson said to check your pulse first. Your injuries weren't as bad as we'd thought. I swear, I've been watching you all night. If you'd gotten any worse . . . I wouldn't have let you die."

"I know that."

She fell silent. Seamus saw the rings under her eyes, the blank and staring fatigue.

"What time is it?" he asked softly.

"Lunchtime, or a bit past. Not really sure. You've been out about twelve hours. I figure you won't take any of Jackson's morphine?"

"Not surprised . . . he's got some stashed away . . . but of course I won't."

She let out a tight breath, turning her face away. "You're not your dad, Seamus. And what am I supposed to do if my best friend doesn't take care of himself?"

He bristled slightly. "It caught me by surprise, but I can deal with this kind of pain—"

Sandra stood up quickly. Seamus braced himself for a punch—she'd never done that before, but if he'd ever deserved a good crack on the jaw from her, he deserved one now—and was quite surprised when she threw her arms around him instead, her breath coming fast, though she was careful not to press on his injuries.

Sandra never cried, but Seamus thought he felt a few drops on his neck. He realized he'd already reached his arms around her, was taking in the smell of coffee and the faint undertone of cedarwood.

"I was so scared, Seamus."

"I—I was too, Sandra. Thought I'd never see you again."

An image came to mind, unbidden: Sandra's lips, warm against his own, and her scarred, perfect body pressed to his in this small cot. His fingers tracing her neck, her thighs, her breath coming faster—

Not that she'd really kiss him back, he reminded himself. He let the image drift away: it was an unworthy thought, now of all times. But he allowed himself that moment of rest in his friend's arms. That much he'd earned.

Then Seamus let her go, silently counted his fingers, and spoke: "There's something I need to tell you about Michael."

"Huh?" She was wiping her eyes. "Look, I know you don't like him—"

"It's something I should have told you a while ago . . . he's been cheating on you, Sandra."

"He—what?" She didn't look angry, just confused, as though she hadn't quite processed the sentence. Then she started to frown, her voice growing sharper. "If this is some kind of joke, Seamus—"

"I wouldn't do that to you." Seamus wanted very badly to look away. He did not. "The night he came to pick you up, he had these strange stains on his neck and shirt. I checked his jacket pockets—" Here Seamus raised a hand against Sandra's beginning of an objection. "I wasn't going to take anything, just keeping in practice. But I found a set of keys with an address I didn't recognize. There was . . . a woman living there, who'd been sleeping with him. She didn't know . . . I think my visit put an end to it."

Sandra's face had gone perfectly still and pale, like she was frozen through. "You—you snuck around. Of course. Like *always*," she said, voice rising, "except this time you've managed to fuck my *entire life*."

"Would you rather not have known?" asked Seamus. "Should I not have told you?"

Sandra wasn't easily hurt; Seamus could count the times he'd seen it on one hand. Seeing it now—watching her finally crumple—was the worst thing that had happened in the last twenty-four hours. Her face was stony now, and her voice was hard: "How long have you known."

It was difficult to meet her eyes. "About ten days. I didn't—"

"You knew. You let me go home to him," she said, the hurt shining in her eyes and her voice, "and share a bed with him. And you didn't tell me. Why didn't you tell me?" Sandra stood, abruptly, and pulled her jacket over her shoulders. Her eyes were dry, blazing with anger.

"I didn't know what to do," said Seamus, where he lay. "I didn't want . . . to hurt you."

"Nice fucking job with that."

"You've been awake all night," he said, struggling to sit up. "Stay for a little while. You don't have to talk to me, but have some food."

"Eating something now?" She let out a short, sharp *hah*. "Only you'd think of that, Seamus. You're your mother's son. All of this—it doesn't bother you, does it? You don't give a shit about anyone else. Or yourself."

Seamus straightened at that and forced his legs over the edge of the cot. His bad leg screamed, but he forced himself to his feet in a brisk, uncompromising motion, showing no pain, and faced Sandra. When he spoke, it was still soft, but there was a hint of steel in his voice. "Is that really what you think, Sandra?"

She held his gaze for a long stretch.

Then she whipped around and ran up the stairs. Seamus couldn't have followed, even if he'd known it was the right thing to do. He collapsed back onto the bed, letting a wave of pain crash over him. He focused on his breathing, the way Ma had taught him, letting the seconds stretch into minutes.

Blackness closed over him, and he didn't fight it.

He woke up alone, unsure of how much time had passed. After what must have been a few hours of half-sleeping, Seamus now felt remarkably worse. His mouth tasted like it'd been packed with sawdust, and the adrenalin had long since burned off, leaving every muscle in his body tense and aching. Seamus sipped some cold water Jackson had brought him and gingerly rubbed the cuts on his face. Sandra must have cleaned them—he could see the faint rusty stains where blood had been dabbed off his clothes and skin.

After a few minutes, Jackson came down to check on him. Above, Seamus could hear the lonely sounds of a mostly empty bar, and Boomtown explaining the finer points of the federal deficit. Seamus sat himself up.

"I'd like to go back to my office."

Jackson wore his usual friendly smile. It had never annoyed Seamus more. "Stay down here and rest a few more days, Seamus. It's warm. And Minnie'll bring you food."

"I'm not even that badly hurt," said Seamus, doing all he could to keep the edge out of his voice. "I appreciate everything you've done, but I'll recover better at home."

"Sandra's pissed at you," said Jackson. "Surprised she didn't break the door when she slammed it on her way out."

Seamus gritted his teeth. "Thank you, Jackson. I noticed."

Jackson was still, unaccountably, smiling. "She'll come around. I've been figuring this would happen for a while, Seamus—you finally told her what was on your mind, huh?"

"Yes, I told her Michael has been cheating on her like the shitspoon he is, thereby derailing her life and shattering her dreams," said Seamus, his voice very dry. The smile slid off Jackson's face. "Unless you've made some brilliant deductions and somehow already knew that, I imagine you're referring to some *other* secret I should have told her. If that's the case, I recommend, with all politeness, that you shut your damn mouth." Seamus paused to draw a slow breath. "So. Are you going to help me to my office, or am I going to crawl?"

Jackson put up the "Back in five" sign in the window, and with his arm to lean on Seamus made it to his office, the bag of evidence stowed safely in his jacket. It was afternoon, and snow had been falling on and off all day, powdering the pavement. The cotton webbing over his leg was sticky with blood, and the bullet wound burned in the cold air, but the round had punched clean through, only damaging soft tissue. He could walk, slowly. Jackson marched beside him looking slightly shamefaced, but mustered a grin as Seamus staggered the final three steps to the front door on his own.

"Didn't think you'd make it. Should've known better, huh?"

Seamus smiled, though pain kept his mouth tight. "Please, Jackson. It'll take more than a few small-calibre rounds to do me a lasting injury."

It required some hopping, but Seamus made it up the stairs too. The office was just as he'd left it, sunlight brightening the frosted glass as he unlocked the door. He leaned hard on his desk, dragging off his jacket and gingerly moving to undo his shirt, hoping to inspect the injuries on his chest before he collapsed. The leg wouldn't kill him, but a drifting shard of rib going through his lung in the middle of the night might.

"If you're taking your shirt off, I'm leaving." Maxwell stepped out of the corner.

"Thought I gave you the day off," said Seamus, straightening.

"Yeah, well, I decided I might as well come here and lose my shit instead of staying home and losing my shit there." She said that lightly and handed him a double-double—Seamus took it and felt her hands tremble through the cup.

"You should've stayed away last night."

Maxwell shook her head. "You would've gotten killed if I weren't there."

"Don't underestimate me," said Seamus with a grin. "But we did make a pretty good team, huh?"

Maxwell nodded, but she didn't say anything.

Seamus, for his part, didn't have much comfort to offer, but he could try. "My advice, Maxwell?" he said. "Don't think about it. You'll have nightmares, in time, and you'll deal with them. You can talk through it with someone trustworthy—or me—when you're ready."

"Is that what you do, boss?"

"No. I count my fingers, and killing people who've earned it has never bothered me much. But I'm not exactly industry standard."

The two of them stood in the half-lit silence of the office, and Seamus found himself thinking. His last suspect had his brains splattered on the floor of the Montmorency, and Seamus didn't know where he could look next. He'd ruled out a rival, a jealous subordinate—what other reason could you have for killing Ryba and Timmy?

The stabbing looked like a crime of opportunity—only because he *happened* to be in the hospital, only because the killer *happened* to have that knife. No one planning ahead would decide to stash a body in an air conditioning vent. The poisoning in the hospital was flamboyant, using some rare and flashy organic compound. And Timmy, the thallium casualty, evidence left at the scene—that seemed almost desperate. The actions of someone who expected to get caught.

Seamus pulled on his gloves, then reached into his coat and took out the evidence he'd gotten from Braydon.

"What's that, boss?"

"A puzzle."

The bag itself was an ordinary plastic grocery bag. The two empty ampules—forensics would be able to source them, but the bright red warning labels were enough for Seamus. Two of them—that wasn't a good sign. Each vial was labelled to contain five grams, more than enough for a lethal dose. If the killer had put both vials into Timmy's beer, they'd wasted good money.

Seamus held the empty vials lightly in his gloved hands—strange how he'd held them, and the knife, days after the killer had. Two steps behind.

He looked at the trophies. The gold chain was obviously Ryba's missing piece of jewellery, and the Montmorency napkin was probably symbolic of Timmy—it was faded, as if pressed flat countless times, worn by a nervous gesture.

The cigarette butt Seamus almost ignored. Braydon's men had dug the bag out of the garbage, after all—most likely it just got mixed in. But Seamus looked closer—the rolling paper was unusually dark, and at the burned end there was a faint glint of gold. Not that Seamus knew much about tobacco, but this looked expensive.

You only confuse yourself. The problem is simple when you forget what's confusing you.

Forget the motive. Rotate the problem in your mind—you're the killer, and you bought twice as much poison as you'd need. Possible justifications: Suicide. Or another intended victim. It was still a very high dosage, higher than you'd need for ingestion if you used all of it. Why would you need a higher dosage? Three grams was enough to kill a normal adult. Maybe if they were very large, or if the method of entry wasn't ideal—

Didn't thallium absorb through the skin?

Always headaches. He break two bones in my neck. Always headaches after that. But I win that match.

That cigarette was a Black Russian. Not many people in Toronto smoked those.

Seamus was on his feet. The leg didn't hurt at all—must've been the adrenalin.

Maxwell glanced up at him. "What's going on?"

With a monumental effort, Seamus focused his eyes on her. "Two murders. The vial of thallium—I know who it was for." Seamus limped for the door.

"Did they hit your leg, boss?"

"Just a flesh wound," he called over his shoulder. "Come on. We're not done yet."

It was frustrating to have to take a cab, but Seamus had his limits, however much he disliked acknowledging them. He could force himself to walk downtown with his injuries or one day have a working leg again, but not both. So he squeezed himself into a grimy cab, using his hands to bend his bad leg as Maxwell slid in beside him.

The driver chewed betel nut with perpetually smacking lips. "Where are you going, sir?"

"Adelaide and Bay."

The driver glanced back at him with a decidedly incredulous look. Seamus hadn't quite cleaned the blood off his clothes, and his face was plastered with bandages.

"You are working like this, sir?"

"Never do anything else. Don't worry, I've got my secretary to keep an eye on me."

The driver shrugged and continued chewing; a plastic bottle of red sloshed at his side as they pulled away from the curb.

"What the hell's on Adelaide?" asked Maxwell.

"An excellent Italian deli, for one thing—"

Maxwell shot him a deadly look.

"And Trelly's house."

"Two questions: Why are we going there, and how the fuck do you know that?"

"That's why I needed your distraction at the range—to see his licence. Always keep track of dangerous people, Maxwell. I'm going to check my hunch first—if I'm wrong, Olexa won't take kindly to our calling an ambulance to Trelly's apartment. But if I'm right, Trelly's lucky we're on our way."

They pulled up in record time, and Seamus limped up to Trelly's apartment complex, caught the main door just as someone was leaving. They gave him and Maxwell a stare as they rushed past—no time for a disguise or an explanation now. Seamus would just have to gamble on the average person's horror of confrontation, which was usually a safe bet. Sure enough, they made it into the building and headed up the elevator with no problem.

Apartment 561. It was a fairly nice building—Olexa kept her men comfortable. Seamus wasted no time, rapped his knuckles hard on the door.

"Trelly, this is Seamus. I think you might be in some trouble. Let me in to talk."

Silence. Maxwell gave him a skeptical look. "Boss, now what—"

Seamus lifted his good leg and kicked the door down. "Trelly! I'm here to help."

No answer. Seamus darted inside, rounding the corner to the kitchen to find the huge man slumped over on his dining room table. Seamus had his gloves on before Maxwell got in the door.

"Boss! What's going on?"

"Poisoning—now's when you call the ambulance."

"Hospital's gonna give me a loyalty card," she muttered as Seamus strained to lower Trelly to the floor.

Seamus surveyed Trelly's long-ago broken nose and crushed ears and listened for his breathing. It was there, but too slow. Seamus's nitrile-coated fingers found the necklace around his neck—a simple cord, with a crucifix and that strange fleck of metal. Under five grams now, Seamus would bet, depending on how much had already been absorbed. Seamus snapped it off, slipped it into an evidence bag. Trelly's eyes snapped open at the sound of the cord breaking. It figured that the old fighter would be alert, even if he was partially comatose.

"Easy, Trelly—"

His hands came up and closed around Seamus's throat. Seamus caught his forearms, but it was like grabbing two telephone poles. Idiot. Trelly's eyes were half-closed—he wasn't fully conscious, but some deep-buried instinct told him he was in danger, and decades' worth of fighting instincts did the rest. Seamus tried to push his hands back—how could a man near-dead from thallium poisoning be so strong?

"Boss!"

Maxwell had dropped her phone and was opposite Seamus, behind Trelly, yanking at his arms. She might've been a mosquito, for all the good it did.

Seamus's vision dipped to black. The colour came back, but muted, and he knew he had maybe ten more seconds before he blacked out. He reached for the gun in his jacket—shame about Trelly, but Seamus wasn't going to die here.

But the pressure on his neck eased, Trelly's fingers relaxed. Seamus finally managed to break Trelly's grip and came up gasping. When the spots stopped dancing across his visual field, he saw Maxwell holding Trelly in the basic rear naked choke he'd taught her, every muscle in her arms straining, her face slick with sweat.

"Boss . . . I think . . . I got him."

"That you do, Maxwell. Now let him go before he has a stroke."

The now *fully* unconscious Trelly was laid out on the cold tile.

"Probably not great for him, huh?"

"They'll be able to fix him up at the hospital," said Seamus, listening to the familiar scream of an approaching ambulance. "As long as they know what the poison was."

Once he'd spoken to the paramedics and convinced Maxwell to go home and try to sleep, Seamus dragged himself back to his office. He was grateful to find it empty—he'd fought hard, but by the time he hobbled to the top of the stairs he could just barely open the door. Slowly, he peeled back his bloody clothes and left them in a heap on the floor. There would be nothing for it but to burn them. All except for his jacket, which he carefully hung up and brushed straight. His leg was bleeding again, staining the fresh bandages to pink damask.

With his last dregs of strength, he dragged together every blanket he owned, piled them on the floor, and collapsed.

Twenty-four hours later, Seamus's eyes flickered open. He wasn't sure if he felt better—he didn't let himself feel too much. Best to eat, use the toilet, and fall back asleep.

The door was still locked, but someone had left a small stack of instant noodles, bottled tea, and green tea Pocky by the door. Seamus was too tired to wonder at this or worry—he chugged down a litre of tea and a dry packet of noodles before he crawled back to bed.

The dreams were not restful, but Seamus knew his nightmares so well there was a certain familiarity to them—Lauren's smile with her lips just a little blue, Thomas Caron wandering through his house like a ghost with his pupils drawn to staring pinpricks, a body slumped over an oak desk. And a brand-new one—Sandra's hand going limp on his, leaving bloody fingerprints. That was the one that managed to wake him.

But Seamus endured, dreaming the fever away, and even as he sweated through the blankets some part of him knew that the pain worming its way through him was right, that it served a purpose. The wounds always closed in the end.

After another two days of half-waking, Seamus got to his feet, able to stand. That meant it was time to get back to work. Seamus bandaged his leg, then pulled on some clean clothes and his oilskin—it wouldn't do to wear his pyjamas to the hospital.

Maxwell seemed to be doing alright—she wasn't curled into the fetal position in bed, and that was about all you could ask of someone who'd just been through a firefight. He found her with a foot kicked up against the wall she was leaning on by the emergency intake doors.

"Hey, boss. Why'd you want to meet me here?"

"Thought I'd pay Trelly a visit," said Seamus. "Considering you shot our last suspect in the head, I've got to do something to pass the time. And maybe he'll have a lead for us." Seamus had been hoping that he'd see an answer during the fever, but he'd gone into that blackness and come out without anything to show for it but a scabbed-over leg.

Maxwell frowned at him. "You really think we're gonna figure out who killed Ryba?"

Seamus limped past her into the hospital and said nothing at all. It was taking all his optimism to stay on his feet—he didn't have any to spare for her.

Trelly was asleep, his breaths rattling the bedframe. But there was someone he hadn't expected to find there as well, and she was awake, jade eyes drawn narrow but watching everything, her back to the wall. Seamus smiled to see her, and he waved to the black-suited guard who reached for his pistol as he and Maxwell walked in.

"Morning, Olexa."

"Detective. Maxwell."

They stood there a moment in silence before Olexa inclined her head to Seamus just slightly.

"The doctors tell me he would've died if you hadn't found him. You have my gratitude."

"That's a valuable thing to have."

"Trelly is my right hand," said Olexa. "My fist. Men will burn for this."

"Who are you planning to burn?"

"I've many enemies. We'll start from the top of the list."

So it would come to open war, and if he or Sandra survived that, it would be on luck alone.

"You're chasing shadows," said Seamus. "There's one person behind all this—not Trelly, but Timmy's betrayal, the Platinum, the poisoning at the hospital: the Angelmaker."

"I will kill him too," said Olexa, and beneath her calm voice was a slow fury. "The Company has weathered storms, and we will again."

"You won't survive this one if you waste your strength hunting small-time rivals," said Seamus. He needed to think, but his mind was slow. The Angelmaker was a threat to all of them, and now Seamus had a target on his back—

"We'll figure out who tried to kill Trelly," said Maxwell, and both Olexa and Seamus turned to stare at her. She'd straightened herself, holding her head as high as she could. "Listen, it'll save you a lot of trouble if you know who you need to go after, right? Seamus can figure that out—he's great at that. And in exchange . . ." Olexa smiled at Maxwell, the way a very old and ancient shark might smile at a small fish swimming by. Maxwell gulped, but she continued. "You're a gangster, right? In exchange, you put us under your protection," she said. "No one comes around to stab us in the middle of the night, no one poisons our drinks. If someone does, you go after them."

"And what do you say, Detective?"

Seamus said nothing, pressed his mouth tight. It was appealing—Olexa's protection carried weight, and his bones told him he'd be needing it. But using the Company for protection was a bit like grabbing a live viper to defend yourself—even if it worked, there would be a risk, and a heavy price to pay. For a moment, Seamus was paralyzed, trying to weigh the advantages and costs, and a moment's hesitation was all it took. Olexa shook her head and turned away.

"You bargain with a name you don't have. And in truth, even that name would not be enough to buy my protection. I protect my men, no one else."

Seamus and Maxwell went back out into the endless sterile corridors, slumped. Maxwell shot him a glare.

"Nice backup there, boss."

"Olexa's not someone for you to toy with," said Seamus, some irritation creeping into his voice. "She could wipe us both out with a word to her men."

"Yeah, that's why I wanted her *on our side*, genius. Besides, I bet you could take down a couple of those guys in suits pretty easily. They look like losers."

Seamus teetered for a breath between anger and amusement before the latter won and he let out a laugh. "You're an excellent secretary, Moscovitz."

A flicker of a smile crossed her lips. "Thanks, boss. You're pretty good at picking lunch spots."

An old instinct told Seamus he ought to keep running, ought to fight, but with no enemy in sight and nowhere to go there was nothing to do but swallow the impulse down, feel the tremor of energy in the bones of his hand. He leaned back against a grey wall, out of sight of any orderlies who might come past, and let his eyes close for a moment.

"Hey, boss. That wasn't the only reason you didn't like the deal, right? You're always doing dangerous shit."

Seamus kept his eyes closed. "Sandra needs protection more than I do," he said. "Back in there, I was thinking that we're headed into a storm. Sandra takes her job seriously—maybe she doesn't always follow regulation, but she does what's right. That's a very dangerous thing with the gangs rolling into war and some madman calling themselves the Angelmaker to deal with."

"But you'll be able to keep her up-to-date on what's going on, right? So she'll be okay."

Seamus just shook his head. "I don't know that she and I will be speaking any time soon."

Maxwell had enough tact not to ask. She stood there a moment, then pushed off the wall. "Well, we ought to get out of here, boss. If that doctor I stole a latte from sees me, she's gonna raise the alarm."

Seamus followed after her, tensing the muscles in his upper leg to avoid having to bend his calf.

"You know, boss, I don't know the specifics, but I think you and Sandra'll work it out. You guys are both fucking weirdos, but you've got each other's backs. You're like family. And let me tell you what I think—if you'd gone down for good back at the Montmorency, she'd have killed the men who did it, no matter what's right or what's by-the-book."

Seamus opened his mouth to say *small comfort*, but the words caught. There was something about Maxwell's words that seemed strangely significant. *She'd have killed the men who did it.*

To remember her son by.

Where had Trelly gotten that necklace? *A funeral gift.*

At a Company funeral.

"There's an answer there," muttered Seamus, coming to a stop.

"Boss?"

He closed his eyes, focusing hard enough that he felt his pulse in his jaw. "Broadly speaking, there're only four reasons people kill other people. What are they?"

"Well, to rob them?"

"Right, that's one, and the most rational. You kill out of fear, or romantic jealousy—I think we can rule both out in this case. I've been assuming that whoever killed Ryba, they're basically rational. They don't want to get caught, and they've something to gain. A rival gang moving against Timmy, or his own men trying to cut him out. But there's nothing rational about gutting someone in the hospital. That takes a particular kind of rage, a special type of hatred. The fourth reason for killing is revenge."

"I get that, but who'd want revenge on all three of them? Timmy, Ryba, and Trelly, all at once . . . what did they all do that you'd want revenge for?"

Seamus was moving, and with a slight noise of frustration Maxwell followed him.

"And I mean, even if Olexa didn't get you, you'd spend the rest of your life rotting in jail."

"What if the rest of your life didn't come to all that much?" Seamus hurried down the corridor, retracing his steps, headed to the palliative care wing. With any luck, they wouldn't have moved her. On second thought, it wouldn't take much luck—he doubted she was stable enough to move. "We've got our killer. Mariah Lopez wanted revenge. Like she told me, her son's death was no accident—Timmy'd been testing Platinum on his own men. Antonio Lopez got a bad batch."

Maxwell stared for a moment, then put a hand on her forehead and leaned back. "How do Trelly and Ryba fit in?"

"Trelly used to be Timmy's handler, spent a lot of time with him. When Mariah's son died, the two of them went to his funeral together. That was her only mistake—she thought Trelly was Timmy's man. That's why she gave him the poisoned necklace. I doubt she planned to take out Ryba, but my guess is she knew who Timmy's lawyer was, recognized him in recovery, and her emotions got the best of her. She probably carried her son's knife with her: a keepsake."

Maxwell's eyes widened.

"So, Mariah tried to kill all three of them. Timmy, his lawyer, Trelly." She let out a harsh breath, staring down the corridor. "Are you gonna call Sandra to come and get her?"

"Of course. As soon as she's had a chance to die quietly, without any policemen or mobsters in the room. She deserves that much, I think."

Seamus found Mariah's room empty, save for some artificial flowers from a church friend and Mariah herself. She'd gone thin and insubstantial in her hospital bed and was sleeping quietly, IV drip humming at her side. Seamus looked around the room—the last rays from the setting sun were coming in through the window, the slanting light red as fire. It would do. He looked at her morphine dosage and nodded to himself. Not that he'd take even an Advil on his deathbed, but Mariah deserved an easy death. She'd fought hard enough to earn it. He had just expected to stand vigil with Maxwell, but after a moment, Mariah's eyes fluttered open.

"Ah, Detective," she said, with a voice like withered leaves.

Seamus smiled and drew close to her bedside. "It's good to see you again, Mariah."

"You came to visit?" The effort of putting the words out showed on her face.

"Of course."

"Thank you."

Seamus shook his head. "It's nothing. Can I get you anything? Some food?"

The corners of her lips pulled back in an attempted smile. "Dying. Lose your appetite. I know it well. But maybe some ice."

Seamus turned and was surprised to see that Maxwell had already swiped some ice chips from the dispenser in the hall. As she came back, she knelt by Mariah's side and wet her lips with the ice, her hands delicate. Mariah managed a smile and took a few slivers of ice in her mouth before she turned her head aside. Seamus joined Maxwell, kneeling at Mariah's side.

"You avenged your son," he said. "Well done."

Mariah's eyes flew open, and she tried and failed to sit up. Seamus shook his head—Maxwell was glaring at him, but everyone deserved to die with some measure of truth.

"I'm not here to arrest you. I just wanted you to know you did well. The same I'd want someone to do for me if I were murdered."

Mariah smiled and raised her wrists, stick-thin and covered with IV bruises. "Handcuffs, ah?" she said.

Seamus laughed and leaned back against the wall. "I don't know, Mrs. Lopez. I'm not sure I could take you alive. You were too slippery for us."

Her eyes lost their focus and drifted towards Maxwell. "A good girl. Let me tell you about my son."

"Uh—of course, Mrs. Lopez," said Maxwell.

"I came to this city a long time ago, in '95. I had been a nurse, in Honduras, but my husband came here to find a job and provide for us. My little Tony was a smart boy—no respect for the law, but not bad. Always he liked his knives, but he never scared anyone with them. He just liked to show off, liked to carve the handles with pictures and give them to his friends. Could have been an artist—he made me the most beautiful paintings too. Still have them. When my husband died . . . I could not be a father and a mother both—I could not watch him as well as I should have." Moisture glinted in her eyes. "Tony didn't spend much time at home, but always—when he did come home—he would bring me a cake, say he was sorry for spending so much time away. He was lost, but he was a good boy. When he was a man, he brought me envelopes of money instead. I never asked where the money came from, never used it—gave it all to the church. Only good thing to do with dirty money.

"The last time my Tony came, he didn't bring anything. He looked confused, walked into things. He wouldn't go to the hospital, kept saying something about Timmy Greene, about an Angelmaker, and I was scared for him. When he left, he was bleeding from the nose. He died on the street that night, just out by that damned bar."

Her voice took on an edge of quiet rage, then, and a strength that belied her wasted body. "My boy, bleeding his life out under the streetlights, not even in his own bed. That bastard . . . Timmy Greene . . ."

"He's paid for what he did," said Seamus softly. "You made sure of that."

Mariah fixed him with a hard look. "He will *never* be finished paying, even with the devil. My son, worth a thousand of him. You know, I had respect for the law. I thought they would catch him—but that lawyer—the man I found in the hospital—he made sure Timmy went free. I felt so lucky when I saw his name on my chart, like my heart was singing. You tell his wife I am sorry for her, but I do not regret it. I used Antonio's favourite knife, so my son could be at peace. I did it because the law couldn't. And the big man, Timmy's man—I met him at my son's funeral. And he took the necklace—that was lucky for me, that he came to visit. He's dead now, yes?"

Seamus said nothing, and Mariah took his silence for agreement. "For Timmy, I waited—I just wanted to get close to the end before I did the work, not to die in jail. You even helped me, Detective, the night I put it in his drink. And that horrible giant, smoking his damned cigarettes while my boy went into the ground—finished. I would have been happy with only Timmy—thanks to God I got all three of them."

She shivered slightly.

"I finished him," she said, the last bit of focus leaving her eyes.

Maxwell nodded, a look of awe in her eyes. "You did the whole world a favour."

Mariah smiled and let her eyes slide closed in the darkening room. "Only . . . what I had to do."

The sun fell by degrees. Mariah didn't open her eyes, and Seamus stood with Maxwell, listening to Mariah's ragged breathing. Maxwell went to walk out but leaned against the door, her hands crossed tight over her chest. After waiting a moment to see that Mariah was resting, Seamus came and spoke quietly to her.

"You don't have to stay, Maxwell. It's a lot of death for a new hire."

"She shouldn't have to be alone, boss."

Seamus considered this, then nodded and pulled a twenty out of his jacket.

"Get us some Tim's, then. Double-double and an old-fashioned plain for me."

Maxwell stared at the bill but finally took it. "I'll be back."

Seamus stayed there, standing vigil. He was still standing when Maxwell returned, hot coffee in hand.

Seamus and Maxwell stood—by some unspoken accord, both of them stayed on their feet—till nine, answering Mariah's muttered questions. It wore on them both, the gurgling breaths and the smell of a body coming apart, but they stood there still, sipping their coffees. At ten, Mariah's eyes flashed open and she gasped, smiled one last time, then lay still. Seamus felt her wrist to be sure—no pulse, and she was already getting cold. In an impulse he couldn't quite make sense of, Seamus pulled her blanket up to her shoulders, then called for the doctors.

Maxwell went home after that, hopefully to sleep. She'd be able to eventually—she'd been running on fear and violence these past few days, but unlike Seamus she wasn't used to it. When her adrenal glands finally stopped dumping stress hormones in her bloodstream, she'd collapse, and probably sleep for a few days. It'd do her good.

Seamus's leg wouldn't bend, and Mariah's death weighed on him like a lead coat, but he couldn't rest. Not yet. He'd realized, watching Mariah's breath slow and stop, that you often told yourself there was nothing more you could do and stopped thinking there. Mariah hadn't fallen into that trap, but he had. There was a storm on the horizon and a mess of danger for him, and for Sandra. But he still had one card left to play, one last stake to lay on the table.

He took a taxi to Olexa's office. The receptionist didn't ask him for the password, just let him pass with a fearful look—he'd been there too often, had become in her eyes another Company man. Just as well.

Olexa had returned and sat behind her desk speaking to one of her men. She was dictating an order for rifles, cut off midway when Seamus came in.

"Here again, Detective? Careful you don't outlast your welcome."

"I'm not too worried about that," said Seamus. "I know who killed Timmy and Ryba. Who tried to kill Trelly."

In an instant Olexa's full concentration was on him, her face a silent mask. The four guards swept out to flank him. "Tell me," she said, and in that room, surrounded by her guards and pinned under her eyes, the command had a physical weight to it. Seamus felt it hit, then grinned at her, and held his chin up high.

"What will you offer me in exchange?"

There was a soft *click* as a pistol was cocked and levelled on his head. Seamus didn't turn, nor did he stop smiling, but he was getting awfully tired of having guns pointed at him.

"Tell your boy to put that down before I take it from him and empty the clip into his head."

"You are brave, Detective. And very foolish."

"I'm neither, actually, I just think things through. See, I'm the only one who can tell you who's responsible for the murders, and if you blow my brains out onto your rug, your men'll have to pick through them to find that name. Not to mention the dry-cleaning bill."

Olexa regarded him a moment, then gestured to the man with the gun, who drew back and replaced it in its holster.

"One million, small bills, all well-cleaned. I can have it in two hours. That's my price, to have that name before your friends the police do."

"No."

"Perhaps there's something else I could do that would convince you. Detective."

Seamus could probably stand up to torture better than most men, but the limit of his endurance was there somewhere, and he had no desire to go looking for it.

"My secretary was on to something. I'd like to buy protection."

Olexa inclined her head. "Not what I'd expected," she said, "but a fair exchange. You and that girl, Maxwell—"

"Not *my* protection. I want everyone on the street, from the kids robbing the 7-Eleven on up to the triad deputies in Chinatown to know that Sandra Blair is under the explicit protection of the Company. Give me that, and I'll give you the name."

Olexa smiled, the expression dying at her eyes. "Remember what I told you about a soft heart, Detective. Why the sudden concern?"

"This was just a sortie. The Angelmaker's still loose, and if my guess is right, there'll be blood in the streets before it's over. I'd rather it wasn't hers."

Olexa paused a moment. "You are right to be afraid. Even if war does not come now, this Angelmaker is dangerous, and they are not beaten."

"Then—"

"I refuse. Protecting the police—it will set us at odds with our own allies, break old alliances. Not worth one name. Not in dangerous times, when we must save our strength."

Seamus nodded. One last bet to stake. "In that case, I have something else to offer you. Same price."

Her eyes glittered. "What else do you have that I can't take from you?"

"My service to the Company."

That got him a moment of silence. Olexa even looked surprised.

"I'll pledge you loyal service, act as one of your own men, when you have need of me. I'm sure you have enough muscle, but you might find yourself in need of a detective in these next few years."

"The same terms?"

"Protection for Sandra and Maxwell. Any injury done to them to be met with the full strength of the Company. With this, of course, as a loyal Company man, I'll tell you who tried to kill Trelly."

Olexa watched him a moment. Then, to his surprise and horror, she began to laugh. It was a grating sound, like an engine that hadn't been turned over in too many winters. And when the laughter guttered out, she opened her desk, set a bottle of Armagnac on the table, then two crystal glasses, and poured a mouthful into each.

"The Surgeon, my own man—you will be useful." She raised her glass. "I accept your service. To honour." Seamus let his breath out. Olexa was watching him—a Company man did what Olexa needed without being asked.

"The killer was named Mariah Lopez."

"Was?"

"She just died at Michael Garron. I was there with her. I'll give you any details you need, but it was revenge. Timmy had used her son as a guinea pig for Platinum, and the drug killed him. Ryba, Timmy, Trelly—they were payback. One last cheque to cash before she died."

"Very interesting. You will tell me everything, later, but if she's dead—no urgency. And Sam Ewe—who killed him?"

It figured that Olexa would already know about that death. The woman had ears everywhere.

"The Angelmaker poisoned him in his bed. I wouldn't be doing this—"

"If you hadn't just made a very dangerous enemy. I see. Poisoned—I'll need to ask one of the men to taste my food, now."

Not a luxury he could afford, thought Seamus with a shiver of discomfort.

"You are injured," said Olexa, with a pointed glance at the leg with the bullet hole Seamus had thought he'd hidden quite well. "My men rest when they're injured so they can serve me better. Take this, and leave."

She took a sip from her glass, then handed him a small satin box. Inside was a finely made five-pointed star, wrought from silver.

"You need not wear this every day," she said. "But when you do, you are a Company man. An extension of my authority, one of my own fingers. Remember that."

Seamus bowed his head and allowed her to pin the badge to his jacket.

"I'm honoured, Ms. Greene. Gentlemen. If you'll excuse me, I need to go home and rest my eyes."

It took time. Seamus knew better than to push, but at lunch on the fourth day Sandra walked into Jackson's, stamped the snow off her boots, and sat down at the bar beside him. Jackson busied himself with some bottles, the soft tinkling sound of glass on glass accompanying the classical station. Neither of them spoke as they drank, but there was a certain comfort in the silence.

"How are you?" asked Seamus, once he'd finished his bourbon.

"A little fucked. Just got my key back from Michael—lots of blubbering. Made me a little nauseous. But I've been worse. You?"

"Healing."

Sandra nodded and sipped her Red Stripe.

"I didn't mean it," she said at last, her gaze still fixed on the bar. "It was a shitty thing to say."

Seamus turned, blade's edge–blue eyes steady on her. "I do care about you, Sandra Blair. If you don't know that—that's my mistake, not yours."

She let out a soft *hah*. "I know you do, Seamus. You just need to make better calls."

"I'm sorry too."

She met his eyes, that old spark of challenge and the echo of a smile dancing on her lips. "What for?"

"For hurting you."

"*You* didn't fuck my fiancé." She showed him the shadow of a smile. "I mean, if you did, I don't wanna hear about it."

Seamus squinted at her. Then— "I should have told you the truth. Immediately."

"Damn straight. Don't do it again."

The silver star in his jacket pocket was suddenly heavy. But that was unavoidable—Seamus had meant what he said. It was high time he'd done something for Sandra, and if his service was the only currency he could buy her safety with, so be it. Seamus didn't think she'd approve, but she didn't have to know about it.

Sandra smiled at him, then smacked a hand on the bar and threw one arm over his shoulder.

"Hey, bartender! What kind of shithole are you running, we don't have wings in front of us?"

Jackson hustled to the back. His grin was slightly broader than usual.

"I do have some good news," said Seamus, "about the Ryba murder. I've got a suspect . . ."

CHAPTER FOURTEEN

Another four days later, they took the afternoon off to go to the funeral. Seamus wore the only black jacket he owned under his oilskin, and Maxwell sat between him and Sandra in the dust and slanted light of the community church. Maxwell wore what she did every day, which was quite suitable for a funeral. Seamus had put in money to pay for the hearse, and, as it turned out, there'd been just enough in Mariah's accounts to pay for the funeral. Mariah had been in all respects methodical.

The Ryba murder had been all over the news that week—it had even made the third page of the *Star*. Mariah Lopez would've had a few more mourners if it weren't for someone at the station leaking the name of the prime suspect. But the opinion of most of her friends remained unshaken. As one tiny, tottering old woman had told Seamus by the coffee urn, *Dear Mariah would never do such a thing, no matter what the police said, and if she had, well, they probably had it coming.*

After the Lord's Prayer, Seamus watched the casket go into the ground, Mariah taking her spot beside her husband and son. Seamus and Sandra stood together, her black dress whipping in the wind and his old coat buttoned tight against it. Seamus figured they matched pretty well, neither of them quite whole, but both still standing.

Maxwell came to stand beside Sandra. "How's the investigation?"

"Off the record," said Sandra, "we don't need much of one. The thallium was easy to trace—she ordered it under her legal name, right to her home address. Never expected to survive to trial, I figure. Still, that woman was stone-cold—didn't even flinch way back when we went to interview her. If all murderers were cool like that, we'd be in trouble."

Seamus looked around, taking in the spare but well-kept church grounds, the cherry trees that'd bloom in the spring. It wouldn't be a bad place for her to rest.

Sandra drove them back, and they listened to songs about summer as snow blew across the highway. Terrible day for it, but Seamus had one last errand to run—he asked her to let him and Maxwell out a few miles north of the city.

"You'll get home on your own?" asked Sandra.

"Yeah. Unless you'd like to pay your respects to the late, great Timmy Greene?"

Sandra spat in the snow by the curb and gunned the Widowmaker heading downtown again.

Timmy's funeral had been delayed on account of the difficulty of finding a mortician skilled enough to reassemble him—Seamus had done his work efficiently, but not very neatly. This church was a stark contrast to the coffee-stained folding tables they'd sat around that morning: all stained glass and vaulted ceilings. As a rule, Seamus liked churches—they were pretty, and even if priests were stubborn about spilling what his marks said in confession, there was nothing easier than bugging a confessional booth.

The church was filled to bursting with black-suited men, most of them wearing silver stars. They nodded when they saw the one he'd pinned to his lapel.

Seamus found his employer, after he'd swiped an entire platter of canapés. Olexa wore a vest as usual, now in solid black, with a gold star on her breast. Six men clustered around her and shuffled back for an audience when Seamus drew close.

"Afternoon, Olexa."

"Detective. I see you're the one bankrupting my caterers."

"Some good has to come of this mess. Why not a free lunch for me?"

Seamus glanced towards the lacquered black casket where Timmy lay, his cheeks stuffed with cotton.

"You know, Olexa, your nephew has made a lot of people very happy this last week. You must be proud."

Olexa drew her lips into an almost-smile. "Detective, I have never been so proud of Timmy Greene as I am today."

EPILOGUE

Seamus had plenty of work to do, and plenty to dump on Maxwell. The bulk of it was breaking the cash from his two cases into enough separate accounts, at enough different banks, to avoid raising too many eyebrows.

Over the course of the winter, a number of Timmy's former associates collapsed with a mysterious degenerative brain disease. Seamus visited them, and hinted at a list of drugs that would limit the damage, though they were all astronomically expensive. He'd heard nothing from the Carletons, which was more or less what he expected—Sandra's friends in narcotics were probably building a case to shove through Alister's heart. Seamus didn't give a damn what happened to *him*, but he hoped Lorraine didn't get caught in the crossfire. She'd been nice enough to feed him pie.

Ruby settled her tab—she crumpled like tissue on an open flame when Seamus told her Mariah, the woman who'd killed her husband, was already dead and beyond the reach of justice. Seamus had taken her money, looked her in the eye, and told her what Mariah had said on her deathbed, that she had no regrets. Ruby had, of course, screamed and slammed the door in his face. Perhaps that had been cruel of him. But rage was the only answer for grief that Seamus knew, the only immediate relief—if she could hate him, it would at least give the emotion an outlet. Seamus didn't speak to her again, but he did check in with the neighbours, and he paid Minnie to send her cakes and fruit and roasted pork while she recovered.

That was the hardest job, but the worst news was that there wasn't any. No seven-victim shooting at the Montmorency, no escaped killers, no panic about a stash of some new drug found at the scene. Nothing, not even through Sandra's channels. Whoever the Angelmaker was, they had connections high enough to make those bodies disappear, or more likely push for them to be tidily filed away as gang-on-gang violence. Something even Olexa would've struggled to pull off, which wasn't exactly comforting. But Seamus had already picked his side—instead of lamenting, he wrote up a list of people the Angelmaker might be leaning on in homicide. It included everyone in the department besides Sandra Blair.

After he'd dusted off a night's worth of accumulated snow, Michael collected his vests and beanies from the sidewalk in front of Sandra's, leaving behind a few cardboard boxes full of verse he evidently hoped would convince her to take him back. Sandra and Seamus took the opportunity to have a bonfire in Jackson's parking lot, for which Jackson donated a bottle of honey bourbon that proved too vile even for Seamus. The bottle was used, instead, to help the damp poetry catch.

Maxwell remained strangely enthusiastic about learning to fight—Seamus trained her up on the slow days, though he had to keep himself from crushing her into a powder with strength and conditioning. It wasn't like she'd actually need the training—still, not a bad skill for his secretary to have. After a few months of practice, she was throwing punches that he could feel the next day.

At a distance, things appeared to return to their usual easy pattern. But as the weather grew warmer, Seamus still kept a revolver at his side while he slept, and he spent most mornings before Maxwell arrived training at the gym or the waterfront. By the time the trees started to bud, the leg still hurt, but his kicks were landing as hard as they ever had.

One night in early spring, Seamus and Sandra bumped into each other on King Street and continued walking in the same direction, talking about nothing in particular, not terribly concerned with where they ended up. They found themselves by food, of course: an ancient hotdog stand, with a proprietor whose skin was sun-parched the same bright red as his wares. As the sky faded grey behind the high-rises, Seamus considered his hotdog.

"Don't think I've ever seen you eat slow before, Seamus."

"I keep thinking about that kid in the hospital—lots of poisonings this winter."

Sandra nodded, looking down at her own hotdog with a wary eye. "You think the street meat man's in on it? A secret agent? The Angelmaker himself?"

"Oh, probably," said Seamus. "We're dead men walking. I'll be damned if it keeps me from enjoying my final meal, though," he said as he tore into his dinner.

Sandra laughed. "Worth dying for, that's for sure." She looked up at the night sky, and Seamus did the same—it was overcast, but the moon was bright enough to paint the whole city with silver. "Hey, you remember the time your Ma wouldn't take you to the hospital?"

Sandra never mentioned her parents, but they could talk about Ma. Seamus grinned. "'It's just in your head, boy.' I thought you were going to deck her."

"I'm surprised *you* remember that at all, with the fever you were running. Had to drive you to the hospital myself."

"Considering you were fourteen at the time, I was more worried about dying when we pulled onto the freeway going the wrong way—"

Sandra punched him in the shoulder. "Hell. Things haven't changed as much as you'd think, huh?"

Seamus nodded, his eyes fixed on the moon. After a moment, he spoke: "Michael was an asshole."

"Yup."

"His poetry is enjoyable the way having your arms split open lengthwise is enjoyable."

Sandra chuckled at that and leaned back against the park bench.

Seamus added one last thing, in a lower voice: "You deserve someone better."

Sandra whipped around at that. "Can I get that in writing, Caron?"

"Mm, did you hear something? Must have been the wind," said Seamus, casually inspecting his napkin. "I certainly didn't say anything."

"Yeah? Well, who knows why I stuck with that fucknugget. He was stable, I guess."

Seamus laughed that one off. "Perhaps you just have catastrophically poor taste in men, Ms. Blair."

"I've known that for twenty years," she said, still grinning slightly, and looking uncharacteristically embarrassed. Seamus, for once, had nothing to say. Instead, he smiled back and looked down.

After a moment, Sandra cleared her throat, clapped him on the back, and stood to leave. "Best be getting back home. I'll see you around, Trouble."

Seamus was on the lookout for new clients—a process which mostly involved hanging around marriage counselling offices and listening for screaming matches. After a fairly fruitless afternoon, he came back to his office and heard a different type of argument as he reached for the knob. When he cracked the door, he found Maxwell with her boots up on his desk, looking quite annoyed at the man standing in front of her. He was thin and pale, dressed in an almost militaristically unfashionable brown sweater, and he was speaking too quickly.

"Are you entirely sure you're not Detective Caron—"

"I told you *three times*, I'm the secretary," snapped Maxwell. Seamus pushed the door open all the way and raised an eyebrow at her.

"Customer service, Maxwell. What can I do for you, sir?"

The man spun around to face him. "I have a case for you, Seamus Caron. My girlfriend is missing. I'm at—you might call them—loose ends . . ."

"Missing person?" said Seamus, settling heavily in his desk chair. "The nearest police station is two blocks north—I'm not one to turn away potential clients, but they're a much better bet for this kind of problem." Most likely she'd just gotten sick of the guy and taken off—in any case, there was little hope for either excitement or profit here.

"But . . . I found this," the thin man said, and handed Seamus a wadded leaf of notebook paper. "It isn't her handwriting."

Maxwell peered over Seamus's shoulder as he unfolded it. "What do we got, boss?"

The message was written in an old-fashioned looping script.

> *"I don't know what is the matter with my wife. She is still in bed, and when I speak to her, she just lies there and won't answer me."*
>
> *"I can well believe it," replied the young man. "Go on back up. And this time, look underneath the bedding."*
>
> *So that's what the miller did. And he discovered his wife had only one hand, and the bed was full of blood.*
>
> *Go find Detective Seamus Caron. Tell him the Angelmaker has great expectations.*

Seamus sprung to his feet, a hard, bright light dancing in his eyes. His heart was beating a good deal faster than was healthy.

"Well, Maxwell, looks like the vacation's over."

"Didn't notice any vacation."